POMPEY
The Little.

FRANCIS COVENTRY

THE HISTORY OF
Pompey the Little

OR

THE LIFE AND ADVENTURES
OF A

LAP-DOG

EDITED WITH AN INTRODUCTION BY
ROBERT ADAMS DAY

LONDON
OXFORD UNIVERSITY PRESS
NEW YORK · TORONTO
1974

Oxford University Press, Ely House, London W.1

GLASGOW NEW YORK TORONTO MELBOURNE WELLINGTON
CAPE TOWN IBADAN NAIROBI DAR ES SALAAM LUSAKA ADDIS ABABA
DELHI BOMBAY CALCUTTA MADRAS KARACHI LAHORE DACCA
KUALA LUMPUR SINGAPORE HONG KONG TOKYO

ISBN 0 19 255354 2

Introduction, Notes, Bibliography, and Chronology
© *Oxford University Press 1974*

PR 3369
.C7H5
1974

FILMSET IN GREAT BRITAIN BY
BAS PRINTERS LIMITED, WALLOP, HAMPSHIRE
AND PRINTED AT THE UNIVERSITY PRESS, OXFORD
BY VIVIAN RIDLER
PRINTER TO THE UNIVERSITY

CONTENTS

06069

BOOK II

INTRODUCTION

═══════

ON 16 February 1752, Lady Mary Wortley Montagu wrote from her Italian exile at Brescia to give her daughter, Lady Bute, the latest news and to thank her for a box of the latest books from London. Lady Mary had begun to read avidly, but was not entirely pleased with her first choices, *Peregrine Pickle* and *The History of Charlotte Summers*. Then,

Candles came, and my Eyes grown weary I took up the next Book meerly because I suppos'd from the Title it could not engage me long. It was Pompey the Little, which has really diverted me more than any of the others, and it was impossible to go to Bed till it was finish'd. It is a real and exact representation of Life as it is now acted in London, as it was in my time, and as it will be (I do not doubt) a Hundred years hence, with some little variation of Dress, and perhaps Government. I found there many of my Acquaintance. Lady T[ownshend] and Lady O[rford] are so well painted, I fancy I heard them talk, and have heard them say the very things here repeated.[1]

Other books followed, but Lady Mary returned in her remarks to *Pompey the Little*: 'I also saw my selfe (as I now am) in the character of Mrs. Qualmsick .... I am now convinc'd I am in no danger of starving, and am oblig'd to little Pompey for this discovery.'[2]

[1] *Complete Letters*, ed. Robert Halsband (1967), iii. 4.
[2] Ibid., pp. 4–5.

The book which had so delighted Lady Mary, no mean critic, was the first and only essay in fiction of a young man named Francis Coventry, a recent graduate of Cambridge who had taken holy orders and was 'perpetual curate' (or vicar) of Edgware, within convenient distance of London. Nephew of the fifth earl of Coventry and cousin of the sixth, he was no stranger to 'Life as it is now acted in London', and his education had given him the insouciant grace of expression and the aristocratic bias that made Lady Mary admire Fielding, while its absence forced her to be ashamed of her partiality for Richardson.[1] This background made Coventry something of an anomaly among the creators of a form of literature that was winning only slow acceptance in the mid-eighteenth century. Yet another anomaly was equally striking. The 'hero' of the book was not a castaway or a Newgate bird, neither a foundling nor a lady's maid, but a Bologna lapdog.

These two extraliterary novelties doubtless had much to do with the book's initial success, as can be seen from the favourable notice given it in the *Monthly Review* for February 1751, shortly after its publication, by John Cleland, author of *Memoirs of a Woman of Pleasure* ('Fanny Hill'), who was no mere pornographer, but a cultivated if impecunious man of letters:

There are, to the great disgust of the public, too many productions of the press, beneath giving a character of: This one is, however, so far of a different kind, that it is not easy to do justice to the merit of it. The author, whose name is not to the work, takes for his subject, a *Bologna* lap-dog, brought from *Italy* to *England*, where he often changes masters, by several accidents, which furnish the writer with a handle to introduce a variety of characters and situations; all painted with great humour, fancy, and wit: and, indeed, he every where displays a perfect knowledge of the world, through all

[1] See Robert Halsband, 'Lady Mary Wortley Montagu and Eighteenth-Century Fiction', *English Studies Today* (Rome, 1966), pp. 330–6.

its ranks, and all its follies. These he ridicules, with a fineness of edge, unknown to the sour satyrist, or the recluse philosopher. Even his negligences are pleasing. The gentleman, in short, breathes throughout the whole performance, and the vein of pleasantry, which runs through it, is every where evenly upheld, from the beginning to the end. He laughs at the world, without doing it the honour to be angry with it. His lashes, however smart, carry with them rather the marks of a benevolent correction, than of the spleen of misanthropy. All his characters are natural. His language easy and genteel.[1]

But writing like a gentleman is no guarantee of literary merit, as hundreds of feeble poems and essays by the noble and gentle authors of the eighteenth century can attest. Coventry, on the other hand, wrote like a minor Fielding. The urbane, intrusive author, the shapely, balanced sentences, the classical learning, the irony which is fully perceived only after a split-second's reflection—these hallmarks of Fielding's manner, though intermittent and not under full control, give *Pompey* an artistic force that almost raises it to the category of major satire.

But apart from its own worth, the circumstances of *Pompey*'s introduction to the world were more than usually auspicious. Whether Ralph Griffiths, the founder and editor of the influential *Monthly Review*, and Cleland, his second-in-command during its first few years, wished to do Coventry a personal favour or were genuinely struck by the book's merit, is unknown; but circumstances combined to give it a publicity campaign unprecedented for such a work at the time. The favourable review quoted above (the *Monthly* had been far less kind to *Peregrine Pickle* and *Charlotte Summers*) appeared as we have seen in the February 1751 number; lack of space forced a

---

[1] *Monthly Review*, iv (article XLV), 316–17. The authorship of the review was indicated by Ralph Griffiths, the editor, in his own marked copy (preserved in the Bodleian Library). See Benjamin C. Nangle, *The Monthly Review: First Series* (1934), p. 125.

series of extracts from it (not uncommon practice in the early days of periodical reviewing) into the March number, where they made up the second article; and an error caused the reprinting of yet more extracts, which had been omitted, in the April number, so that the reading public was reminded of the book for three consecutive months, with samples of its contents totalling three entire chapters and part of a fourth, and occupying sixteen of the *Monthly*'s pages.[1] Griffiths' interest in the book is further evinced by the fact that in marking up his master copy of the *Monthly* for a possible reprinting, he indicated that the passages appearing in the April number should be moved back into their proper place, and gave *Pompey* a cross-reference in the table of contents.[2]

Whether because of this puffing or not, it appears that the book rapidly became, if not the talk of the town, at least a subject of considerable interest among those who corresponded on literary matters. The first edition was anonymous, as befitted the maiden effort of a novelist who was not a hack; but at least one reader, and probably more, was sure that Fielding was its author. By May, Shenstone had heard of it and wanted to borrow it of Lady Luxborough; in replying she remarked that 'Fielding you know cannot write without humour'.[3] Other admirers included Mrs. Delany, who from Ireland inquired after the book's reception in England only a month after its publication (though she thought it a mere trifle),[4] Richardson's friend Lady Bradshaigh, who found it 'both well designed and well executed,'[5] and the erudite printer William Bowyer, who wrote to a friend on 1 August

[1] *Monthly Review*, iv (Articles XLVIII and LXVI), 329–37, 457–65.

[2] MS annotations in the Bodleian copy, pp. 11, 321, 329.

[3] *Letters written by the Late Right Honourable Lady Luxborough, to William Shenstone, Esq.* (1775), p. 265 (27 May 1751).

[4] *The Autobiography and Correspondence of Mary Granville, Mrs. Delany*, ed. Lady Llanover (1861), iii. 26 (16 March 1751).

[5] *The Correspondence of Samuel Richardson*, ed. Anna L. Barbauld (1804), iv. 159 (*c.* March 1752).

1751: 'You do me much honour in ascribing "Pompey the Little" to me. I am obliged to you; and shall be glad never to be suspected of a worse thing.'[1] Horace Walpole purchased a copy of the first edition,[2] and evidently wrote to his friend Thomas Gray at Cambridge to ask for details, since the latter part of the book is set in Cambridge and includes portraits of a seclusive scholar, a do-nothing don, and a frivolous undergraduate, among other Cambridge characters. Gray, hardly an indiscriminate snapper-up of unconsidered trifles, may have been attracted to *Pompey* by hearing of its merits; but he was personally acquainted with its author and with his cousin Henry Coventry, who had been a Fellow of Magdalene College since 1730 and a close friend of Walpole when the latter was an undergraduate.[3] He therefore wrote to Walpole, only a few weeks after *Pompey* was first published: '*Pompey* is the hasty production of a Mr. Coventry (cousin to him you knew), a young clergyman: I found it out by three characters, which once made part of a comedy that he showed me of his own writing.'[4] And it is thought that nearly two years later Arthur Murphy was counting on the associations which the name Pompey would arouse when, satirizing the hack writer and physician 'Sir' John Hill in the *Gray's Inn Journal*, he converted him into Lady Fidget's lapdog Pompey, who has a sanguinary encounter in the park with five other dogs.[5]

[1] John Nichols, *Biographical and Literary Anecdotes of William Bowyer, Printer, F. S. A.* (1782), p. 326n.

[2] See Allen T. Hazen, *A Catalogue of Horace Walpole's Library* (1969), i. 411.

[3] John Nichols, *Literary Anecdotes of the Eighteenth Century* (1815), v. 564–9; ix. 801. Many years before as a Cambridge freshman Gray had sent Walpole a humorous description of Cambridge characters, reminiscent of Coventry's; see *Horace Walpole's Correspondence with Thomas Gray* (Yale Edition, ed. W. S. Lewis, *et al.*, 1948), i. 58–60 (letter of 31 October 1734).

[4] *Horace Walpole's Correspondence with Thomas Gray*, ii. 48 (letter of 3 March 1751).

[5] *The Gray's Inn Journal*, No. 7 (2 December 1752). Hill had satirized Mountefort Brown, who retaliated by caning and kicking him at Ranelagh. Hill published an account in which he represented himself as having been set upon by five bullies, and grossly exaggerated his injuries. See Gerard E. Jensen, ed., *The Covent Garden Journal* (New Haven, 1915), i. 73–4, 81.

At any rate, the 'more favourable reception than its writer had any reason to expect'[1] led to a revised third edition, which was prepared in the autumn of 1751, and for which the bookseller Dodsley paid Coventry the amazing fee (for a mere work of fiction by a new author) of thirty pounds.[2] Now sure of himself, and not unaware of the advantage of enrolling himself among the followers of such a literary lion, Coventry affixed his name to the third edition's laudatory dedication to Fielding. Here he clearly indicated his admiration for the manner of writing which Fielding represented by classing him as first among living novelists.

English fiction in the second half of the eighteenth century, if we except the late 'Gothic' romance and the whimsical imitations of Sterne, can be seen as deriving ultimately from the influence either of Richardson or of Fielding—that is, to put it crudely, having a bias toward either satire or sentiment. The taste of readers was divided in like manner, and the initial success of *Pompey the Little* was lasting. It had the honour of being twice pirated in Dublin; it ran to at least ten English editions by 1824. It was translated into French in 1752 and Italian in 1760, and in 1753 it was even mentioned (albeit inaccurately and unfavourably) in the literary newsletter which Friedrich Melchior von Grimm circulated among the crowned heads of Europe.

M. Toussaint . . . s'est occupé . . . à traduire quelques ouvrages qui ne devaient pas sortir des ténèbres dont ils avaient été entourés dès leur naissance: telle est la traduction d'un mauvais roman d'une chienne qu'il nous donna il y a environ deux ans [but *Pompey* is bracketed with '*William*' *Pickle*].[3]

[1] See p. xlv, below.
[2] See p. xxvi, below.
[3] *Correspondance littéraire*, ed. Maurice Tourneux (Paris, 1877), ii. 267 (1 August 1753).

But the most significant measure of *Pompey*'s success, and its importance to the history of fiction, lies in the fact that it may be said to have originated, or at least prepared the public to receive, a sub-genre of fiction which flourished for fifty years or more—the satirical story in which a non-human 'hero' (a dog, cat, hackney-coach, flea, banknote, rupee, monkey, and many more) passed rapidly from hand to hand and underwent as many varied adventures as the author was disposed to invent. Perhaps the most famous example in its day was the notorious *Chrysal* (1760–5) of Charles Johnstone, in which a golden guinea fell into the hands of a galaxy of characters including George II himself, and in which the 'secret histories' of many well-known persons were scandalously revealed. Several dozen such works appeared, and various comments toward the end of the century indicate that this form of satire was taken for granted, however much it might be deplored. Even Smollett, almost certainly established as the author of the anonymous *History and Adventures of an Atom* (1769), would seem to have sensed the value of the device in constructing a savage and all-inclusive attack on the conduct of public affairs in the last years of George II. *Pompey* had started a fashion, but it had also established a literary technique.

Pompey the Little is very much a young man's book; if the comparison is admissible, he came to it like Swift to *A Tale of a Tub*, 'his invention at the height, and his reading fresh in his head'. His prejudices have not had time to mellow, the collegian's desire to display his classical attainments is all too obvious, and the giddy alterations in style between the sublime and the ridiculous have not been smoothed over by a concern for overall symmetry. The narrative is totally episodic; scenes are finished either by being brought to a natural outcome or by mere accident— whatever first comes to the author's mind. The text bristles with learned quotations and allusions, but no

less with the slang and the local allusions of London in
1750. (It is remarkable how many nonce-words of the
time in the *Oxford English Dictionary* give *Pompey* as their
sole source.) But it is precisely this 'unfinished' quality of
Pompey that conveys the flavour of its time and place,
elements which would have been subdued in a more
polished work. The point is easily established by comparing
Pompey as to specific details with the far greater novels of
Fielding which it professedly imitates. If the comparison
lowers our estimation of Coventry's work, it also points
up *Pompey*'s ability to achieve a legitimate end of fiction
(what Mary McCarthy indeed has called its most essential
quality, Diderot's 'petites choses' or her own 'thinginess')
which Fielding, by the classical requirements of his art,
was forced to renounce. Dr. Johnson's famous comparison
of Fielding as a man who could tell time by the face of a
watch to Richardson as a man who understood its interior
mechanisms is relevant here: the works of the watch
(though Johnson of course meant the subtle shadings of
emotion and thought displayed in Richardson's novels)
are laid open in *Pompey*'s linguistic texture and knowing
references as they cannot be on the larger, more generalized
surfaces of *Tom Jones*.

But pointing out this fact serves only to give Coventry
the virtues of his defects. If one were asked to sum up
the furniture of his mind as he commenced novelist,
the task would be simple—it is not too reductive to say,
'Swift, Pope, and Fielding'. Coventry alludes constantly
to the three, he continually quotes or perhaps merely lifts
passages from them (and in the context of his literary
milieu it is impossible to decide which—Pope was not
plagiarizing from Addison when he modified one of the
latter's well-known couplets with a satirical effect that
would not be lost on his audience). Like all three Coventry
is firmly oriented politically with the Tory or Country
party (though this, considering his family background

and ecclesiastical hopes, is the reverse of astonishing). But it is Fielding in particular on whom Coventry seems to be consciously modelling himself.

The larger virtues of Fielding were and are perhaps inimitable, but Coventry showed himself fully aware of his master's idiosyncrasies. The archaic 'hath' and 'doth' that Fielding (and Swift) affected, the addressing of the reader as 'thou', the false-innocent irony, the author's intrusive reflections on life and manners in his own voice, the constant comment on the fact that the writer is constructing a story and manipulating the reader, all are consciously adopted. Likewise the ironic, impudent, or tantalizing chapter-titles ('What the Reader will Know if he Reads it') represent an attempt to proceed in the manner of Fielding. In fact, the only aspect of Fielding's art which is intensively rather than generally examined and evaluated in the anonymous *Essay upon the New Species of Writing* (1751; generally attributed to Coventry) is the handling of chapter titles (pp. 21–7). The author comments on the damage done to the vital quality of suspense by giving too much away in chapter titles, and this discussion is the best reason for ascribing the pamphlet to Coventry. Fielding, who had a copy of *Pompey* in his library, must have been pleased by the compliment of imitation.

But clearly *Pompey the Little* is no *Tom Jones*; and while Coventry could hardly have chosen better contemporary models to form his thought than Swift, Pope, and Fielding, literary mimicry is not originality. There remains the central device of the novel—the use of a non-human protagonist. Most of Coventry's readers, to be sure, would have found this a striking novelty, though modern scholars would quickly cite among English occurrences the medieval *Owl and the Nightingale*, Chaucer's *Nun's Priest's Tale*, William Baldwin's satirical prose tale *Beware the Cat* (1561) and many more. But a University man of

Coventry's day would have known other works ready to hand and more to the purpose. There existed as model the *Metamorphoses* (or '*Golden Ass*') of Apuleius, in which the narrator-turned-ass is bandied about by a congeries of rascals in high and low life and of both sexes; there was *Le Diable boiteux* of Le Sage, translated early in the century, in which a demon flits about Madrid, unroofing houses to reveal vice. One of the *Tatlers* had used the idea of narrating the adventures of a shilling to hold together several satirical portraits,[1] and an anonymous novel called *The Tell-Tale* (1711) had introduced a spirit who darted from one boudoir to another to report on amorous intrigues. The 'secret history' was of course nothing new; the undeservedly infamous Mrs. Mary Manley and Mrs. Eliza Haywood were among many who had enlivened the first third of the century with their reports on the alleged misbehaviour of the great. But these fictions, most of which Coventry undoubtedly knew, could have furnished him only with the general direction of his satire. There were, nevertheless, direct ancestors of *Pompey*. In 1741 Robert Goadby had published his translation of *Two Humorous Novels* of Cervantes (republished 1747); one of these was 'A Diverting Dialogue between Scipio and Berganza', two dogs which have been granted the power of speech for a night. Scipio, sententious and garrulous, loves to quote the classics (he has accompanied his young master to a Jesuit academy), and he laments the treatment he has undergone from various masters, including shepherds, beggars, a butcher, and a sorceress. The novella, in short, is a picaresque tale with a dog as *picaro*. Even closer to *Pompey* were two works of fiction by the hack writer and opponent of Pope, Charles Gildon: not novels, but rather narrative satires. In the first, *The Golden Spy* (1709) a golden *louis d'or*

---

[1] No. 249 (11 November 1710).

exemplifies the proverb 'money talks' in a manner indicated by the full title,

The Golden Spy: or, a Political Journal of the British Nights Entertainments of War and Peace, and Love and Politics: Wherein are laid open, The Secret miraculous Power and Progress of Gold, in the Courts of Europe. Intermix'd with Delightful Intrigues, Memoirs, Tales, and Adventures, Serious and Comical.

In the second, *The New Metamorphosis* (1724), the 'editor' presents a 'Vatican manuscript ... of *Fumoso de la Fantasia*,' and speaks of the latter's

transformation into a *Bologna* Lap-Dog; a Form more opportune for the Discovery of the Secrets and Intrigues of Ladies and great Men, than that of an Ass, who could not be admitted beyond the very Stable, or at most to a nearer View of the Affairs of the Mob.[1]

Gildon made little and feeble use of the device, and we cannot know whether Coventry knew the book, but authors are not prone to take their inventions out of the air.

The mere use of a dog as hero, however, would have mattered little if Coventry had not made it in a sense organic to the conduct of his novel. It clearly occurred to him at a very early stage, as his first chapter shows, that the use of a dog (and a toy dog at that) offered an admirable vehicle for the mock-heroic mode that was so central to the satire of his models, Swift, Pope, and Fielding. The text of *Pompey* shows that Coventry knew *The Rape of the Lock* very well, and there we find

Now Lap-Dogs give themselves the rouzing Shake,
And sleepless Lovers, just at Twelve, awake.   (i, 15–16)

Not louder Shrieks to pitying Heav'n are cast,   (iii, 157–8)
When Husbands, or when Lap-Dogs, breathe their last.

[1] P. 3 (copy in the Houghton Library, Harvard University).

Nay, *Poll* sate mute, and *Shock* was most Unkind! (iv, 164)

Sooner let Earth, Air, Sea to Chaos fall;
Men, Monkies, Lap-Dogs, Parrots, perish all! (iv, 119–20)

The lapdog is as much a citizen of the belle's toy-world of inverted humane values as is the man (who is not a man, but a 'husband' or a 'beau'). Here certainly is the principal *reason* for the use of little Pompey in the novel; Coventry is writing the 'life' of a lapdog, just as Conyers Middleton wrote the life of Cicero and Colley Cibber the life of himself; the author will be just as precisely pedantic about minute facts, just as eloquent in describing the data of character, as they (it should be remembered that both are attacked in *Joseph Andrews* and by Pope), and the inversion of values and wasted effort revealed in the painstaking dating of Pompey's birth and death will point up the waste and inversion of Christian and humanistic values that Coventry sees in the life and letters of his day. In the world of Pompey, a dog is of course more important than a man, or should be, and Coventry could not foresee a time when humanitarianism should have eroded humanism to such an extent that a critic could in effect complain that the 'character' of Pompey was not handled in the manner of Black Beauty or Greyfriars Bobby.[1] The fact that Lady Tempest, and perhaps the lady of fashion she stood for, and her friends, could and did place dogs above men was for Coventry, a late Augustan and a son of Pope, a sufficient symptom of the decay of values in society to be used as a pivot around which his satire could circle.

But Coventry was no Swift or Fielding, and he did not make the dog-man inversion the centre of his book. (Indeed, at several points there are as eloquent pleas against the mistreatment of animals as any modern

[1] See Arundell del Re's introduction to the Golden Cockerel edition of *Pompey* (1926), p. xii.

crusader for the prevention of cruelty to animals could wish.) Coventry does not attempt to create a unified fiction, and throughout most of the book the 'character' of Pompey serves merely as a string on which the satiric episodes can be threaded. And this point brings one to a final question: what can be said of *Pompey the Little* as a work of art; what is its value for the reader of today?

Pompey is not a novel, if by 'novel' one means anything more than a fictional prose narrative of a certain length. It is certainly not a novel about a dog in the manner of Jack London. The question of complex characterization in the protagonist cannot be raised except paradoxically; there are no minor characters, only portraits. There is no unification of tone or point of view, at least in the demanding modern sense. As for plot, Pompey's loose skein of episodes cannot be mentioned in the same context as, for instance, *Pamela*, to say nothing of the elaborate symmetries of *Tom Jones*. It is these 'deficiencies', no doubt, that have brought about the almost total absence of comment on the book in the older standard histories of fiction, oriented as they have been to a concept of the 'rise of the novel' borrowed from the somewhat misapprehended theory of biological evolution. But more recent treatments of fiction have been led to discard the idea of its painful development in the direction, say, of George Eliot and Henry James in favour of an attempt to see what authors were trying to do in their own times and their own terms. Notable among these is that of Ronald Paulson,[1] who examines certain eighteenth-century fictions as though they were offshoots in narrative prose of the formal poetic satire in the tradition of Juvenal. Such a scheme offers a perfect characterization of *Pompey*—the problems of handling the Juvenalian protagonist as a believable human being are solved by making

[1] *Satire and the Novel in Eighteenth-Century England* (New Haven, 1967), pp. 21–3.

him non-human; the catalogue of vices is metamorphosed into a journey with its incidents and adventures; the fact that formal satire is essentially 'the middle of a story' is rendered less troublesome by making the story that of a dog, whose life can have no plot; the unconventional or shocking approaches of satire to its subjects, and its concrete detail, fit easily into the succession of vivid unrelated scenes permitted by the dog's random movements from master to master.

Here is an adequate accounting for what *Pompey* does; the question of what it *is* involves the idea of genre. Although as we have seen it may be regarded as the work that established a briefly flowering sub-genre, the humorous narrative with a non-human protagonist, this sub-genre has been given no name. But it might be regarded historically as the fusion of two already well established forms—the secret history or 'spy' novel and the picaresque narrative. Like the spy novel (examples would be Montesquieu's *Lettres persanes* and the *Turkish Spy*) *Pompey* offers a protagonist who is in some way detached from uncritical acceptance of the life around him, and through whom the author can criticize the mores, politics, religious practices, or personal eccentricities he encounters. The picaresque novel carried its protagonist through all levels of society, but often failed in the attempt to make him believable, a sympathetic human being who would engage the reader, as Smollett's criticism of Le Sage's *Gil Blas* pointed out.[1] Such a novel as *Pompey* eliminated certain artistic liabilities of its predecessors, but incurred others: the 'spy' could have infinite and rapid social mobility and did not have to be characterized in detail; but on the other hand the author's richness of humour and satire would suffer if he set himself the problem of conscientiously representing how a non-human spectator of society might think and react. Thus

[1] In the introduction to *Roderick Random*.

Pompey the Little can be regarded, if one wishes, as almost an inevitable development from several forms of fiction that had arisen before it, an attempt to rectify several of their literary shortcomings by compromise, though clearly at the expense of warm humanity. But then satire, narrative or not, has seldom been noted for its human warmth.

The modern reader, unless his interests include the scholarly, will first be interested in *Pompey*, or any novel, as merely something to read; and its value as entertainment should not be in question after a few pages. Though its comedy flickers in intensity it never goes out. But the reader who desires something beyond entertainment to justify his interest may reflect that *Pompey* is perhaps the best example of a form of English fiction that is at the very least historically important, and that deserves to be better known. Its verbal texture affords a more authentic and wide-ranging voice of its era than can be found in the more impressive contemporary novels that were polished either by an artistic conscience or in a mistaken pursuit of gentility and delicacy. Its satire, *mutatis mutandis*, is applicable to the social climbers, the adherents of gurus, the fashionable swindlers, and the well-heeled delinquents of our own day. Its scenes of both high and low life are filled with the specific details that inform as well as amuse. Lastly, and by no means the worst recommendation for a novel, it still gives the reader what it gave Lady Mary Wortley Montagu two hundred and twenty years ago: 'Life . . . as it was in my time, and as it will be . . . a Hundred years hence.'

ACKNOWLEDGEMENTS

═══════════

I WISH TO thank the Trustees of the Houghton Library, Harvard University, for permission to quote an unpublished document in its collection. The staffs of the British Museum, the Lambeth Palace Library, the Guildhall Library, the Cambridge University Library, the Bodleian Library, the Middlesex Records Office, the Public Record Office, and the Burnt Oak Public Library, Edgware, have been more than professionally helpful; and I wish especially to thank Miss Carolyn Jakeman of the Houghton Library for her assistance. For their patience and kindness in responding to queries and searching records, I have to thank the Archivist of Magdalene College, Cambridge; the Revd. Canon W. E. Watts, of Henley-on-Thames; the Revd. Prebendary Gordon Harman, of Edgware; the Revd. Christopher Spencer, of Stanmore, and the diocesan archivists of Ely and Lincoln. Mr. Alan Carr greatly assisted in research; and Mr. Milton Malkin patiently pointed out errors and furnished valuable information.

NOTE ON THE TEXT

The first edition of *Pompey the Little* was printed 'for M. Cooper at the Globe'. Mary Cooper was associated with the far more notable bookseller Robert Dodsley,[1] and it was she who had also sold Coventry's poem *Penshurst* in 1750, though it was listed as 'printed for R. Dodsley'. Given the extremely dubious status of fiction at the time (in comparison with poetry, history, or sermons, and with the exception of such luminaries as Richardson, Fielding, and Smollett) it is reasonable to suppose that Dodsley regarded this first venture of an unknown young man from the University as a risky undertaking and chose to let Mrs. Cooper assume the hazards of printing and distributing the three-shilling duodecimo. It is also probable either that a very small edition was printed and the type left standing in case the book did well, or that only a portion of the sheets were bound, the rest remaining available for a 'second edition' if required, as it soon was.[2]

---

[1] H. R. Plomer *et al.*, *A Dictionary of the Printers and Booksellers ... from 1726 to 1775* (1930), pp. 60–1.

[2] For the prevalence of such practices see William B. Todd, 'Bibliography and the Editorial Problem in the Eighteenth Century', *Bibliography and Textual Criticism*, ed. O. M. Brack, Jr., and Warner Barnes (1969), pp. 141–2. The 'second edition' (1751; copy in the University Library, Cambridge) differs in no way from the first except that the words '*The* SECOND EDITION' have been inserted within horizontal rules between the Latin mottoes and the printer's name on the title-page.

Pompey, however, attracted a considerable amount of attention, and may even have been briefly 'the talk of the Town' (see pp. xii–xiii, above), so that by the end of 1751 there could be no doubt of its commercial value. This is confirmed by a document now in the Houghton Library of Harvard University, which reads:

Rec^d Nov^{br} the 2^d 1751 of M^r. Dodsley the Sum of thirty Pounds for the Alterations in the third Edition of Pompey the Little in consideration of which, together with what I have before receiv'd, I do assign over to the s^d Robt Dodsley all my right and Property in ye Copy of the said Book

Francis Coventry[1]

It should be remembered that authors in general did not receive royalties, but sold the copy to the printer for a lump sum, usually only a few pounds for minor fiction; that authors were paid separately for revisions (it was said that Defoe deliberately turned bad texts over to the printers so that he could realize the maximum profit for revising); that Dodsley's consenting at all to revisions for a fictional text testifies that he had promoted *Pompey* from a minor to a major work; and that thirty pounds, according to Dr. Johnson, could maintain a single man of frugal habits for a year.[2]

The nature of Coventry's revisions, however, militates against the common editorial rule that the last edition published during the author's life (if there is evidence for revision) should ordinarily be taken as the copy-text. The first edition of *Pompey* consisted of two books, the first having fourteen chapters, the second eighteen. In his revision Coventry dropped a number of chapters altogether and added others, the result being two books of eighteen and fifteen chapters respectively.

[1] Printed with the permission of the Trustees of the Houghton Library, Harvard University.

[2] For a general discussion of the economics of minor fiction at the time see R. A. Day, *Told In Letters* (Ann Arbor, Michigan, 1966), ch. IV.

Book I

DROPPED

   X. The Genealogy of a Cat.

ADDED

   X. A matrimonial dispute.

   XI. A stroke at the methodists.

   XVI. The history of a highwayman.

   XVII. Adventures at the *Bath*.

   XVIII. More adventures at *Bath*.

Book II

DROPPED

   I. A Dissertation upon *Nothing*.

   V. Relating the History of a *Milliner*.

   VII. A sad Disaster befalls Sir *Thomas Frippery* in the Night, and a worse in the Day.

   XI. Shewing the ill Effects of Ladies having the Vapours.

   XIV. Another College-Character.

ADDED

   VII. Matrimonial amusements.

   IX. A poetical feast, and squabble of authors.

The dedicatory epistle to Henry Fielding was also added.

When the new chapters were written is impossible to tell. If Coventry wrote the anonymous *Essay on the New Species of Writing founded by Mr. Fielding* (1751) he may thereby have been emboldened to add the dedicatory essay to Fielding; his satire of the Methodists may have been motivated by his new status as perpetual curate of Edgware and a desire to appear zealous in the defence of the Established Church. But it is equally possible that the added chapters were written earlier and withheld from the first edition from considerations of space. The 'Dissertation on Nothing', which could be seen as partly plagiarized from Fielding's essay on nothing in his *Miscellanies* (1743), and the character of the old doctor at Cambridge, were perhaps withdrawn lest they prove offensive. The adventures of Sir Thomas Frippery are mildly bawdy, but no less so than some of the new material. And in conclusion, it is entirely possible that Coventry undertook the revision largely for money, that he had to produce a new book of approximately the same size as the old one, and that, not wishing to sacrifice his new chapters, he merely discarded such of the old as he felt had least merit.

Unfortunately the modern reader is apt to feel that the third edition is not an improvement on the first. The new chapters are entertaining and lively, but no more so than the missing ones; the style has not been bettered. In adding his new chapters Coventry inserted a few bridging passages and made the smallest possible number of slight modifications in the text needed to accommodate the new material; he also, in fewer than one hundred places, mostly in the first book, made small changes in wording. But, like Richardson before him,[1] he was not happy in his second thoughts. The style of the first edition is on the whole lively and crisp; the altered passages are nearly all more abstract, over-concerned with avoiding 'low' expressions, unfunnily inflated or pompous, and in some cases where Coventry is clearly trying to parody the orotund period of rhetoric he succeeds merely in giving an imitation of it.

For these reasons (and the even more cogent one that editorial procedures developed for masterpieces are not necessarily relevant to minor literature) the present text represents a departure from the usual editorial method; it is a 'practical' edition. The text of the first edition has been retained, but the new chapters from the third have been added at the points where the author placed them. A very few brief passages from the first edition have

---

[1] See M. Kinkead-Weekes, 'Clarissa Restored?' *Review of English Studies*, x (1959), 156–71.

necessarily been deleted as therefore resulting in re-
dundancy; these deletions are indicated by full points
within brackets. A scene from the first edition has been
relegated to an appendix. A few passages and chapters
from the third edition have been incorporated into the
text as representing substantial improvement in content;
these passages are enclosed within brackets, as are the
titles of the chapters inserted entire from the third
edition.

The text is printed from the British Museum copies
of the first and third editions. It is unmodified, with the
following exceptions: the long 's' has been eliminated,
as have the running inverted commas in the left margin
indicating dialogue; obvious misprints, and a few eccentric
spellings which would confuse the reader, have been
silently corrected.

SELECT BIBLIOGRAPHY

───────────

Pompey the Little was first published in London in January or early February, 1751, and in the same year by George Faulkner in Dublin (presumably pirated). The 'second edition' of 1751 is merely an issue, and either consisted of sheets of the first with a new title-page, or was printed from the undistributed type set for the first. The revised third edition appeared in 1752, and in 1753 there was a Dublin edition, called the fourth, again printed by Faulkner. Dodsley's fourth edition appeared in 1761, the fifth in 1773, and others in 1785, 1799, 1800, 1810, and 1824. (*Pompey* was included in the *Novelist's Magazine* [1785] and in Mrs. Barbauld's *British Novelists* in 1810.) A limited edition from the Golden Cockerel Press (a reprint of the fourth edition), with an introduction by Arundell del Re, appeared in 1926.

A French version of *Pompey*, *La Vie et les avantures du petit Pompée . . . traduit de l'anglois par M. Toussaint*, appeared in two volumes in 1752. In 1784, J. H. D. Briel produced a *Histoire du petit Pompée . . . imité de l'anglois*. An Italian version, perhaps by Gasparo Gozzi, was published in 1760 with the title *Avventure di Lillo cagnuolo Bolognese . . . tradotta dall'inglese*. And numerous works evidently derived from *Pompey* are listed in the various bibliographies of eighteenth-century European fiction.

BIBLIOGRAPHY. See the section 'Minor Fiction' in the *New Cambridge Bibliography of English Literature*, ii (1971) for English works in the tradition of *Pompey*; a more specialized listing is in Richard K. Meeker, 'Bank Note, Corkscrew, Flea and

Sedan: A Checklist of Eighteenth-Century Fiction', *The Library Chronicle* (University of Pennsylvania), Winter-Spring 1969.

CRITICISM. There is no extended critical discussion of *Pompey the Little*, though it is briefly mentioned in George Saintsbury's *The English Novel* (1913) p. 145, J. M. S. Tompkins, *The Popular Novel in England, 1770–1800* (1932) p. 49, Sir Walter Raleigh, *The English Novel* (1903) p. 192, and Ernest A. Baker's *History of the English Novel* (1934) v, 53–4. The reader is referred to Arundell del Re's introduction to the Golden Cockerel Press edition (1926); the Augustan Reprint Society's facsimile of *An Essay on the New Species of Writing founded by Mr. Fielding* (No. 95, 1962, ed. A. D. McKillop), which is attributed to Coventry; the extracts from this reprinted in *Henry Fielding: The Critical Heritage* (1969, ed. Ronald Paulson and Thomas Lockwood). Two brief articles dealing with *Pompey* have recently appeared: Toby A. Olshin, '*Pompey the Little*: A Study in Fielding's Influence', *Revue des langues vivantes*, xxxvi (1970), 117–24; William Scott, 'Francis Coventry's "Pompey the Little", 1751 and 1752,' *Notes & Queries*, n. s. xv (1968), 215–19.

A CHRONOLOGY OF FRANCIS COVENTRY

BIOGRAPHICAL NOTE

Whatever promise *Pompey* might augur for its author was
not fulfilled, for Coventry died young. Although the

materials for his life are extremely scanty, much of the information in print being inaccurate, a rudimentary biography can be pieced together from various sources, as follows.[1]

William Francis Walter Coventry belonged to a family which had given London a Lord Mayor in the fifteenth century, Charles I a Lord Keeper, Charles II a secretary of state and a member of the Privy Council, and William III a Lord Privy Seal in the person of the celebrated George Savile, Marquess of Halifax. They also belonged to that group of merchants become landed gentry and Court bureaucrats which had given rise to such figures as James Brydges, the princely Duke of Chandos. Coventry's father, Thomas, described as 'a Turkey merchant', and therefore as a member of the powerful Levant Company no doubt enjoying the opulent ease of a Walter Shandy, was the younger brother of William, fifth earl of Coventry, who succeeded to the title in 1719 on the death of the fourth Earl (of another branch of the family) without an heir. Thomas married Mary Green, heiress of the manor of Mill End, in the Desborough hundred of Buckinghamshire, by whom he had a son, Thomas (later an M.P.), and a daughter, Mary. On her death he married Gratia (Grace?)-Anna-Maria, daughter of the Rev. Thomas Brown, of Polston, Wilts.,

---

[1] The entries in the *Dictionary of National Biography*, Venn's *Alumni Cantabrigienses*, Collins's *Complete Peerage*, and Nichols's *Literary Anecdotes*, all of which are inaccurate in most particulars, have been corrected and supplemented from the following original documents: parish records of Hambleden, Buckinghamshire; matriculation register of Magdalene College, Cambridge; a manuscript volume containing the earliest records of the Cambridge Tripos (Cambridge University Library, shelfmark Exam. L. 4; records of election to fellowships, Magdalene College, Cambridge; parish records of Edgware, Middlesex; the wills of Francis Coventry and his cousin Henry (transcripts in the Public Record Office); a manuscript history of the parish of Edgware containing transcripts of parish records, compiled by Mr. Harold G. Geikie and deposited in the public library at Burnt Oak; parish records of Little Stanmore.

by whom he had two sons, Francis and George, and three daughters. Francis was born on or about 15 July 1725, at Mill End, and was baptized on 18 July at the parish church of Hambleden. It may be assumed from the family's position that he was educated at home by tutors. From 1742 to 1744 he was at Eton (having entered as a considerably older boy than was usual); here he seems to have formed a friendship with Wilmot Vaughan, the future earl of Lisburne, to whom he later addressed a poetical epistle that was published post-humously in the fourth volume of Dodsley's Miscellany.[1] On 7 March 1746, he was admitted as a pensioner at Magdalene College, Cambridge; while there he wrote a comedy as we have seen, and may have written all or part of *Pompey the Little*. He must also have pursued his studies to good effect, however, for when he proceeded B.A. *in Comitiis Prioribus* (a degree ceremony for the most distinguished candidates) on 9 February 1749, he was designated second wrangler, there being twenty-two Senior Optimes, as is recorded in the first extant list preserved in the earliest Cambridge Tripos book. Since his cousin Henry had been made a Fellow of Magdalene in 1730 and would therefore have been in regular residence, Coventry's undergraduate career must have been smooth-ed by his being taken under his cousin's wing; and he knew Gray well enough to show him his comedy. In 1750 his poem *Penshurst* was brought out by Dodsley. It is a flat and cliché-ridden piece in two hundred-odd octo-syllabic couplets, in the topographical-descriptive-medi-tative tradition of Ben Jonson's *Penshurst* and Marvell's *Upon Appleton-House*, but more clearly influenced by Dyer's *Grongar Hill* and similar topographical poems of the mid-eighteenth century; it also borrows from Milton's *Il Penseroso*. This 'tour of house and garden', in the words

[1] A copy in the British Museum, owned by Horace Walpole, contains his MS identification of Vaughan (p. 61).

of a modern critic, 'shows the formula [of the *genius loci*] in its explicit form.'[1] But it clearly testifies to the young man's social connections by speaking of happy days at Penshurst in the company of its dedicatees, his relatives William Perry and the Hon. Elizabeth Perry, heiress of the estate and of the famous Sidney family. Coventry may have been ordained in 1749 or 1750; at any rate, as the parish registers show, in 1751 he was established as the perpetual curate (the term has now been replaced by 'vicar') of the parish of Edgware, not far from his birthplace. He was presented to the living by 'his relative the Earl of Coventry'. But his duties were not burdensome (the parish register shows a total of twenty-five baptisms, marriages, and burials in 1751), and he had plenty of time for literary and social activities. *Pompey the Little* was announced in the *General Advertiser* for 12 February 1751, and in the same year was published *An Essay on the New Species of Writing founded by Mr. Fielding*, which has been ascribed to Coventry. During 1751 he revised *Pompey the Little*, finishing it by November, and in 1752 the third edition appeared. In the same year Coventry received his M.A. from Cambridge, and on 25 March he made his will, bequeathing his entire possessions to his sister Anne. On 29 December 1752, his cousin Henry Coventry died, having left to Francis his gold watch, his gold sleeve-buttons, and the copyright to his unfinished *Philemon to Hydaspes*, a lengthy work in dialogue form dealing with the various errors of the pagan religions. The dialogues had appeared separately between 1736 and 1744, and William (later Bishop) Warburton had accused Henry of plagiarism in the fourth of them.[2] Whether from a sense of family duty or a desire to enhance his reputation for literature and orthodoxy, Francis published the collected dialogues in

[1] Geoffrey H. Hartman, *Beyond Formalism* (New Haven and London, 1970), p. 326.

[2] See Nichols, *Literary Anecdotes*, v. 564–9.

one volume in 1753, with a dedication to his cousin George William, who had succeeded to the title in 1751 as sixth earl and had married the famous beauty Maria Gunning the next year. In his dedication Coventry defends Henry's religious views, declaring the dialogues free from any taint of Shaftesburian freethinking, for which they had recently been attacked. The year 1753 also saw the publication in *The World*, a journal with Dodsley as publisher and Chesterfield as patron (his ill-fated essays on Johnson's Dictionary appeared in it), of an essay by Coventry on taste in gardening.[1] It is liberally sprinkled either with quotations or plagiarisms from Pope's *Epistle to Burlington*, and like it advocates the informality of the *jardin anglais*. (At the time the famous 'Capability' Brown was redesigning the Earl of Coventry's seat at Croome.) This closes the list of Coventry's works; but for a man of twenty-eight he had made no mean beginning. The last fact of his career is an entry in the parish register of St. Lawrence's Church, Little Stanmore, formerly the site of Cannons, the palatial villa of the Duke of Chandos, a few miles from his parish:

1754 January 9th. The Rev^d Mr. Francis Coventree (Vicar of Edgware in the County of Middlesex) was buried in the vault under the Communion Table on the east side, the foot of the coffin next the hole that drains the vault, upon two oaken trussels.

Coventry is said to have died of smallpox.[2] There is no stone or memorial tablet either at Little Stanmore or at Edgware.

---

[1] No. xv (12 April 1753), pp. 85–90. Horace Walpole may have provided the essay's impetus by some remarks in No. vi; Coventry refers to a forthcoming treatise by Hogarth which will contain the famous 'line of beauty', an S-curve. (*The Analysis of Beauty* appeared later in the year.)

[2] *Gentleman's Magazine*, xlvi (1776), 64.

THE
HISTORY
OF
Pompey the Little :
OR, THE
LIFE and ADVENTURES
OF A
LAP-DOG

—gressumque Canes comitantur herilem.

VIR. Æn.[1]

——mutato nomine de te
Fabula narratur.

HOR.[2]

TO

Henry Fielding, Esq ;

SIR,

M Y DESIGN BEING to speak a word or two in behalf of novel-writing, I know not to whom I can address myself with so much propriety as to yourself, who unquestionably stand foremost in this species of composition.

To convey instruction in a pleasant manner, and mix entertainment with it, is certainly a commendable undertaking, perhaps more likely to be attended with success than graver precepts; and even where amusement is the chief thing consulted, there is some little merit in making people laugh, when it is done without giving offence to religion, or virtue, or good manners. If the laugh be not raised at the expence of innocence or decency, good humour bids us indulge it, and we cannot well laugh too often.

CAN one help wondering therefore at the contempt, with which many people affect to talk of this sort of composition? they seem to think it degrades the dignity of their understandings, to be found with a novel in their hands, and take great pains to let you know that they never read them. They are people of too great importance, it seems, to misspend their time in so idle a manner, and much too wise to be amused.

Now, tho' many reasons may be given for this ridiculous and affected disdain, I believe a very principal one, is the pride and pedantry of learned men, who are willing to monopolize reading to themselves, and therefore fastidiously decry all books that are on a level with common understandings, as empty, trifling and impertinent.

THUS the grave metaphysician for example, who after working night and day perhaps for several years, sends forth at last a profound treatise, where *A.* and *B.* seem to contain some very deep mysterious meaning; grows indignant to think that every little paltry scribbler, who paints only the characters of the age, the manners of the times, and the working of the passions, should presume to equal him in glory.

THE politician too, who shakes his head in coffee-houses, and produces now and then, from his fund of observations, a grave, sober, political pamphlet on the good of the nation; looks down with contempt on all such idle compositions, as lives and romances, which contain no strokes of satire at the ministry, no unmannerly reflections upon *Hannover*, nor any thing concerning the balance of power on the continent. These gentlemen and their readers join all to a man in depreciating works of humour: or if they ever vouchsafe to speak in their praise, the commendation never rises higher than, 'yes, 'tis well enough for such a sort of a thing;' after which the grave observator retires to his news-paper, and there, according to the general estimation, employs his time *to the best advantage*.

BUT besides these, there is another set, who never read any modern books at all. They, wise men, are so deep in the learned languages, that they can pay no regard to what has been published within these last thousand years. The world is grown old; men's geniuses are degenerated; the writers of this age are too contemptible for their notice, and they have no hopes of any better to succeed them. Yet these gentlemen of profound erudition will contentedly read any trash, that is disguised in a learned language, and the worst ribaldry of *Aristophanes*, shall be critiqued and commented on by men, who turn up their noses at *Gulliver* or *Joseph Andrews*.

BUT if this contempt for books of amusement be carried a little too far, as I suspect it is, even among men of science and learning, what shall be said to some of the greatest triflers of the times, who affect to talk the same language? these surely have no right to express any disdain of what is at least equal to their understandings. Scholars and men of learning have a reason to give; their application to severe studies may have destroyed their relish for works of a lighter cast, and consequently it cannot be expected that they should approve what they do not understand. But as for beaux, rakes, petit-maitres and fine ladies, whose lives are spent in doing the things which novels record, I do not see why they should be indulged in affecting a contempt of them. People, whose most earnest business is to dress and play at cards, are not so importantly employed, but that they may find leisure now and then to read a novel. Yet these are as forward as any to despise them; and I once heard a very fine lady, condemning some highly finished conversations in one of your works, sir, for this curious reason—'because,' said she, ''tis such sort of stuff as passes every day between me and my own maid.'

I DO not pretend to apply any thing here said in behalf of books of amusement, to the following little work, of which I ask your patronage: I am sensible how very imperfect it is in all its parts, and how unworthy to be ranked in that class of writings, which I am now defending. But I desire to be understood in general, or more particularly with an eye to your works, which I take to be master-pieces and complete models in their kind. They are, I think, worthy the attention of the greatest and wisest men, and if any body is ashamed of reading them, or can read them without entertainment and instruction, I heartily pity their understandings.

THE late editor of Mr. *Pope*'s works, in a very ingenious note, wherein he traces the progress of romance-writing, justly observes, that this species of composition is now brought to maturity by Mr. *De Marivaux* in *France*, and Mr. *Fielding* in *England*.[1]

I HAVE but one objection to make to this remark, which is, that the name of Mr. *De Marivaux* stands foremost of the two; a superiority I can by no means allow him. Mr. *Marivaux* is indeed a very amiable, elegant, witty and penetrating writer. The reflections he scatters up and down his *Marianne* are highly judicious, *recherchées*, and infinitely agreeable. But not to mention that he never finishes his works,[2] which greatly disappoints his readers, I think, his *characters* fall infinitely short of those we find in the performances of his *English* cotemporary. They are neither so original, so ludicrous, so well distinguished, nor so happily contrasted as your own: and as the characters of a novel principally determine its merit, I must be allowed to esteem my countryman the greater author.

THERE is another celebrated novel writer,[3] of the same kingdom, now living, who in the choice and diversity of his characters, perhaps exceeds his rival Mr. *Marivaux*, and would deserve greater commendation, if the extreme libertinism of his plans, and too wanton drawings of nature, did not take off from the other merit of his works; tho' at the same time it must be confessed, that his genius and knowledge of mankind are very extensive. But with all due respect for the parts of these two able *Frenchmen*, I will venture to say they have their superior, and whoever has read the works of Mr. *Fielding*, cannot be at a loss to determine who that superior is. Few books of this kind have ever been written with a spirit equal to *Joseph Andrews*, and no story that I know of, was ever invented with more happiness, or conducted with more art and management than that of *Tom Jones*.

As to the following little piece, sir, it pretends to a

very small degree of merit. 'Tis the first essay of a young author, and perhaps may be the last. A very hasty and unfinished edition of it was published last winter,[1] which meeting with a more favourable reception than its writer had any reason to expect, he has since been tempted to revise and improve it, in hopes of rendering it a little more worthy of his readers' regard. With these alterations he now begs leave, sir, to desire your acceptance of it; he can hardly hope for your approbation; but whatever be its fate, he is proud in this public manner to declare himself

Your constant reader,

and sincere admirer.

THE HISTORY OF

Pompey the Little.

BOOK I

CHAPTER I

A Panegyric upon Dogs, together with some Observations on modern Novels and Romances.

VARIOUS and wonderful, in all Ages, have been the Actions of Dogs; and if I should set myself to collect, from Poets and Historians, the many Passages that make honourable mention of them, I should compose a Work much too large and voluminous for the Patience of any modern Reader. But as the Politicians of the Age, and Men of Gravity may be apt to censure me for misspending my Time in writing the Adventures of a Lap-dog, when there are so many *modern Heroes*, whose illustrious Actions call loudly for the Pen of an Historian; it will not be amiss to detain the Reader, in the Entrance of this Work, with a short Panegyric on the *canine Race*, to justify my undertaking it.

AND can we, without the basest Ingratitude, think ill of an Animal, that has ever honoured Mankind with his Company and Friendship, from the Beginning of the

World to the present Moment? While all other Creatures
are in a State of Enmity with us, some flying into Woods
and Wildernesses to escape our Tyranny, and others
requiring to be restrained with Bridles and Fences in
close Confinement; Dogs alone enter into voluntary
Friendship with us, and of their own accord make their
Residence among us.

NOR do they trouble us only with officious Fidelity,
and useless Good-will, but take care to earn their Liveli-
hood by many meritorious Services: they guard our
Houses, supply our Tables with Provision, amuse our
leisure Hours, and discover Plots to the Government.[1]
Nay, I have heard of a Dog's making a Syllogism; which
cannot fail to endear him to our two famous Universities,
where his Brother-Logicians are so honoured and distinguished for their Skill in that *useful* Science.

AFTER these extraordinary Instances of Sagacity and
Merit, it may be thought too ludicrous, perhaps, to
mention the Capacity they have often discovered, for
playing at Cards, Fiddling, Dancing, and other polite
Accomplishments; yet I cannot help relating a little
Story, which formerly happened at the Play-house in
Lincolns-Inn-Fields.[2]

THERE was, at that Time, the same Emulation between
the two Houses, as there is at present between the great
Common-wealths of *Drury-Lane* and *Covent-Garden*;[3] each
of them striving to amuse the Town with various Feats
of Activity, when they began to grow tired of Sense, Wit,
and Action. At length, the Managers of the House at
Lincolns-Inn-Fields, possessed with a happy Turn of
Thought, introduced a Dance of Dogs; who were dressed
in *French* Characters, to make the Representation more
ridiculous, and acquitted themselves for several Evenings
to the universal Delight and Improvement of the Town.
But one unfortunate Night, a malicious Wag behind the
Scenes, threw down among them the Leg of a Fowl, which

he had brought thither in his Pocket for that Purpose. Instantly all was in Confusion; the Marquis shook off his Peruke, Mademoiselle dropp'd her Hoop-petticoat, the Fidler threw away his Violin, and all fell to scrambling for the Prize that was thrown among them.—But let us return to graver Matter.

If we look back into ancient History, we shall find the wisest and most celebrated Nations of Antiquity, as it were, contending with one another, which should pay the greatest Honour to Dogs. The old Astronomers denominated Stars after their Name; and the *Egyptians* in particular, a sapient and venerable People, worshipped a Dog[1] among the principal of their Divinities. The Poets represent *Diana*, as spending great Part of her Life among a Pack of Hounds, which I mention for the Honour of the Country Gentlemen of *Great Britain*; and we know that the illustrious *Theseus* dedicated much of his Time to the same Companions.[2]

Julius Pollux[3] informs us, that the Art of dying purple and scarlet Cloth was first found out by *Hercules*'s Dog, who roving along the Sea-coast, and accidentally eating of the Fish *Murex*, or *Purpura*, his lips became tinged with that Colour; from whence the *Tyrians* first took the Hint of the purple Manufacture, and to this lucky Event our fine Gentlemen of the Army are indebted for the scarlet, with which they subdue the Hearts of so many fair Ladies.

But nothing can give us a more exalted Idea of these illustrious Animals, than to consider, that formerly, in old *Greece*, they founded a Sect of Philosophy; the Members whereof took the Name of *Cynics*, and were gloriously ambitious of assimilating themselves to the Manners and Behaviour of that Animal, from whom they derived their Title.

And that the Ladies of *Greece* had as great a Fondness for them as the Men, may be collected from the Story

which *Lucian* relates[1] of a certain Philosopher; who in
the Excess of his Complaisance to a Woman of Fashion,
on whom he depended for Support, took up her *favourite
Lap-Dog* one Day, and attempted to caress and kiss it;
but the little Creature, not being used to the rude Gripe
of philosophic Hands, found his Loins affected in such
a manner, that he was obliged to water the Sage's Beard,
as he held him to his Mouth; which so discomposed that
principal, if not only Seat of his Wisdom, as excited
Laughter in all the Beholders.

SUCH was the Reverence paid to them among the
Nations of Antiquity; and if we descend to later Times,
we shall not want Examples in our own Days and Nation,
of great Men's devoting themselves to Dogs. King *Charles*
the Second, of pious and immortal Memory, came always
to the Council-board accompanied with a favourite
Spaniel; who propagated his Breed, and *scattered his
Image through the Land*,[2] almost as extensively as his Royal
Master. His Successor, King *James*, of pious and immortal
Memory likewise, was distinguished for the same Attachment to these four-footed Worthies; and 'tis reported of
him, that being once in a dangerous Storm at Sea, and
obliged to quit the Ship for his Life, he roar'd aloud with
a most vehement Voice, as his principal Concern, *to save
the Dogs* [and colonel *Churchill*].[3] But why need we
multiply Examples? The greatest Heroes and Beauties
have not been ashamed to erect Monuments to them in
their Gardens, nor the greatest Wits and Poets to write
their Epitaphs.[4] Bishops have intrusted them with their
Secrets, and Prime-Ministers deigned to receive Information from them, when Treason and Conspiracies were
hatching against the Government.[5] Islands likewise,[6] as
well as Stars, have been called after their Names; so that
I hope no one will dare to think me idly employed in
composing the following Work: or if any should, let him
own himself ignorant of ancient and modern History, let

him confess himself an Enemy to his Country, and ungrateful to the Benefactors of *Great Britain*.

AND as no Exception can reasonably be taken against the Dignity of my Hero, much less can I expect any will arise against the Nature of this Work, which one of my Cotemporaries declares to be an *Epic Poem in Prose*;[1] and I cannot help promising myself some Encouragement, in this *Life-writing Age* especially, where no Character is thought too inconsiderable to engage the public Notice, or too abandoned to be set up as a Pattern of Imitation. The lowest and most contemptible Vagrants, Parish-Girls, Chamber-Maids, Pick-Pockets, and Highwaymen, find Historians to record their Praises, and Readers to wonder at their Exploits: Star-Gazers, superannuated Strumpets, quarrelling Lovers, all think themselves authorized to appeal to the Publick, and to *write Apologies* for their Lives. Even the Prisons and Stews are ransacked to find Materials for Novels and Romances. [Thus we have seen the memoirs of a lady of pleasure, and the memoirs of a lady of quality; both written with the same public-spirited aim, of initiating the unexperienced part of the female sex into the hidden mysteries of love; only that the former work has rather a greater air of chastity, if possible, than the latter.][2] Thus, I am told, that illustrious *Mimic* Mr. *F—t*, when all other Expedients fail him, and he shall be no longer able to raise a Kind of Tax, if I may so call it, from Tea, Coffee, Chocolate, and Marriages,[3] designs, as the last Effort of his Wit, to oblige the World with an accurate History of his own Life; with which View one may suppose he takes care to chequer it with so many extraordinary Occurrences, and selects such Adventures as will best serve hereafter to amaze and astonish his Readers.

THIS then being the Case, I hope the very Superiority of the Character here treated of, above the Heroes of common Romances, will procure it a favourable Reception, altho' perhaps I may fall short of my great Cotemporaries in the Elegance of Style, and Graces of Language. For when such Multitudes of Lives are daily offered to the Publick, written *by the saddest Dogs*, or *of the saddest Dogs* of the Times, it may be considered as some little Merit to have chosen a Subject worthy the Dignity of History; and in this single View I may be allowed to paragon myself with the incomparable Writer of the Life of *Cicero*,[1] in that I have deserted the beaten Track of Biographers, and chosen a Subject worthy the Attention of polite and classical Readers.

HAVING detained the Reader with this little necessary Introduction, I now proceed to open the Birth and Parentage of my Hero.

CHAPTER II

The Birth, Parentage, Education, and Travels of a Lap-Dog.

POMPEY, the Son of *Julio* and *Phyllis*, was born A. D. 1735 at *Bologna* in *Italy*, a Place famous for Lap-Dogs and Sausages. Both his Parents were of the most illustrious Families, descended from a long Train of Ancestors, who had figured in many Parts of Europe, and lived in Intimacy with the greatest Men of the Times. They had frequented the Chambers of the proudest Beauties, and had Access to the Closets of the greatest Princes; Cardinals, Kings, Popes, and Emperors were all happy in their Acquaintance; and I am told the elder Branch of the Family now lives with his present Holiness in the papal Palace at *Rome*.

BUT *Julio*, the Father of my Hero, being a younger Brother of a numerous Family, fell to the Share of an *Italian* Nobleman at *Bologna*; from whom I heard a Story of him, redounding so much to his Credit, that it would be an Injury to his Memory not to relate it; especially as it is the Duty of an Historian to derive his Hero from honourable Ancestors, and to introduce him into the World with all the Eclat and Renown he can.

I T seems the City of *Bologna* being greatly over-stocked with Dogs, the Inhabitants of the Place are obliged at certain Seasons of the Year to scatter poisoned Sausages up and down the Streets for their Destruction; by which Means the Multitude of them is reduced to a more tolerable Number. Now *Julio* having got abroad one Morning by the Carelessness of Servants into the Streets, was unwisely tempted to eat of these pernicious Cates;[1] which immediately threw him into a violent Fit of Illness: But being seasonably relieved with Emetics, and having a good Constitution, he struggled thro' the Distemper; and ever afterwards remembering what himself had escaped, out of Pity to his Brethren, who might possibly undergo the same Fate, he was observed to employ himself during the whole Sausage-Season, in carrying these poisonous Baits away one by one in his Mouth, and throwing them into the River that runs by the City. But to return.

T HE *Italian* Nobleman above-mentioned had an Intrigue with a celebrated Courtesan of *Bologna*, and little *Julio* often attending him when he made his Visits to her, (as it is the Nature of all Servants to imitate the Vices of their Masters,) he also commenced an Affair of Gallantry with a Favourite little Bitch named *Phyllis*, at that Time the Darling of this *Fille de Joye*. For a long while she rejected his Courtship with Disdain, and received him with that Coyness, which Beauties of her Sex know very well how to counterfeit; but at length in a little Closet devoted to *Venus*, the happy Lover accomplished his Desires, and *Phyllis* soon gave Signs of Pregnancy.

I HAVE not been able to learn whether my Hero was

introduced into the World with any Prodigies preceding
his Birth; and tho' the Practice of most Historians might
authorize me to invent them, I think it most ingenuous
to confess, as well as most probable to conclude, that
Nature did not put herself to any miraculous Expence
on this Occasion. Miracles are unquestionably ceased
in this Century, whatever they might be in some former
ones; there needs no Dr. *Middleton* to convince us of
this; and I scarce think Dr. *Ch——n*[1] himself would have
the Hardiness to support me, if I should venture to relate
one in the present Age.

BE it sufficient then to say, that on the 25th of May
N. S.[2] 1735, *Pompey* made his first Appearance in the
World at *Bologna*; on which Day, as far as I can learn,
the Sun shone just as usual, and Nature wore exactly the
same Aspect as upon any other Day in the Year.

ABOUT this Time an *English* Gentleman, who was
making the Tour of *Europe*, to enrich himself in foreign
Manners and foreign Cloaths, happened to be residing
at *Bologna*. And as one great End of modern Travelling
is the Pleasure of intriguing with Women of all Nations
and Languages, he was introduced to visit the Lady
above-mentioned, who was at that Time the fashionable
and foremost Courtesan of the Place. Little *Pompey*
having now opened his Eyes and learnt the Use of his
Legs, was admitted to frolic about the Room, as his
Mistress sat at her Toilet or presided at her Tea-Table.
On these Occasions her Gallants never failed to play
with him, and many pretty Dialogues often arose concerning him which perhaps might make a Figure in a
modern Comedy. Every one had something to say to
the little Favourite, who seemed proud to be taken Notice
of, and by many significant Gestures would often make
believe he understood the Compliments that were paid
him.

BUT nobody distinguished himself more on this

Subject than our *English Hillario*; who had now made a considerable Progress in the Affections of his Mistress: For partly the Recommendation of his Person, but chiefly the Profusion of his Expences made her think him a very desireable Lover; and as she saw that his ruling Passion was Vanity, she was too good a Dissembler, and too much a Mistress of her Trade, not to flatter this Weakness for her own Ends. This so elated the Spirits of *Hillario*, that he surveyed himself every Day with Increase of Pleasure at his Glass, and took a Pride on all Occasions to shew how much he was distinguished, as he thought, above any of her antient Admirers. Resolving therefore to out-do them all as much in Magnificence, as he imagined he did in the Success of his Love, he was continually making her the most costly Presents, and among other Things, presented Master *Pompey* with a Collar studded with Diamonds. This so tickled the little Animal's Vanity, being the first Ornament he had ever worn, that he would eat Biscuit from *Hillario*'s Hands with twice the Pleasure, with which he received it from any other Person's; and *Hillario* made him the Occasion of conveying indirect Compliments to his Mistress. Sometimes he would swear, *he believed it was in her Power to impart Beauty to her very Dogs*, and when she smiled at the Staleness of the Conceit,[1] he, imagining her charmed with his Wit, would grow transported with Gaiety, and practise all the fashionable Airs that Custom prescribes to an Intrigue.

BUT the Time came at length that this gay Gentleman was to quit this Scene of his Pleasures, and go in quest of Adventures in some other Part of *Italy*. Nothing delayed him but the Fear of breaking his Mistress's Heart, which his own great Love of himself, joined with the seeming Love she expressed for him, made him think a very likely Consequence. The Point therefore was to reveal his Intentions to her in the most tender Manner, and to

reconcile her to this terrible Event as well as he could.
They had been dining together one Day in her Apartments, and *Hillario* after Dinner, first inspiring himself
with a Glass of Tokay, began to curse his Stars for obliging
him to leave *Bologna*, where he had been so divinely
happy; but he said, he had received News of his Father's
Death, and was obliged to go to settle *cursed Accounts*
with his Mother and Sisters, who were in a Hurry for
their *confounded Fortunes*; and after many other Flourishes,
concluded his Rhapsody with requesting to take little
Pompey with him as a Memorial of their Love. The Lady
received this News with all the artificial Astonishment
and counterfeited Sorrow that Ladies of her Profession
can assume whenever they please; in short she played
the Farce of Passions so well, that *Hillario* thought her
very Life depended on his Presence: She wept, intreated,
threatened, swore, but all to no Purpose; at length she
was obliged to submit on Condition that *Hillario* should
give her a Gold-watch in Exchange for her Favourite
Dog, which he consented to without any Hesitation.

THE Day was now fixed for his Departure, and having
ordered his Post-Chaise to wait at her Door, he went in
the Morning to take his last Farewell. He found her at
her Tea-Table ready to receive him, and little *Pompey*
sitting innocently on the Settee by his Mistress's Side,
not once suspecting what was about to happen to him,
and far from thinking himself on the Point of so long a
Journey. For neither Dogs nor Men can look into Futurity,
or penetrate the Designs of Fate. Nay, I have been told
that he eat his Breakfast that Morning with more than
usual Tranquillity; and tho' his Mistress continued to
caress him, and lament his Departure, he neither understood the Meaning of her kisses, nor greatly returned her
Affection. At length the accomplished *Hillario* taking out
his Watch, and cursing Time for intruding on his Pleasures,
signified he must be gone that Moment. Ravishing

therefore an hundred Kisses from his Mistress, and taking up little *Pompey* in his Arms, he went off humming an *Italian* Tune, and with an Air of affected Concern threw himself carelessly into his Chaise. From whence looking up with a melancholy Shrug to her Window, and shewing the little Favourite to his forsaken Mistress, he was interrupted by the Voice of the Postilion, desiring to be informed of the Route he was to take; which little Particular this well-bred Gentleman had in his Hurry forgot, as thinking it perhaps of no great Consequence. But now cursing the Fellow for not knowing his Mind without putting him to the Trouble of explaining it, *Damn you*, cries he, *drive to the Devil if you will, for I shall never be happy again as long as I breathe*. Recollecting himself upon second Thoughts, and thinking it as well to defer that Journey to some future Opportunity, he gave his Orders for ——; and then looking up again at the Window, and bowing, the Post Chaise hurried away, while his Charmer stood laughing and mimicking his Gestures.

As her Affection for him was wholly built on Interest, of course it ended the very Moment she lost sight of his Chaise; and we may conclude his for her had not a much longer Continuance; for notwithstanding the Protestations he made of keeping her Dog for ever in Remembrance of her, little *Pompey* had like to have been left behind in the very first Day's Stage. *Hillario* after Dinner had reposed himself to sleep on a Couch in the Inn; from whence being waked with Information that his Chaise was ready and waited his Pleasure at the Door, he started up, discharged his Bill, and was proceeding on his Journey without once bestowing a Thought on the neglected Favourite. His Servant however, being more considerate, brought him and delivered him at the Chaise Door to his Master; who cried indolently, *Begad that's well thought on*, called him *a little Devil for giving so much*

Trouble, and then drove away with the utmost Unconcernedness. This I mention to shew how very short-lived are the Affections of protesting Lovers.

CHAPTER III

Our Hero arrives in England. *A Conversation between two Ladies concerning his Master.*

B UT as it is not my Design to follow this Gentleman through his Tour, we must be contented to pass over great part of the Puppyhood of little *Pompey*, till the Time of his Arrival at *London*: only it may be of Importance to remember, that in his Passage from *Calais* to *Dover* he was extremely Sea-sick, and twice given over by a Physician on board; but some medicinal Applications, together with a Week's Confinement in his Chamber, after he came to Town, restored him to his perfect Health.

HILLARIO was no sooner landed, than he dispatched his *French* Valet to *London*, with Orders to provide him handsome Lodgings in *Pall Mall*, or some other great Street near the Court; and himself set forwards the next Day with his whole Retinue. Let us therefore imagine him arrived and settled in his new Apartments; let us suppose the News-writers to have performed their Duty, and all the important World of Dress busy, as usual, in reporting from one to another, *that* Hillario *was returned from his Travels*.

As soon as his Chests and Baggage were arrived in Town, his Servants were all employed in setting forth to View in his Anti-chamber, the several valuable Curiosities he had collected; that his Visiters might be detained as they passed through it, in making Observations on the Elegance of his Taste. For tho' Dress and

Gallantry were his principal Ambition, he had con-
descended, in Compliance with the Humour of the Times,
to consult the *Ciceroni* at *Rome*, and other Places, as to
what was proper to be purchased, in order to establish a
Reputation for *Vertù*:[1] and they had furnished him
accordingly, at a proportionable Expence, with all the
necessary Ingredients of modern Taste; that is to say,
with Fingers and Toes of ancient Statues, Medals bearing
the Name of *Roman* Emperors on their Inscriptions, and
copied-original Pictures of all the great Masters and
Schools of *Italy*. They had likewise taught him a Set of
Phrases and Observations proper to be made, whenever
the Conversation should turn upon such Subjects;
which, by the Help of a good Memory, he used with
tolerable Propriety: he could descant in Terms of Art,
on Rusts and Varnishes; and describe the Air, the Manner, the Characteristic of different Painters, in Language
almost as learned as the ingenious Writer of a late Essay.[2]
'Here, he would observe, the Drawing is incorrect; there
the Attitude ungraceful—the *Costume*[3] ill-preserved, the
Contours harsh, the Ordonnance irregular—the Light
too strong—the Shade too deep,'—with many other
affected Remarks, which may be found in a very grave
sententious Book of Morality.

But Dress, as we before observed, was his darling
Vanity, and consequently, his Rooms were more plentifully scattered with Cloaths than any other Curiosity.
There all the Pride of *Paris* was exhibited to View; Suits
of Velvet and Embroidery, Sword-hilts, red-heel'd Shoes,
and Snuff-boxes, lay about in negligent Confusion, yet
all artfully disposed to catch the Eyes of his Female
Visiters. Nor did he appear with less Eclat without
Doors; for he had now shewn his gilt Chariot and bay
Horses in all the Streets of gay Resort, and was allowed
to have the most splendid brilliant Equipage in *London*.
The Club at *White's*[4] soon voted him a Member of their

Fraternity, and there began a kind of Rivalry among the Ladies of Fashion, who should first engage him to their Assemblies. At all Toilettes and Parties in the Morning, who but *Hillario*? At all Drums[1] and Diversions in the Evening, who but *Hillario*? No-body came into the Side-box at a Play-house with so graceful a Negligence; and it was on all Hands confessed, that he had the most accomplished Way of talking Nonsense of any Man of Quality in *London*.

As the fashionable Part of the World are glad of any fresh Topic of Conversation, that will not much fatigue their Understandings; and the Arrival of a new Fop, the Sight of a new Chariot, or the Appearance of a new Fashion, are all Articles of the highest Importance to them; it could not be otherwise, but that the Shew and Figure, which *Hillario* made, must supply all the polite Circles with Matter for Commendation or Censure. As a little Specimen of this kind of Conversations may, per-haps, not be disagreeable, I will beg the Reader's Patience a Moment, to relate what passed on this Subject between *Cleanthe* and *Cleora*, two Ladies of Eminence and Distinction in the Commonwealth of Vanity. The former was a young Lady of about Fifty, who had out-lived many Generations of Beauties, yet still preserved the Airs and Behaviour of Fifteen; the latter a celebrated Toast now in the Meridian of her Charms, and giddy with the Admiration she excited. These two Ladies had been for some Time past engaged in a strict *Female Friendship*, and were now sitting down to Supper at Twelve o' Clock at Night, to talk over the important Follies of the Day. They had play'd at Cards that Evening at four different Assemblies, left their Names each of them at near Twenty Doors, and taken half a Turn round *Ranelagh*,[2] where the youngest had been engaged in a very smart Exchange of Bows, Smiles, and Compliments with *Hillario*. This had been observed by *Cleanthe*, who was at the same

Place, and envied her the many Civilities she received from a Gentleman so splendidly dress'd, whose Embroidery gave a peculiar Poignancy to his Wit. Wherefore at Supper she began to vent her Spite against him, telling *Cleora*, she wondered how she could listen to the Impertinence of such a Coxcomb: 'Surely, said she, 'you cannot admire him; for my Part, I am amazed at People for calling him handsome—do you really think him, my Dear, so agreeable as the Town generally makes him?' *Cleora* hesitating a Moment, replied, 'She did not well know what Beauty was in a Man: To be sure, added she, if one examines his Features one by one, one sees nothing very extraordinary in him; but altogether he has an Air, and a Manner, and a Notion of Things, my Dear—he is lively, and airy, and engaging, and all that—and then his Dresses are quite charming.' 'Yes, said *Cleanthe*, that may be a very good Recommendation of his Taylor, and if one designs to marry a Suit of Velvet, why No body better than *Hillario*—How should you like him for a Husband, *Cleora*?' 'Faith, said *Cleora* smiling, I never once thought seriously upon the Subject in my Life; but surely, my Dear, there is such a thing as Fancy and Taste in Dress; in my Opinion, a Man shews his Parts in nothing more than in the Choice of his Cloaths and Equipage.' 'Why to be sure, said *Cleanthe*, the Man has something of a Notion at Dress, I confess it—yet methinks I could make an Alteration for the better in his Liveries.' Then began a very curious Conversation on Shoulder-knots,[1] and they ran over all the Liveries in Town, commending one, and disliking another, with great Nicety of Judgment. From Shoulder-knots they proceeded to the Colour of Coach-horses, and *Cleanthe*, resolving to dislike *Hillario*'s Equipage, asked her if she did not prefer Greys to Bays? *Cleora* answered in the Negative, and the Clock struck one before they had decided this momentous Question; which was contested with so much Earnestness, that both of them were beginning to grow angry, and to say ill-natured Things, had not a new Topic arisen to divert the Discourse. His Chariot came next under Consideration, and then they returned to speculate his Dress; and when they had fully exhausted all the external Accomplishments of a Husband, they vouchsafed, at last, to come to the Qualities of the Mind. *Cleora* preferred a Man who had travelled; 'Because, said she, he has seen the World, and must be ten thousand times more agreeable and entertaining than a dull home-bred Fellow, who has never improved himself by *seeing Things*:' But *Cleanthe* was of a different Opinion, alledging that this would only give him a greater Conceit of himself, and make him less manageable by a Wife. Then they fell to abusing Matrimony, numbered over the many unhappy Couples of their Acquaintance, and both of them for a Moment resolved to live single: But those Resolutions were soon exploded; 'For though, said *Cleanthe*, 'I should prefer a Friendship with an agreeable Man far beyond marrying him, yet you know, my Dear, *we Girls* are under so many Restraints, that one must wish for a Husband, if it be only for the Privilege of going into public Places, without Protection of a married Woman along with one, to give one Countenance.' *Cleora* rallied the Expression of *we Girls*, which again had like to have bred a Quarrel between them; and soon afterwards happening to say, she should like to dance with *Hillario* at the next Ridotta,[1] *Cleanthe* could not help declaring, that she should be pleased also to have him for a Partner. This stirred up a warmer Altercation than any that had yet arisen, and they contended with such Vehemence for this distant imaginary Happiness, which perhaps might happen to neither of them, that they grew quite unappeaseable, and in the End, departed to Bed with as much Malice and Enmity, as if the one had made an Attempt on the other's Life.

CHAPTER IV

Another Conversation between Hillario *and a celebrated Lady of Quality.*

IF the foregoing Dialogue appears impertinent and foreign to this History, the ensuing one immediately concerns the Hero of it; whose Pardon I beg for having so long neglected to mention his Name. He was now perfectly recovered from the Indisposition hinted at in the Beginning of the preceding Chapter, and pretty well reconciled to the Air of *England*; but as yet he had made few Acquaintances either with Gentlemen of his own or a different Species; being seldom permitted to expatiate beyond the Anti-chamber of *Hillario*'s Lodgings; where his chief Amusement was to stand with his Fore paws up in the Window, and contemplate the Coaches that passed through the Street.

BUT Fortune, who had destined him to a great Variety of Adventures, no sooner observed that he was settled and began to grow established in his new Apartments, than she determined, according to her usual Inconstancy, to beat up his Quarters,[1] and provide him a new Habitation.

AMONG the many Visiters that favour'd *Hillario* with their Company in a Morning, a Lady of Quality, who had buried her Husband, and was thereby at liberty to pursue her own Inclinations, was one Day drinking Chocolate with him. They were engaged in a very interesting Conversation on the *Italian* Opera, which they declared to be the most sublime Entertainment in Life; when on a sudden little *Pompey* came running into the Room, and leapt up into his Master's Lap. Lady *Tempest* (for that was her Name) no sooner saw him, than addressing herself to *Hillario* with the Ease and Familiarity of modern Breeding; '*Hillario*, said she, 'where the devil

did you get that pretty Dog? That Dog, Madam! cries
Hillario, Oh *l'Amour*! thereby hangs a Tale—That Dog,
Madam, once belonged to a Nobleman's Wife in *Italy*,
the finest Creature that ever my Eyes beheld—such a
Shape and such an Air—*O quelle mine! quelle delicatesse!*'
Then ran he into the most extravagant Encomiums of
her Beauty, and after dropping many Hints of an Intrigue,
to awaken Lady *Tempest*'s Curiosity, and make her enquire
into the Particulars of the Story, concluded with desiring
her Ladyship to excuse him from proceeding any farther,
for he thought it the highest Injury to betray a Lady's
Secrets. 'Nay, said Lady *Tempest*, it can do her Reputation
no hurt to tell Tales of her in *England*; and besides,
Hillario, if you acquitted yourself with Spirit and Gallantry
in the Affair, who knows but I shall like you the better
after I have heard your Story?' 'Well, said he, on that
Condition, my dear Countess! I will confess the Truth
——I had an Affair with this Lady, and, I think, none
of my Amours ever afforded me greater Transport: But
the Eyes of a Husband will officiously be prying into
things that do not concern them; her jealous-pated Booby
surprized me one Evening in a little familiar Dalliance,
and sent me a Challenge the next Morning.' 'Bless us!
said Lady *Tempest*, and what became of it?' 'Why, cries
Hillario, I wou'd willingly have washed my Hands of
the Fellow if I could, for I thought it but a silly Business
to hazard one's Life with so ridiculous an Animal; but,
curse the Blockhead, he could not understand Ridicule—
You must know, Madam, I sent him for Answer, with
the greatest Ease imaginable—quite composed as I am
at this Moment—that I had so prodigious a Cold, it
wou'd be imprudent to fight abroad in the open Air; but
if he wou'd have a Fire in his best Apartment, and a
Bottle of *Burgundy* ready for me on the Table after I had
gone thro' the Fatigue of killing him, I was at his Service
as soon as he pleased—meaning, you see, to have turned

the Affair off with a Joke, if the Fellow had been capable
of tasting Ridicule.' 'But that Stratagem, replied Lady
Tempest, I am afraid did not succeed—the Man I doubt
was too dull to apprehend your Raillery.' 'Dull as a
Beetle, Madam, said *Hillario*; the Monster continued
obstinate, and repeated his Challenge.—When therefore
I found nothing else wou'd do, I resolved to meet him
according to his Appointment; and there—in short, not
to trouble your Ladyship with a long, tedious Description
—I ran him through the Body.' Lady *Tempest* burst out
a laughing at this Story, which she most justly concluded
to be a Lie; and after entertaining herself with many
pleasant Remarks upon it, said with a Smile, 'But what
is this to the Dog, *Hillario*?' 'The Dog, Madam! answered
he, O pardon me, I am coming to the Dog immediately.—
Come hither *Pompey*, and listen to your own Story.—This
Dog, Madam, this very little Dog, had at that time the
Honour of waiting on the dear Woman I have been
describing, and as the Noise of my Duel obliged me to
quit *Bologna*, I sent her private Notice of my Intentions,
and begged her by any means to favour me with an
Interview before my Departure. The Monster her
Husband, who then lay on his Death-bed, immured her
so closely, that you may imagine it was very difficult to
gratify my Desires; but Love, immortal Love, gave her
Courage; she sent me a private Key to get Admission into
her Garden, and appointed me an Assignation in an
Orange-Grove at Nine in the Evening. I flew to the dear
Creature's Arms, and after spending an Hour with her
in the bitterest Lamentations, when it grew dangerous
and impossible for me to stay any longer, we knelt down
both of us on the cold Ground, and saluted[1] each other
for the last time on our Knees.——Oh how I cursed
Fortune for separating us! but at length I was obliged
to decamp, and she gave me this Dog, this individual
little Dog, to carry with me as a Memorial of her Love.

The poor, dear, tender Woman died, I hear, within three Weeks after my Departure; but this Dog, this divine little Dog, will I keep everlastingly for her Sake.'

WHEN the Lady had heard him to an End, 'Well, said she, you have really told a very pretty Story, *Hillario*; but as to your Resolutions of keeping the Dog, I swear you shall break them; for I had the Misfortune t'other Day to lose my favourite black Spaniel of the Mange, and I intend you shall give me this little Dog to supply his Place.' 'Not for the Universe, Madam, replied *Hillario*; I should expect to see his dear injured Mistress's Ghost haunting me in my Sleep to Night, if I could be guilty of such an Act of Infidelity to her.' 'Pugh! said the Lady, don't tell me of such ridiculous superstitious Trumpery.—You no more came by the Dog in this manner, *Hillario*, than you will fly to the Moon to Night—but if you did, it does not signify; for I positively must and will take him home with me.' 'Madam, said *Hillario*, this little Dog is sacred to Love! he was born to be the Herald of Love, and there is but one Consideration in Nature than can possibly induce me to part with him.' 'And what is that? said the Lady. 'That, Madam, cries *Hillario*, bowing, is the Honour of visiting him at all Hours in his new Apartments—he must be the Herald of Love wherever he goes, and on these Conditions—if you will now and then admit me of your Retirements, little *Pompey* waits your Acceptance as soon as you please.' 'Well, said the Lady, smiling, you know I am not inexorable, *Hillario*, and if you have a mind to visit your Little Friend at my Ruelle,[1] you'll find him ready to receive you—though, faith, upon second Thoughts, I know not whether I dare admit you or not. You are such a Killer of Husbands, *Hillario*, that 'tis quite terrible to think on; and if mine was not conveniently removed out of the Way, I should have the poor Man sacrificed for his Jealousy.' 'Raillery! Raillery! returned *Hillario*; but as you say, my dear

Countess, your Monster is commodiously out of the way, and therefore we need be under no Apprehensions from that Quarter, for I hardly believe he will rise out of his Grave to interrupt our Amours.'—'Amours! cried the Lady, lifting her Voice, pray what have I said that encourages you to talk of Amours?'—

FROM this time the Conversation began to grow much too loose to be reported in this Work: They congratulated each other on the Felicity of living in an Age, that allows such Indulgence to Women, and gives them leave to break loose from their Husbands, whenever they grow morose and disagreeable, or attempt to interrupt their Pleasures. They laughed at Constancy in Marriage as the most ridiculous thing in Nature, exploded the very Notion of matrimonial Happiness, and were most fashionably pleasant in decrying every thing that is serious, virtuous and religious. From hence they relapsed again into a Discourse on the *Italian* Opera, and thence made a quick Transition to Ladies' Painting. This was no sooner started than *Hillario* begged leave to present her with a Box of *Rouge*, which he had brought with him from *France*, assuring her that the Ladies were arrived at such an Excellency of using it at *Paris*, as to confound all Distinction of Age and Beauty. 'I protest to your Ladyship, continued he, it is impossible at any Distance to distinguish a Woman of Sixty from a Girl of Sixteen; and I have seen an old Dowager in the opposite Box at their Playhouse, make as good a Figure, and look as blooming as the youngest Beauty in the Place. Nothing in Nature is there required to make a Woman handsome but Eyes.——If a Woman has but Eyes, she may be a Beauty whenever she pleases, at the Expence of a Couple of Guineas.—Teeth and Hair and Eye-brows and Complexions are all as cheap as Fans and Gloves and Ribbons.'

WHILE this ingenious Orator was pursuing his

eloquent Harangue on Beauty, Lady *Tempest*, looking at her Watch, declared it was time to be going; for she had seven or eight Visits more to make that Morning, and it was then almost Three in the Afternoon. Little *Pompey*, who had absented himself during great part of the preceding Conversation, as thinking it perhaps above the Reach of his Understanding, was now ordered to be produced; and the Moment he made his Appearance, Lady *Tempest* catching him up in her Arms, was conducted by *Hillario* into her Chair, which stood at the Door waiting her Commands. Little *Pompey* cast up a wishful Eye at the Window above; but the Chairmen were now in Motion, and with three Footmen fore-running his Equipage, he set out in Triumph to his new Apartments.

CHAPTER V

The Character of Lady Tempest, *with some Particulars of her Servants and Family.*

THE sudden Appearance of this Lady, with whom our Hero is now about to take up his Residence, may perhaps excite the Reader's Curiosity to know who she is; and therefore, before we proceed any farther in our History, we shall spend a Page or two in bringing him acquainted with her Character.[1] But let me admonish thee, my gentle Friend, whosoever thou art, that shalt vouchsafe to peruse this little Treatise, not to be too forward in making Applications, or to construe Satire into Libel. For we declare here once for all, that no Character drawn in this Work is intended for any particular Person, but meant to comprehend a great Variety; and therefore, if thy Sagacity discovers Likenesses that were never intended, and Meanings that were never meant, be so good to impute it to thy own Ill-nature, and accuse not the humble Author of these Sheets. Taking this Caution along with thee, candid Reader, we may venture to trust thee with a Character, which otherwise we should be afraid to draw.

LADY *Tempest* then was originally Daughter to a private Gentleman of a moderate Fortune, which she was to share in common with a Brother and two other Sisters; But her Wit and Beauty soon distinguished her among her Acquaintance, and recompensed the Deficiences of Fortune. She was what the Men call *a sprightly jolly Girl*, and the Women *a bold forward Creature*; very chearful in her Conversation, and open in her Behaviour; ready to promote any Party of Pleasure, (for she was a very Rake at Heart)[1] and not displeased now and then to be assistant in a little Mischief. This made her Company courted by Men of all Sorts; among whom her Affability and Spirit, as well as her Beauty, procured her many Admirers. At length she was sollicited in Marriage by a young Lord, famous for nothing but his great Estate, and far her Inferior in Understanding: But the Advantageousness of the Match soon prevailed with her Parents to give their Consent, and the Thoughts of a Title so dazzled her own Eyes, that she had no Leisure to ask herself whether she liked the Man or no that wore it. His Lordship married for the sake of begetting an Heir to his Estate; and married her in particular, because he had heard her toasted as a Beauty by most of his Acquaintance. She, on the contrary, married because she wanted a Husband; and married him, because he could give her a Title and a Coach and Six.

BUT, alas! there is this little Misfortune attending Matrimony, that People cannot live together any Time, without discovering each other's Tempers. Familiarity soon draws aside the Masque, and all that artificial Complaisance and smiling Good-humour, which make so agreeable a Part of Courtship, go off like *April* Blossoms, upon a longer Acquaintance. The Year was scarce ended before her young Ladyship was surprized to find she had married *a Fool*; which little Circumstance her Vanity had concealed from her before Marriage, and the Hurry and Transport she felt in a new Equipage did not suffer her to attend to for the first Half-year afterwards. But now she began to doubt whether she had not made a foolish Bargain for Life, and consulting with some of her Female Intimates about it (several of whom were married) she received such Documents from them, as, I am afraid, did not a little contribute to prepare her for the Steps she afterwards took.

HER Husband too, tho' not very quick of Discernment, had by this Time found out, that his Wife's Spirit and romantic Disposition were inconsistent with his own Gloom; which gave new Clouds to his Temper, and he often cursed himself in secret for marrying her.

THEY soon grew to reveal these Thoughts to one another, both in Words and Actions; they sat down to Meals with Indifference; they went to Bed with In-difference; and the one was always sure to dislike what the other at any Time seemed to approve. Her Ladyship had Recourse to the common Expedient in these Cases, I mean the getting a Female Companion into the House with her, as well to relieve her from the Tediousness of sitting down to Meals alone with her Husband, as chiefly to hear her Complaints, and spirit her up against her Fool and Tyrant; the Names by which she usually spoke of her Lord and Master. When no such Female Companions, or more properly *Toad-eaters*,[1] happened to be present, she chose rather to divert herself with a little favourite Dog, than to murder any of her precious Time in conversing with her Husband. This his Lordship observed, and besides many severe Reflexions and cross Speeches, at length he wreak'd his Vengeance on the little Favourite, and in a Passion put him to Death. This

was an Affair so heinous in the Lady's own Esteem, and
pronounced to be *so barbarous, so shocking, so inhuman* by all
her Acquaintance, that she resolved no longer to keep
any Terms with him, and from this Moment grew
desperate in all her Actions.

FIRST then, she resolved to supply the Place of one
Favourite with a great Number, and immediately procured as many Dogs into the Family as it could well
hold. His Lordship, in return, would order his Servant
to hang two or three of them every Week, and never
failed kicking them down Stairs by Dozens, whenever
they came in his Way. When this and many other
Stratagems had been tried, some with good and some
with bad Success, she came at last to play the great Game
of Female Resentment, and by many Intimations gave
him to mistrust, that a Stranger had invaded his Bed.
Whether this was real, or only an Artifice of Spite, his
Lordship could never discover, and therefore we shall
not indulge the Reader's Curiosity, by letting him into
the Secret; but the bare Apprehension of it so inflamed
his Lordship's Choler, that her Company now became
intolerable to him, and indeed their Meetings were
dreadful to themselves, and terrible to all Beholders.
Their Servants used to stand at the Door to listen to
their Quarrels, and then charitably disperse the Subjects
of them throughout the Town; so that all Companies
now rang of Lord and Lady *Tempest*. But this could not
continue long; for Indifference may sometimes be borne
in a married State, but Indignation and Hatred I believe
never can; and 'tis impossible to say what their Quarrels
might have produced, had not his Lordship very seasonably died, and left his *disconsolate Widow* to bear about
the Mockery of Woe to all public Places for a Year.

SHE now began the World anew on her own Foundation, and set sail down the Stream of Pleasure, without
the Fears of Virginity to check her, or the Influence of a

Husband to controul her. Now she recover'd that
Sprightliness of Conversation and Gaiety of Behaviour,
which had been clouded during the latter Part of her
Cohabitation with her Husband; and was soon cried up
for the greatest Female Wit in *London*. Men of Gallantry,
and all the World of Pleasure, had easy Access to her,
and malicious Fame reports, that she was not over-hard-
hearted to the Sollicitations of Love; but far be it from us
to report any such improbable Scandal. What gives her
a Place in this History is her Fondness for Dogs, which
from her Childhood she loved exceedingly, and was
seldom without a little Favourite to carry about in her
Arms: But from the Moment that her angry Husband
sacrificed one of them to his Resentment, she grew more
passionately fond of them than ever, and now constantly
kept Six or Eight of various Kinds in her House. About
this Time, one of her greatest Favourites had the Misfortune to die of the Mange, as was above commemorated,
and when she saw little *Pompey* at *Hillario*'s Lodgings, she
resolved immediately to bestow the Vacancy upon him,
which that well-bred Gentleman consented to on certain
Conditions, as the Reader has seen in the foregoing
Chapter.

SHE returned Home from her Visit just as the Clock
was striking Four, and after surveying herself a Moment
in the Glass, and a little adjusting her Hair, went directly
to introduce Master *Pompey* to his Companions. These
were an *Italian* Grey-hound, a *Dutch* Pug, two black
Spaniels of King *Charles*'s Breed, a Harlequin Grey-
hound, a spotted *Dane*, and a mouse-colour'd *English*
Bull-dog. They heard their Mistress's Rap at the Door,
and were assembled in the Dining-room, ready to receive
her: But on the Appearance of Master *Pompey*, they set
up a general Bark, perhaps out of Envy; and some of
them treated the little Stranger with rather more Rudeness than was consistent with Dogs of their Education.

However, the Lady soon interposed her Authority, and commanded Silence among them, by ringing a little Bell, which she kept by her for that Purpose. They all obeyed the Signal instantly, and were still in a Moment; upon which she carried little *Pompey* round, and obliged them all to salute their new Acquaintance, at the same Time commanding some of them to ask Pardon for their unpolite Behaviour; which whether they understood or not, must be left to the Reader's Determination. She then summoned a Servant, and ordered a Chicken to be roasted for him; but hearing that Dinner was just ready to be served up, she was pleased to say, he must be contented with what was provided for herself that Day, but gave Orders to the Cook to get ready a Chicken to his own Share against Night.

HER Ladyship now sat down to Table, and *Pompey* was placed at her Elbow, where he received many dainty Bits from her fair Hands, and was caressed by her all Dinner-time, with more than usual Fondness. The Servants winked at one another, while they were waiting, and conveyed many Sneers across the Table with their Looks; all which had the good Luck to escape her Ladyship's Observation. But the Moment they were retired from waiting, they gave Vent to their Thoughts with all the scurrilous Wit and ill-manner'd Raillery, which distinguishes the Conversation of those parti-coloured Gentlemen.[1]

AND first, the Butler out of Livery served up his Remarks to the House-keeper's Table; which consisted of himself, an elderly fat Woman the House-keeper, and my Lady's Maid, a saucy, forward, affected Girl, of about Twenty. Addressing himself to these second-hand Gentlewomen, as soon as they were pleased to sit down to Dinner, he informed them, *that their Family was in-creased, and that his Lady had brought home a new Companion.* Their Curiosity soon led them to desire an Explanation,

and then telling them that this new Companion was a
new Dog, he related minutely and circumstantially all
her Ladyship's Behaviour to him, during the Time of his
Attendance at the Side-board, not forgetting to mention
the Orders of a roasted Chicken for the Gentleman's
Supper. The House-keeper launched out largely on the
Sin and Wickedness of feeding *such Creatures with Christian
Victuals*, declared it was flying in the Face of Heaven,
and wondered how her Lady could admit them into her
Apartment, for she said *they had already spoiled all the
crimson Damask-chairs in the Dining-room.*

BUT my Lady's Maid had a great deal more to say
on this Subject, and as it was her particular Office to
wait on these four-footed Worthies, she complained of
the Hardship done her, with great Volubility of Tongue.
'Then, says she, there's a new Plague come home, is
there? he has got the Mange too, I suppose, and I shall
have him to wash and comb To-morrow Morning. I am
sure I am all over Fleas with tending such nasty poisonous
Vermin, and 'tis a Shame to put a Christian to such
Offices.—I was in Hopes when that little mangy Devil
died t'other Day, we should have had no more of them;
but there is to be no End of them I find, and for my
Part, I wish with all my Heart some-body would poison
'em all—I can't endure to see my Lady let them kiss her,
and lick her Face all over as she does. I am sure I'd see
all the Dogs in *England* at *Jericho*, before I'd suffer such
Poulcat[1] Vermin to lick my Face. Fogh! 'tis enough to
make one sick to see it; and I am sure, if I was a Man,
I'd scorn to kiss a Face that had been licked by a Dog.'

THIS was Part of a Speech made by this delicate,
mincing Comb-brusher, and the rest we shall omit, to
wait upon the inferior Servants, who were now assembled
at Dinner in their common Hall of Gluttony, and exercising
their Talents likewise on the same Subject. *John* the
Footman here reported what Mr. *William* the Butler had

done before in his Department, that their Lady had brought home a new Dog. 'Damn it, cries the Coachman, with a surly brutal Voice, what signifies a new Dog? has she brought home ever a new Man?' which was seconded with a loud Laugh from all the Company. Another swore, that he never knew a Kennel of Dogs kept in a Bed-chamber before; which likewise was applauded with a loud and boisterous Laugh: but as such kind of Wit is too low for the Dignity of this History, tho' much affected by many of my Cotemporaries, I fancy I shall easily have the Reader's Excuse, if I forbear to relate any more of it.

My Design in giving this short Sketch of Kitchen-Humour, is only to convey a Hint to all Masters and Mistresses, if they chuse to receive it, not to be guilty of any Actions, that will expose them to the Ridicule and Contempt of their Servants. For these ungrateful Wretches, tho' receiving ever so many Favours from you, and treated by you in general with the greatest Indulgence, will shew no Mercy to your slightest Failings, but expose and ridicule your Weakness in Ale-houses, Nine-pin-alleys, Gin-shops, Cellars, and every other Place of dirty Rendezvous. The Truth is, the lower Sort of Men-servants are the most insolent, brutal, ungenerous Rascals on the Face of the Earth: they are bred up in Idleness, Drunkenness and Debauchery, and instead of concealing any Faults they observe at home, find a Pleasure in vilifying and mangling the Reputations of their Masters.

CHAPTER VI

Our Hero becomes a Dog of the Town, and shines in High-life.

POMPEY was now grown up to Maturity and Dog's Estate, when he came to live with Lady *Tempest*; who soon ushered him into all the Joys and Vanities of the Town. He quickly became a great Admirer of Mr. *Garrick*'s acting at the Play-house, grew extremely fond of Masquerades, passed his Judgment on Operas, and was allowed to have a very nice and distinguishing Ear for *Italian* Music. Nor did he lie under the Censure which fell on many other well-bred People of a different Species, I mean the Absurdity of admiring what they did not understand; for as he had been born in *Italy*, 'tis probable he was a little acquainted with the Language of his native Country.

As he attended his Mistress to all Routs, Drums, Hurricanes, Hurly-burlys and Earthquakes,[1] he soon established an Acquaintance and Friendship with all the Dogs of Quality, and of course affected a most hearty Contempt for all of inferior Station, whom he would never vouchsafe to play with, or pay them the least Regard. He pretended to know at first Sight, whether a Dog had received a good Education, by his Manner of coming into a Room, and was extremely proud to shew *his Collar at Court*; in which again he resembled certain other Dogs, who are equally vain of their Finery, and happy to be distinguished in their *respective Orders*.[2]

IF he could have spoken, I am persuaded he would have used the Phrases so much in fashion, *Nobody one knows*, *Wretches dropt out of the Moon*, *Creatures sprung from a Dunghil*; by which are signified all those who are not born to a Title, or have not Impudence and Dishonesty enough to run in debt with their Taylors for Laced Cloaths.

AGAIN, had he been to write a Letter from *Bath* or *Tunbridge*, he wou'd have told his Correspondent *there was not a Soul in the Place*, tho' at the same time he knew there were above two Thousand; because perhaps none of the Men wore Stars and Garters, and none of the Women were bold enough to impoverish their Families by playing at the noble and illustrious Game of Brag.[1] As to his own Part, his Lady was at the Expence of a Master, perhaps the great Mr. *H——le*, to teach him to play at Cards; and so forward was his Genius, that in less than three Months he was able to sit down with her Ladyship to Piquet,[2] whenever Sickness or the Vapours confined her to her Chamber.

As he was now become a Dog of the Town, and perfectly well-bred, of course he gave himself up to Intrigue, and had seldom less than two or three Amours on his Hands at a time with *Bitches of the highest Fashion*: In which Circumstances he again lamented the Want of Speech, for by that means he was prevented the Pleasure of boasting of the Favours he received. But his Gallantries were soon divulged by the Consequences of them; and as several very pretty Puppies had been the Offspring of his Loves, it was usual for all the Acquaintance of Lady *Tempest* to solicit and cultivate his Breed. And here I shall beg leave to insert two little *Billets* of a very extraordinary Nature, as a Specimen of what it is that engages the Attention of Ladies of Quality in this refined and accomplished Age. Lady *Tempest* was sitting at her Toillette one Morning, when her Maid brought her the following little Scroll, from another Lady, whose Name [will be seen at the bottom of her Letter.]

Dear Tempest,

MY favourite little *Veny*[3] is at present troubled with certain amorous Infirmities of Nature, and wou'd not be displeased with the Addresses of a Lover. Be so good

therefore to send little *Pompey* by my Servant who brings
this Note, for I fancy it will make a very pretty Breed,
and when the Lovers have transacted their Affairs, he
shall be sent home incontinently. Believe me, dear
Tempest,

Yours affectionately [, RACKET.]

LADY *Tempest*, as soon as she had read this curious
Epistle, called for Pen and Ink, and immediately wrote
the following Answer, which likewise we beg leave to
insert.

Dear [*Racket*,]
INFIRMITIES of Nature we all are subject to, and
therefore I have sent Master *Pompey* to wait upon Miss
Veny, begging the Favour of you to return him as soon as
his Gallantries are over. Consider, my Dear, no modern
Love can, in the Nature of Things, last above three Days,
and therefore I hope to see my little Friend again very
soon.

Your affectionate friend,
TEMPEST.

[In consequence of these letters, our hero was conducted
to Mrs. *Racket*'s house, where he was received with the
civility due to his station in life, and treated on the
footing of a gentleman who came a courting in the family.
Mrs. *Racket* had two daughters, who had greatly improved
their natural relish for pleasure in the warm climate of
a town education, and were extremely solicitous to inform
themselves of all the mysteries of love. These young
ladies no sooner heard of *Pompey*'s arrival, than they went
down stairs into the parlour, and undertook themselves
to introduce him to miss *Veny*: for love so much engrossed
their thoughts, that they could not suffer a lap-dog in
the house to have an amour without their privity. Here,

while they were solacing themselves with innocent
speculation, a young gentleman, who visited on a
familiar footing in the family, was introduced somewhat
abruptly to them. They no sooner found themselves
surprized, than they ran tittering to a corner of the parlour, and hid their faces behind their fans; while their
visiter, not happening to observe the *Hymeneal* rites that
were celebrating, begged to know the cause of their mirth.
This redoubled their diversion, and they burst out afresh
into such immoderate fits of laughter, that the poor man
began to look exceedingly foolish, imagining himself to
be the object of their ridicule. In vain he renewed his
entreaties to be let into the secret of their laughter; the
ladies had not the power of utterance, and he would still
have continued ignorant, had he not accidentally cast his
eye aside, and there beheld master *Pompey* with the most
prevailing sollicitation making love to his four-footed
mistress. This at once satisfied his curiosity, and he was
no longer at a loss to know the reason of that uncommon
joy and rapture which the ladies had expressed.]

THUS was our Hero permitted to indulge himself in
all the Luxuries of Life; but in the midst of these Felicities,
caressed as he was by his Mistress, and courted by her
Visiters, some Misfortunes every now and then fell to
his Share, which served a little to check his Pride in the
midst of Prosperity. He had once a most bloody Battle
with a Cat, in which terrible Rencontre he was very near
losing his Right Eye: at another Time he was frightened
into a Canal by a huge overgrown Turky-cock, and had
like to have been drowned for want of timely Assistance
to relieve him. Besides these unlucky Accidents, he was
persecuted by all the Servants for being a Favourite, and
particularly by the Waiting-gentle-woman abovementioned, who was pleased one Day to run the Comb into
his Back; where two of the Teeth remained infixed, and
his Mistress was obliged to send for a Surgeon to extract

them. But Mrs. *Abigail*[1] had good Reason to repent of her Cruelty, for she was instantly discarded with the greatest Passion, and afterwards refused a Character, when she applied for one to recommend her to a new Service.

YET, notwithstanding these accidental Misfortunes, from which no Condition is free, he may be said to have led a Life of great Happiness with Lady *Tempest*. He fed upon Chicken, Partridges, Wildfowl, Ragouts, Fricassees, and all the Rarities in Season; which so pampered him up with luxurious Notions, as made some future Scenes of Life the more grievous to him, when Fortune obliged him to undergo the Hardships that will hereafter be recorded.

CHAPTER VII

[*Relating a curious dispute on the immortality of the soul, in which the name of our hero will but once be mentioned.*]

NOTHING is more common on the stage, than to suspend the curiosity of an audience in the most interesting scenes of a play, and *relieve* them (as it is called) with a dance of ghosts, or devils, or furies, or other outlandish beings. In imitation of this laudable custom, before the reader proceeds any farther in *Pompey*'s history, he is desired to relieve himself with a curious dispute on the immortality of the soul, which passed one day in our hero's presence.

LADY *Tempest*, about this time, being indisposed with some trifling disorder, kept her chamber, and was attended by two physicians. These gentlemen were now making their morning visit, and had just gone through the examinations, which custom immemorial prescribes— as, 'how did your ladyship sleep last night?—do you find

any drowth,[1] madam?—pray let me look at your ladyship's tongue,' and many other questions which I have
not leisure now to record; when on a sudden, a violent
rap at the door, and shortly afterwards the appearance
of a visiter interrupted their proceedings. The lady, who
now arrived, came directly up to lady *Tempest*, and made
her compliments; then being desired to sit down, she
fell into some common chit-chat on the news of the town;
in the midst of which, without any thing preparatory to
such a subject, addressing herself on a sudden to one of
the physicians, with a face of infinite significance and
erudition, she asked him, 'if he believed in the immortality of the soul?'—but before we answer this extraordinary question, or relate the conversation that ensued
upon it, it will be for the reader's ease to receive a short
sketch of her character.

IN many respects this lady was in similar circumstances
with lady *Tempest*; only with this difference, that the one
had been separated from her husband by his death, the
other divorced from hers by act of parliament; the one
was famous for wit, and the other affected the character
of wisdom. Lady *Sophister*, (for that was her name)[2] as
soon as she was released from the matrimonial fetters,
set out to visit foreign parts, and had displayed her
charms in most of the courts in *Europe*. There, in many
parts of her tour, she had cultivated an acquaintance
with *Literati*, and particularly in *France*, where the ladies
affect a reputation of science, and are able to discourse
on the profoundest questions of theology and philosophy.
The labyrinths of a female brain are so various and
intricate, that it is difficult to say what first suggested the
opinion to her, whether caprice or vanity of being singular;
but all on a sudden her ladyship took a fancy into her head
to disbelieve the immortality of the soul, and never came
into the company of learned men without displaying her
talents on this wonderful subject. This extraordinary

principle, to shew that she did not take up her notions lightly and wantonly, she was able to demonstrate; and could appeal to the greatest authorities in defence of it. She had read *Hobbes*, *Malbranche*, *Locke*, *Shaftsbury*, *Woollaston*,[1] and many more; all of whom she obliged to give testimony to her paradox, and perverted passages out of their works with a facility *very easy to be imagined*. But Mr. *Locke* had the misfortune to be her principal favourite, and consequently it rested chiefly upon him to furnish her with quotations, whenever her ladyship pleased to engage in controversy. Such was the character of lady *Sophister*, who now arrived, and asked the sur-prizing question above-mentioned, concerning the im-mortality of the soul.

DOCTOR *Killdarby*,[2] to whom she addressed herself, astonished at the novelty of the question, sat staring with horror and amazement on his companion; which lady *Tempest* observing, and guessing that her female friend was going to be very absurd, resolved to promote the conversation for her own amusement. Turning herself therefore to the doctor, she said with a smile, 'don't you understand the meaning of her ladyship's question, Sir? She asks you, if you believe in the immortality of the soul?'

'Believe in the immortality of the soul, madam!' said the doctor staring, 'bless me, your ladyships astonish me beyond measure—Believe in the immortality of the soul! Yes undoubtedly, and I hope all mankind does the same.'

'Be not too sure of that, Sir,' said lady *Sophister*; 'pray have you ever read Mr. *Locke*'s controversy with the bishop of *Worcester*?'[3]

'Mr. *Locke*'s controversy, madam!' replied the doctor— 'I protest I am not sure; Mr. *Locke*'s controversy with the bishop of *Worcester*! Let me see, I vow I can't recollect— My reading has been very multifarious and extensive—

Yes, madam, I think I have read it, tho' I protest I can't be sure whether I have read it or no.'

'HAVE you ever read it, doctor *Rhubarb*?'[1] said she, addressing herself to the other physician.

'O yes, madam, very often,' replied he; ''tis that fine piece of his where—Yes, yes, I have read it very often; I remember it perfectly well——but pray, madam, is there any passage (I beg your ladyship's pardon if I am mistaken) but is there any passage, I say, in that piece, which tends to confirm your ladyship's notion concerning the immortality of the soul?'

'WHY pray, Sir,' said the lady, with a smile of triumph, 'what do you esteem the soul to be? Is it air, or fire, or æther, or a kind of quintessence, as *Aristotle* observed,[2] and composition of all the elements?'

DOCTOR *Rhubarb* quite dumb-founded with so much learning, desired first to hear her ladyship's opinion of the matter. 'My opinion,' resumed she, 'is exactly the same with Mr. *Locke*'s. You know Mr. *Locke* observes, there are various kinds of matter—well—but first we should define matter, which you know the logicians tell us, is an extended solid substance—Well, out of this matter, some you know is made into roses and peach-trees; then the next step which matter takes, is animal life; from whence you know we have lions and elephants, and all the race of brutes. Then the last step, as Mr. *Locke* observes, is thought and reason and volition, from whence are created men, and therefore you very plainly see, 'tis impossible for the soul to be immortal.'

'PARDON me, Madam,' said *Rhubarb*; 'Roses and peach-trees, and elephants and lions! I protest I remember nothing of this nature in Mr. *Locke*.' 'Nay Sir, cried she, can you deny me this? If the Soul is fire, it must be extinguished; if it is air, it must be dispersed; if it be only a modification of matter, why then of course it ceases, you know, when matter is no longer modified—

if it be any thing else, it is exactly the same thing, and therefore you must confess—indeed Doctor, you must confess, that 'tis impossible for the Soul to be immortal.'

DOCTOR *Killdarby*, who had sat silent for some time to collect his thoughts, finding what a learned antagonist he had to cope with, began now to harangue in the following manner. 'Madam,' said he, 'as to the nature of the soul, to be sure there have been such opinions as your ladyship mentions about it——many various and unaccountable opinions. Some called it *divinum cæleste*; others *quinta essentia*, as your ladyship observes; and others *inflammata anima*, that is, madam, inflamed air. *Aristoxenus*, an old musician, as I remember, imagined the soul to be a musical tune;[1] and a mathematician that I have heard of, supposed it to be like an æquilateral triangle. *Descartes*, I think, makes its residence to be the pineal gland of the brain, where all the nerves terminate; and *Borri*,[2] I remember, the *Milanese* physician, in a letter to *Bartholine, de ortu cerebri & usu medico*, asserts, that in the brain is found a certain very subtil fragrant juice (which I conceive may be the same as the nervous juice or animal spirits) and this he takes to be the residence or seat of the soul; the subtilty or fineness of which he supposes to depend, madam, on the temperature of this liquor—— but really all these opinions may very probably be false; we do but grope in the dark, madam, we do but grope in the dark, and it would be better to let the subject entirely alone. The concurrent opinions of all mankind have ever agreed in believing the immortality of the soul; and this, I confess, is to me an unanswerable argument of its truth. You see, madam, I purposely wave[3] the topic of revelation.'

'OH, Sir, as to that matter,' cries the lady, interrupting him, 'as to revelation, Sir'——and here she ran into much common-place raillery at the expence only of christianity and the gospel; till lady *Tempest* cut her short, and desired her to be silent on that head; for this good lady believed all the doctrines of religion, and was contented, like many others, with the trifling privilege only of disobeying all its precepts.

LADY *Sophister* however resolved not to quit the field of battle, but rallied her forces, and once more fell on her adversaries with an air of trimph. 'You say, I think, Sir,' resumed she, 'that a multitude of opinions will establish a truth. Now you know all the *Indians* believe that their dogs will go to heaven along with them;[1] and if a great many opinions can prove any thing to be true, what say you to that, Sir? *India* you know, doctor, is a prodigious large wide tract of continent, where the *Gymnosophists* lived,[2] and all that—Pray, lady *Tempest*, let us look at your globes.'

'MY globes, madam,' said lady *Tempest*, 'what globes of mine does your ladyship desire to see?'

'WHAT globes,' replied the disputant; 'why your celestial and terrestrial globes to be sure; I want to look out *India* in the map, and shew the doctor what a prodigious wide tract of continent it is in comparison of our *Europe*—however, come, I believe we can do without them—as I was saying therefore, Sir, the *Indians* you know believe their dogs will bear them company to heaven; and if a great many opinions can establish the truth of an hypothesis——you understand me, I hope, because I would fain speak to be understood—I say, if a great many opinions can prove any thing to be true, what say you to that, Sir? For instance now, there's lady *Tempest*'s little lap-dog'——'My dear little creature,' said lady *Tempest*, catching him up in her arms, 'will you go to heaven along with me? I shall be vastly glad of your company, *Pompey*, if you will.' From this hint both their ladyships had many bright sallies, till lady *Sophister*, flushed with the hopes of this argument, recalled her adversary to the question, and desired to hear his reply.

'Come, Sir,' said she, 'you have not yet responsed to my argument, you have not answered my last syllogism——I think I have gravelled you now; I think I have done for you; I think I have demolished you, doctor.'

'NOT at all, madam,' said *Killdarby*; 'really as to that matter, that is neither here nor there——Opinions, madam, vague irregular opinions will spring up and float in people's brains, but we were talking of the dictates of sense and reason. Savages, madam, will be savage, but *Indians* have nothing to do with *Europeans*. The reply to what your ladyship has advanced, would be easy and obvious; but really I must beg to be excused—my profession does not oblige me to a knowledge of such subjects—I came here to prescribe as a physician, and not to discuss topics of theology. Come, brother, I believe we only interrupt their ladyships, and I am obliged to call upon my lord—and Sir *William*—and lady *Betty*, and many other people of quality this morning.' Dr. *Rhubarb* declared that he likewise had as many visits to make that morning; whereupon, taking their leaves (and their fees) the two gentlemen retired with great precipitation, leaving her ladyship in possession of the field of battle; who immediately reported all over the town, that she had out-reasoned two physicians, and obliged them by dint of argument to confess that the soul is not immortal.

AND now begging the reader's pardon for this digression, let us return to our hero, who I am afraid is going to suffer a great revolution in his life.

CHAPTER VIII

Containing various and sundry Matters.

POMPEY had now lived two Years with Lady *Tempest*, in all the Comforts and Luxuries of Life, fed every Day with the choicest, most expensive Dainties that *London* could afford, and caressed by all the People of Fashion that visited his Mistress:

> - - - - - - - *sed scilicet ultima semper*
> *Expectanda dies* - - - - *dicique beatus*
> *Ante obitum nemo supremaque funera debet.*[1]

A moral Reflection, no less applicable to Dogs than to Men! for they both alike experience the Inconstancy of Fortune, of which our Hero was a great Example, as all the following Pages of his History will very remarkably evince.

LADY *Tempest* was walking in *St. James's Park* one Morning in the Spring, with little *Pompey*, as usual, attending her, for she never went abroad without taking him in her Arms. Here she set him down on his Legs, to play with some other Dogs of Quality, that were taking the Air that Morning in the *Mall*; giving him strict Orders, however, not to presume to stray out of her Sight. But in spite of this Injunction, something or other tempted his Curiosity beyond the Limits of the *Mall*; and there, while he was rolling and indulging himself on the green Grass, a Pleasure by Novelty rendered more agreeable to him, it was his Misfortune to spring a Bird; which he pursued with such Eagerness and Alacrity, that he was got as far as *Rosamond's Pond*[2] before he thought proper to give over the Chace. His Mistress, in the mean while, was engaged in a warm and interesting Dispute on the Price of Silk, which so engrossed her

Attention, that she never missed her Favourite; nay,
what is still more extraordinary, she got into her Coach,
and drove home without once bestowing a Thought upon
him. But the Moment she arrived in her Dining-room,
and cast her Eyes on the rest of her four-footed Friends,
her Guilt immediately flew in her Face, and she cried
out with a Scream, *As I am alive, I have left little* Pompey
behind me. Then summoning up two of her Servants in an
Instant, she commanded them to go directly, and search
every Corner of the Park with the greatest Diligence,
protesting she shou'd never have any Peace of Mind, 'till
her Favourite was restored to her Arms. Many Times
she rang her Bell, to know if her Servants were returned,
before it was possible for them to have got thither; but
at length the fatal Message arrived, that *Pompey* was no
where to be found. And indeed it would have been next
to a Miracle, if he had; for these faithful Ambassadors
had never once stirred from the Kitchen Fire, where,
together with the rest of the Servants, they had been
laughing at the Folly of their Mistress, and diverting
themselves with the Misfortunes of her little Darling.
And the Reason why they denied their Return sooner,
was because they imagined a sufficient Time had not
then elapsed, to give a Probability to that Lie, which
they were determined to tell. Yet this did not satisfy their
Lady; she sent them a second Time to repeat their
Search, and a second Time they returned with the same
Story, that *Pompey* was to be found *neither high nor low*. At
this again the Reader is desired not to wonder; for tho'
her Ladyship saw them out of the House herself, and
ordered them to bring back her Favourite, under Pain
of Dismission, the farthest of their Travels was only to
an Ale-house at the Corner of the Street, where they had
been entertaining a large Circle of their parti-colour'd
Brethren, with much Ribbaldry, at the Expence of their
Mistress.

TENDERNESS to this Lady's Character makes me pass over much of the Sorrow she vented on this Occasion; but I cannot help relating, that she immediately dispatched Cards to all her Acquaintance, to put off a Drum which was to have been held at her House that Evening, giving as a Reason, that she had lost her darling Lap-dog, and could not see Company. She likewise sent an Advertisement to the News-Papers, of which we have procured a Copy, and beg leave to insert it.

Lost in the Mall *in* St. James's Park, *between the Hours of Two and Three* in the Morning,[1] *a beautiful* Bologna *Lap-dog, with black and white Spots, a mottled Breast, and several Moles upon his Nose, and answers to the Name of* Pomp, *or* Pompey. *Whoever will bring the same to Mrs.* La Place's, *in* Duke-street, Westminster, *or Mrs.* Hussy's, *Mantua-maker in the* Strand, *or to* St. James's *Coffee-house, shall receive two Guineas Reward.*

THIS Advertisement was inserted in all the Papers for a Month, with Increase of the Reward, as the Case grew more desperate; yet neither all the Enquiries she made, nor all the Rewards she offered, ever restored little *Pompey* to her Arms. We must leave her therefore to receive the Consolations of her Friends on this afflicting Loss, and return to examine after our Hero, of whose Fortune the Reader, perhaps, may have a Desire to hear.

HE had been pursuing a Bird, as was before described, as far as *Rosamond's Pond*, and when his Diversion was over, galloped back to the *Mall*, not in the least doubting to find his Lady there at his Return. But alas! how great was his Disappointment! he ran up and down, smelling to every Petticoat he met, and staring in every female Face he saw, yet neither his Eyes, or Nose, gave him the Information he desired. Seven Times he coursed from *Buckingham-house*[2] to the *Horse-guards*, and back again, but all in vain: At length, tired, and full of Despair, he sat himself down, disconsolate and sorrowful, under a Tree, and there turning his Head aside, abandoned himself to much mournful Meditation. In this evil Plight, while he was ruminating on his Fate, and, like many other People in the *Park*, unable to divine where he should get a Dinner; he was spied by a little Girl, about eight Years old, who was walking by her Mother's Side in the *Mall*. She no sooner perceived him, than she cried out, *La! Mamma! there's a pretty Dog!——I have a good Mind to call to it, Mamma! Shall I, Mamma? Shall I call to it, Mamma?* Having received her Mother's Assent, she applied herself, with much Tenderness, to sollicit him to her; which the little Unfortunate no sooner observed, than breaking off his Meditations, he ran hastily up, and saluting her with his Fore-paws (as the Wretched are glad to find a Friend) gave so many dumb Expressions of Joy, that Speech itself could hardly have been more eloquent. The young Lady, on her Side, charmed with his ready Compliance, took him up in her Arms, and kissed him with great Delight; then turning again to her Mother, and asking her, if she did not think him a charming Creature, 'I wonder, says she, whose Dog it is, Mamma! I have a good mind to take it home with me, Mamma! Shall I, Mamma? Shall I take it home with me, Mamma?' To this also her Mother consented, and when they had taken two or three more Turns, they retired to their Coach, and *Pompey* was conducted to his new Lodgings.

As soon as they alighted at home, little Miss ran hastily up Stairs, to shew her Brother and Sisters the Prize she had found, and he was handed about from one to the other with great Delight and Admiration of his Beauty. He was then introduced to all their Favourites; which were a Dormouse, two Kittens, a *Dutch* Pug, a Squirrel, a Parrot, and a Magpye. To these he was presented with many childish Ceremonies, and all the innocent Follies, that are so important to the Happiness of this happiest Age. The Parrot was to make a Speech to him, the Squirrel to make him a Present of some Nuts, the Kittens were to dance for his Diversion, the Magpye to tell his Fortune, and all enjoined to contribute something to the Entertainment of the little Stranger. And 'tis inconceivable how busy they were in the Execution of these Trifles, with all their Spirits up in Arms, and their whole Souls laid out upon them.

In a few Days, little *Pompey* began to know his Way about the House alone, and I am sorry to say it, in less than a Week he had quite forgot his former Mistress. Here I know not how to excuse his Behaviour. Had he been a Man, one should not have wondered to find him guilty of Ingratitude, a Vice deeply rooted in the Nature of that wicked Animal; and accordingly, we see in all the Revolutions at Court, how readily a new Minister is acknowledged and embraced by all the Subalterns and dependent Flatterers, who fawn with the same Servility on the new Favourite, as before they practised to the old; but that a Dog—a Creature famous for Fidelity, should so soon forget his former Friend and Benefactor, is, I confess, quite unaccountable, and I would willingly draw a Veil over this Part of his Conduct, if the Veracity of an Historian did not oblige me to relate it.

CHAPTER IX

Containing what the Reader will know, if he reads it.

Although the Family, into which *Pompey* now arrived, are almost too inconsiderable for the Dignity of History, yet as they had the Honour of entertaining our Hero for a Time, we shall explain some few Circumstances of their Characters.

The Master of it was Son of a wealthy Trader in the

City,[1] who had amassed together an immense Heap of Riches, merely for the Credit of leaving so much Money behind him. He had destined his Son to the same honourable Pursuit, and very early initiated him into all the Secrets of Business; but the young Gentleman, marrying as soon as his Father died, was prevailed upon by his loving Spouse, whose Head ran after genteel Life, to quit the dirty Scene of Business, and take a House within the Regions of Pleasure. As neither of them had been used to the Company they were now to keep, and both utterly unacquainted with all the Arts of Taste, their Appearance in the polite World plainly manifested their Original, and shewed how unworthy they were of those Riches they so awkardly enjoy'd. A clumsy, inelegant Magnificence prevailed in every Part of their Œconomy, in the Furniture of their Houses, in the Disposition of their Tables, in the Choice of their Cloaths, and in every other Action of their Lives. They knew no other Enjoyment but profuse Expence, and their Country-house was by the Road-side at *Highgate*. It may be imagined such awkard Pretenders to High-Life, were treated with Ridicule by all the People of Genius and Spirit; but immoderate Wealth, and a Coach and Six, opened them a Way into Company, and few refused their Visits, tho' all laughed at their Appearance. For to tell the Reader a Secret, Money will procure its Owners Admittance any where; and however People may pride themselves on the Antiquity of their Families, if they have not Money to preserve a Splendor in Life, they may go a begging with their Pedigrees in their Hands; whereas lift a Grocer into a Coach-and-Six, and let him attend publick Places, and make grand Entertainments, he may be sure of having his Table filled with People of Fashion, tho' it was no longer ago than last Week that he left off selling Plumbs and Sugar.

THE Fruits of their Marriage were three Daughters

and a Son, who seemed not to promise long Life, or at least were likely to be made wretched by Distempers. For as the Father was much afflicted with the Gout, and the Mother pale, unhealthy and consumptive, the Children inherited the Diseases of their Parents, and were ricketty, scrophulous,[1] sallow in their Complexions, and distorted in their Limbs. Nor were their Minds at all more amiable than their Bodies, being proud, selfish, obstinate and cross-humoured; and the whole Turn of their Education seemed calculated rather to improve these Vices than to eradicate them. For this Purpose, instead of sending them to Schools, where they would have been whipt out of many of their Ill-tempers, and perhaps by Conversation with other Children, might have learnt a more open generous Disposition, they were bred up under private Teachers at home, who never opposed any of their Humours, for fear of offending their Parents. Thus little Master, the Mother's Darling, was put under the Care of a domestic Tutor, partly because she cou'd not endure to have him at a Distance from her Sight, and partly because she had heard it was genteel to educate young Gentlemen at home.

THE Tutor selected for this Purpose, had been dragged out of a College-Garret at Thirty, and just seen enough of the World to make him impertinent and a Coxcomb. For being introduced all at once into what is called *Life*, his Eyes were dazzled with the Things he beheld, and without waiting the Call of Nature, he made a quick Transition from College-reservedness to the pert Familiarity of a *London* Preacher. He soon grew to despise the Books he had read at the University, and affected a Taste for polite Literature—that is, for no Literature at all; by which he endeared himself so much to the Family he lived in, by reading Plays to them, bringing home Stories from the Coffee-house, and other Arts, that they gave him the Character of the *entertainingest*, *most facetious*, *best-*

humoured Creature that ever came into a House. As his Temper led him by any Means to flatter his Benefactors, he never failed to cry up the Parts and Genius of his Pupil, as a Miracle of Nature; which the fond Mother, understanding nothing of the Matter, very easily believed. When therefore any of her female Visiters were commending little Master *for the finest Child they ever beheld*, she could not help adding something concerning his Learning, and wou'd say on such Occasions, 'I assure you, Madam, his Tutor tells me he is forwarder than ever Boy was of his Age. He has got already, it seems, into his *Syntax*—I don't know what the *Syntax* is Ma'am, but I dare say 'tis some very good moral Book, otherwise Mr. *Jackson* wou'd not teach it him; for to be sure, there never was a Master that had a better Manner of teaching than Mr. *Jackson*——What is the *Syntax*, my Dear? Tell the Ladies what the *Syntax* is, Child!' 'Why, Mamma, cries the Boy, the *Syntax* is—it is at the End of the *As in Præsenti*,[1] and teaches you how to parse.' 'Ay, ay, said the Mother, I thought so my dear; 'tis some very good Book I make no doubt, and will improve your Morals as well as your Understanding. Be a good Boy, Child, and mind what Mr. *Jackson* says to you, and I dare say, you'll make a great Figure in Life.'

THIS is a little Specimen of the young Gentleman's Education, and that of the young Ladies fell short of it in no Particular: For they were taught by their Mother and Governesses to be vain, affected, and foppish; to disguise every natural Inclination of the Soul, and give themselves up to Cunning, Dissimulation, and Insincerity; to be proud of Beauty they had not, and ashamed of Passions they had; to think all the Happiness of Life consisted in a new Cap or a new Gown, and no Misfortune equal to the missing a Ball.

BESIDES many inanimate Play-things, this little Family had likewise, as we before observed, several living

Favourites, whom they took a Delight to vex and torture for their Diversion. Among the Number of these, little *Pompey* had the Misfortune to be enrolled; I say Misfortune, for wretched indeed are all those Animals, that become the Favourites of Children. For a good while he suffered only the Barbarity of their Kindness, and was persecuted with no other Cruelties than what arose from their extravagant Love of him; but when the Date of his Favour began to expire (and indeed it did not continue long) he was then taught to feel how much severer their Hate could be than their Fondness. Indeed he had from the first two or three dreadful Presages of what might happen to him, for he had seen with his own Eyes the two Kittens, his Play-fellows, drowned for some Misdemeanor they had been guilty of, and the Magpy's Head chopt off with the greatest Passion, for daring to peck a Piece of Plumb-cake that laid in the Window, without Permission; which Instances of Cruelty were sufficient to warn him, if he had any Foresight, of what might afterwards happen to himself.

But he was not left long to entertain himself with Conjectures, before he felt in Person and in reality the mischievous Disposition of these little Tyrants. Sometimes they took it into their Heads that he was full of Fleas, and then he was dragged thro' a Canal till he was almost dead, in order to kill the Vermin that inhabited the Hair of his Body. At other Times he was set upon his hinder Legs with a Book before his Eyes, and ordered to read his Lesson; which not being able to perform, they whipt him with Rods till he began to exert his Voice in a lamentable Tone, and then they chastised him the more for daring to be sensible of Pain.

Much of this Treatment did he undergo, often wishing himself restored to the Arms of Lady *Tempest*, when Fortune taking pity of his Calamities, again resolved to change his Lodgings. An elderly Maiden Lady, Aunt to

this little Brood and Sister to their Papa, was one Day
making a Visit in the Family, and by great good Luck
happened to be Witness of some of the Ill-usage, which
Pompey underwent: For having committed some imaginary
Fault he was brought down to be tormented in her Presence. Her righteous Spirit immediately rose at this
Treatment; she declared it was a Shame to persecute
poor dumb Creatures in that barbarous manner, wondered their Mamma would suffer it, and signified that
she would take the Dog home with her to her own House.
Tho' the little Tyrants had long been tired of him, yet
mere Obstinacy set them a crying, when they found he
was to be taken from them; but there was no contending;
their Aunt was resolute, and thus *Pompey* was happily
delivered from this House of Inquisition.

CHAPTER X

*The Genealogy of a Cat, and other odd Matters, which the
great Critics of the Age will call improbable and unnatural.*

A QUITE new Scene of Life now opened on our Hero,
who from frequenting Drums and Assemblies with
Lady *Tempest*, from shining conspicuous in the Side
boxes of the Opera and Play-house, was now confined
to the Chambers of an old Maid, and obliged to attend
Morning and Evening Prayers. 'Tis true the Change
was not altogether a sudden one, since his last Place had
a good deal reduced his aspiring Notions; but still his
Genius for Gallantry and High-life continued, and he
found it very difficult to compose himself to the sober
Hours and orderly Deportment of an ancient Virgin.
Sometimes indeed he would turn up his Ear and seem
attentive, while she was reading *Tillotson*'s Sermons;[1]
but if the Truth were known, I believe he had much

rather have been listening to a Novel or a Play-book.

PEOPLE who have been used to much Company, cannot easily reconcile themselves to Solitude, and the only Companion he found here, was an ancient tabby Cat, whom he despised at first with a most fashionable Disdain, tho' she solicited his Acquaintance with much Civility, and shewed him all the Respect due to a Stranger. She took every Opportunity of meeting him in her Walks, and tried to enter into Conversation with him; but he never returned any of her Compliments, and as much as possible declined her Haunts. At length, however, Time reconciled him to her, and frequent Meetings produced a strict Friendship between them.

THIS Cat, by name *Mopsa*, was Heiress of the most ancient Family of Cats in the World. There is a Tradition, which makes her to be descended from that memorable *Grimalkin* of Antiquity, who was converted into a Woman at the Request of her Master, and is said to have leapt out of Bed one Morning, forgetting her Transformation, in pursuit of a fugitive Mouse: From which Event all Moralists have declaimed on the Impossibility of changing fixed Habits, and *L'Estrange* in particular observes, *that Puss, tho' a Madam, will be a Mouser still*.[1]

IT is very difficult to fix the precise Time of her Family's first Arrival in *England*, so various and discordant are the Opinions of our Antiquaries on that Subject. Many are persuaded they came over with *Brute* the *Trojan*; others conjecture they were left by *Phœnician* Merchants, who formerly traded on the Coast of *Cornwal*. The great *B—n W—ll—s* insists, that *Julius Cæsar*, in his second Expedition to *Britain*, brought over with him a Colony of *Roman* Cats to people the Island, at that time greatly infested with Mice and Rats. The learned and ingenious Dr. *S—k—y*,[2] disliking all these Opinions, undertakes to prove, that they were not in *England* till the Conquest, but that they came over in the same Ship with the Duke

of *Normandy*, afterwards *William* the First. Which of
their Conjectures is the truest, these ingenious Gentlemen
must decide among themselves; which I apprehend will
not be done without many Volumes of Controversy; but
they are all unanimous in supposing the Family to be
very ancient and of foreign Extraction.

ANOTHER of her great Ancestors, whose Name likewise is considerable in History, was that immortal Cat,
who made the Fortune of Mr. *Whittington*, and advanced
him to the Dignity of a Lord-Mayor of *London*, according
to the Prophecy of a Parish-Steeple to that effect. There
are likewise many others well known to Fame, as *Gridelin
the Great*, and *Dina the Sober*, and *Grimalkin the Pious*,[1] and
the famous Puss that wore Boots, and another that had a
Legacy left her in the last Will and Testament of her
deceased Mistress; of which satirical Mention is made in
the Works of our *English Horace*.[2] But leaving the Deduction
of her Genealogy to the great Professors of that Science,
and recommending it to them as a Subject quite new,
and extremely worthy of their sagacious Researches, I
shall proceed to Matters of greater Consequence to this
History.

'TIS observed by an old *Greek* Poet, and from thence
copied into the *Spectator*, that there is a great Similitude
between Cats and Women.[3] Whether the Resemblance
be just in other Instances, I will not pretend to determine,
but I believe it holds exactly between ancient Cats and
ancient Maids; which I suppose is the Reason why Ladies
of that Character are never without a grave Mouser in
their Houses, and generally at their Elbows.

MOPSA had now lived near a dozen Years with her
present Mistress, and being naturally of a studious,
musing Temper, she had so improved her Understanding
from the Conversation of this aged Virgin, that she was
now deservedly reckoned the most philosophic Cat in
England. She had the Misfortune some Years before to

lose her favorite Sister *Selima*, who was unfortunately drowned in a large China Vase; which sorrowful Accident is very ingeniously lamented in a most elegant little Ode, which I heartily recommend to the Perusal of every Reader, who has a Taste for Lyric Numbers and poetical Fancy; and it is to be found in one of the Volumes of Mr. *Dodsley*'s Collection of *Miscellany Poems*.[1] This Misfortune added much to *Mopsa*'s Gravity, and gave her an Air of Melancholy not easily described. For a long while indeed her Grief was so great, that she neglected the Care of her Person, neither cleansing her Whiskers, nor washing her Face as usual; but Time and Reflection at length got the better of her Sorrow, and restored her to the natural Serenity of her Temper.

WHEN little *Pompey* came into the Family, she saw he had a good Disposition at the bottom, tho' he was a *wild*, *thoughtless*, *young Dog*, and therefore resolved to try the Effects of her Philosophy upon him. If therefore at any time he began to talk in the Language of the World, and flourished upon Balls, Operas, Plays, Masquerades, and the like, she would take up the Discourse, and with much Socratical Composure prove to him the Folly and Vanity of such Pursuits. She would tell him how unworthy it was of a Dog of any Understanding to follow the trivial Gratification of his Senses, and how idle were the Pageants of Ambition compared with the sober Comforts of Philosophy. This indeed he used to ridicule with great Gaiety of Spirit (if the Reader will believe it) and tell her by way of Answer, that her Contempt of the World arose from her having never lived in it. But when he had a little wore off the Relish of Pleasure, he began to listen every Day to her Arguments with greater Attention, till at length she absolutely convinced him that Happiness is no where so perfect, as in Tranquillity and retired Life.

FROM this Time their Friendship grew stricter every

Day; they used to go upon little Parties of innocent Amusement together, and it was very entertaining to see them walking Side by Side in the Garden, or lying couchant under a Tree to surprize some little Bird in the Branches. Malicious Fame no sooner observed this Intimacy, than with her usual Malice she published the Scandal of an Amour between them; but I am persuaded it had no Foundation, for *Mopsa* was old enough to be *Pompey*'s Grand-mother, and besides he always behaved to her, rather with the Homage due to a Parent than the ardent Fondness of a Lover.

BUT Fortune, his constant Enemy, again set her Face against him. The two Friends one Day in their Mistress's Closet, had been engaged in a very serious Dispute on the *Summum Bonum*, or chief Good of Life; and both of them had delivered their Sentiments very gravely upon it; the one contending for an absolute Exclusion of all Pleasure, the other desirous only to intermix some Diversions with his Philosophy. They were seated on two Books, which their Mistress had left open in her Study; to wit, *Mopsa* on *Nelson*'s *Festivals*, and *Pompey* on *Baker*'s *Chronicles*;[1] when alas—how little things often determine the greatest Matters! *Pompey*, in the Earnestness of his Debate, did something on the Leaves of that sage Historian, very unworthy of his Character, and improper to be mentioned in explicit Terms. His Mistress unfortunately entered the Room at that Moment, and saw the Crime he had been guilty of; which so enraged her, that she resolved never to see his Face any more, but ordered her Footman to dispose of him without delay.

[....]

[Pompey now enters the household of Captain Vincent, a man of fashion.]

CHAPTER XI

[What the reader will know if he reads it.]

CAPTAIN *Vincent* of the guards, was an exceeding handsome man, about thirty years old, tall and well-proportioned in his limbs; but so entirely devoted to the contemplation of his own pretty person, that he never detached his thoughts one moment from the consideration of it. Conscious of being a favourite of the ladies, among whom he was received always with eyes of affection, he thought the charms of his figure irresistible wherever he came, and seemed to shew himself in all public places as an object of public admiration. You saw for ever in his look a smile of assurance, complacency, and self-applause; he appeared always to be wondering at his own accomplishments, and especially when he made a survey now and then of his dress and limbs, 'twas as much as to say to his company, 'gentlemen and ladies, look on me if you can without admiration.' The reputation of two or three affairs which fame had given him with women of fashion, still contributed to encrease his vanity, and authorized him, as he thought, to bestow more time and pains on the beautifying and adorning so successful a figure. In short, after many real or pretended amours, which made him insufferably vain, he married at last a celebrated town-beauty, a woman of quality, who was in all respects equal to, and worthy of such a husband.

LADY *Betty Vincent*, the wife of this gentleman, was one of those haughty nymphs of quality, who presume so much on the merit of a title, that they never trouble themselves to acquire any other. She was proud, expensive, insolent and unmannerly to her inferiors; vain of her rank, and still vainer of her person; full of extravagant airs, and tho' exceedingly silly, conceited of an imaginary wit and smartness. As she set out in life with a full persuasion that her prodigious beauty, merit, and accomplishments, must soon procure her the title of *her grace*, she rejected several advantageous matches that offered, because they did not in all points come up to the height of her ambition. At length finding her charms begin to decay, in a fit of lust, disappointed pride, and opposition to her mother, with whom she had then a quarrel, she patched up a marriage with captain *Vincent* of the guards, contrary to the advice and remonstrances of all her friends and relations.

As the captain had no revenue beside the income of his commission, and her ladyship's fortune did not exceed seven thousand pounds, it may be concluded, when the honey-moon of love was over, this agreeable couple did not find the matrimonial fetters sit perfectly easy upon them. To retrench in any article, they found it impossible; to retire into the country, still more impossible; that was horrors, death, and despair—her ladyship could not hear of such a thing with patience—she was ready to swoon at the mention of it; and indeed the captain, who was equally attached to *London*, never made the proposal in earnest.

WHAT then could they do in these embarrassing circumstances? Why, they took a little house in *Hedge-lane*,[1] near the bottom of the *Hay-Market*, which being in the center of public diversions, served to keep them a little in countenance; and there they supported their spirits as well as they could, with reflecting that they still lived in the world, tho' their apartments were not so commodious as they could wish.

FETTERED pride is sure to turn into peevishness, and spleen is the daughter of mortified vanity. Finding themselves cramped with want, they grew uneasy, discontented, jealous of each other's extravagance, and were scarce ever alone without reproaching one another on the article of expence. The lady powted at the captain for going to *White*'s, and the captain recriminated on his wife for playing at Brag; and then followed a long contention, which of them spent the most money.

To compleat their misfortunes, her ladyship took to breeding, which introduced a thousand new expences; and they must absolutely have starved in the midst of pride and vanity, had they not been seasonably relieved now and then by some handsome presents from lady *Betty*'s mother, my old lady *Harridan*, who was still alive, and in possession of a considerable jointure.

THE devotion which the captain paid to his beautiful figure, has already been described; nor was her ladyship one jot behind him in idolizing and adoring her own charms. She prided herself in a more particular manner on the *lovely bloom* and *charming delicacy of her complexion*, which had procured her the envy of one sex, and the admiration of the other; tho' perhaps if her enviers and admirers had known the following little story, both these passions would have considerably abated in them.

IT was our hero's custom, whenever he came into a new family, to gratify his curiosity as soon as possible, with a general survey of the house. On his arrival here, his little owners were so fond of him the first day, that they lugged him about in their arms, and never permitted him to stray one moment out of their sights; but being left more at his own liberty the next morning, he thought it was then a convenient time for making his tour. After examining all the rooms above ground, he descended intrepidly into the kitchen, and began to look about sharp for a breakfast; for to say the truth, he had hitherto met with very thin commons in his new apartments. At last a blue and white dish, which stood on the dresser, presented itself to his eye. This immediately he determined to be a lawful prey, and perceiving nobody present to interrupt him, boldly made a spring at it; but happening unluckily to leap against the dish, down it came, and its contents ran about the kitchen. Scarce had this happened, when my lady's maid appeared below stairs, and began to scream out in a very shrill accent, 'why who has done this now? I'll be whipped if this *owdacious* little dog has not been and thrown down my lady's backside's breakfast;' after which she fell very severely on the cook, who now entered the kitchen, and began to reprimand her in a very authoritative tone, for not taking more care of her dressers; 'but let the 'pothecary,' added she, 'come and mix up his nastiness himself an he will, for deuce fetch me if I'll wait on her ladyship's backside in this manner: If she will have her clysters,[1] let the clyster-pipe doctor come and minister them himself, and not put me to her filthy offices.——O Lord bless us! well, rather than be at all this pains for a complexion, I'd be as brown as a berry all my life-time. The finest flowers, I have heard say, are raised from dung, and perhaps it may be so—I am sure 'tis so at our house, for my lady takes physic twice a week, and treats her backside with a clyster once a fortnight, and all this to preserve a complexion.'

WHILE the waiting-gentlewoman was haranguing thus at the expence of her mistress, the captain's valet also came into the kitchen, and hearing his fellow-servant very loud and vociferous, enquired what was the matter. 'Matter,' cries she, 'matter enough o'conscience! don't you see there? This plaguy little devil of a dog has been and flung down my lady's backside's breakfast.' 'Bless us, a prodigious disaster indeed!' replied the valet; 'why, what shall we do now, Mrs. *Minikin?* I am afraid your lady's complexion will want its bloom to day.' 'Hang her complexion,' said *Abigail*,[2] 'I wish her complexion was at the bottom of her own close-stool; she need be so generous to her backside indeed—I am sure she is not so over-and-above generous to her servants, and her trades-folks.' 'True,' cries the valet, 'if she would treat us with a breakfast now and then, as well as her backside, methinks it would not be amiss, for deuce take me, if I ever saw such house-keeping in any family that ever I lived in, in my days. They dress plaguy fine both of 'em, and cut a figure abroad, while their servants are starving at home.' 'Yes, yes,' said Mrs. *Minikin*, ''tis all shew and no substance at our house. There's your pretty master, the captain, has been smugging up his pretty face, and cleaning his teeth for this hour, before the looking-glass this morning. I wonder he does not clyster for a complexion too. Tho', thank heaven, he's coxcomb enough already, and wants no addition to his pride; he seems to think no woman can look him in the face without falling in love with him, with his black solitaire,[1] and his white teeth, and his frizzled hair, and his fopperies. O Lord have mercy upon us! well, every one to their liking, but hang me if I would not marry a monkey as soon as such a powdered scaramouch,[2] were I a woman of quality.—Get out you little nasty devil of a dog; hang me if I don't brain you, and let the little vixens your mistresses say what they please.'

HAVING said this, she set out full of rage in pursuit of poor *Pompey*, who took to his heels with great precipitation, and fled for his life; but not being nimble enough he was overtaken, and smarted severely for the trespass he had committed.

CHAPTER XII

[*A matrimonial dispute.*]

LADY *Betty Vincent* had a mother still living, as we hinted in the preceding chapter; who having worn out her life in vanity, cards, and all sorts of luxury, was now turned methodist at seventy, and thought by presenting heaven with the dregs of her age, to atone for all the riot and lasciviousness of her youth. For this purpose she had renounced all public diversions, put herself under the tuition of the two great field-preaching apostles,[1] and was become one of the warmest votaries of that prevailing sect.

BUT besides the self-mortification she was pleased to undergo, her ladyship had likewise an additional stratagem to procure her pardon above, which she thought impossible to fail her; and this was to take her eldest grand-daughter out of the temptations of a wicked seducing age into her own family, and breed her up a methodist: the merit of which laudable action she hoped would compensate all her own miscarriages, and effectually restore her to the divine favour.

HAVING thus laid the scheme of compounding matters with heaven, and making the virtues of the grand-daughter balance as it were and set off the sins of the grand-mother, she now thought only of putting it in execution. In the first place she communicated her design to the two apostles, and the moment she was assured of their approbation, she dispatched a message to her daughter, desiring an hour's conversation with her the first time she was at leisure.

LADY *Betty*, who had great dependance on her mother, did not fail to answer the summons, and was with her very early the next morning; *so very early*, that the clock had but just struck one; which she said was an instance of *her uncommon filial obedience*. It may be imagined the two ladies soon came to agreement; lady *Betty* being as glad to get rid of a charge, as lady *Harridan* to acquire a companion, which she represented as the motive that induced her to take her grand-daughter into her family.

MATTERS being thus settled, lady *Betty* returned home to dinner; where she observed a sullen silence till the cloth was removed, and the servants were carrying

away the last things. Then it was that she pleased to
open her mouth, and bade one of the footmen 'tell
Minikin to get *Sally*'s cloaths and linnen packed up against
the evening.' There happened at this time to be a *miff*
subsisting between her ladyship and the captain, and
they had glowted[1] at one another for several days without
exchanging a word. She did not therefore vouchsafe to
ask her husband's consent in the step she was taking, nor
even to inform him of it in direct terms, but left him to
extract it as well as he could from this oblique message,
which she sent to her maid. The captain, who saw
plainly that some mystery was contained under these
orders, had at first a mind to be revenged by affecting
not to hear them; but curiosity prevailing over his resentment, he submitted at length to ask whither his
daughter was going?

'WHY, if you will spend all your life at *White*'s, and
lose all your money in play, (replied the lady with an air
of disdain) I must dispose of my children as well as I can,
I think.'

'BUT what connexion is there, in the name of God,'
said the captain, 'between my playing at *White*'s, and
your packing up your daughter's cloaths?—Unless
perhaps you are going to send your daughter to the
Foundling-Hospital.'

'YES, perhaps I am,' cries she with a toss of her head;
'if one can't maintain one's children at home, they must
e'en come upon the parish, and there's an end of it.'

STILL the captain remained unenlightened.; not a
ray of information transpired through these dark speeches,
and indeed there seemed to be no likelihood of an eclaircissement; for in this manner they continued to play at
cross-purposes with one another for several minutes. At
last, his patience being utterly exhausted, he insisted
very earnestly, and somewhat angrily, to know what
was going to be done with his daughter. 'Why, mamma

has a mind to take the girl to live with her, if you must know,' replied her ladyship, 'and that is going to be done with your daughter. If you will get children, without being able to maintain them, you may be thankful methinks to find there is somebody in the world that will take them off your hands.' 'Oh Madam!' cries the captain, 'as to the article of begetting children, I apprehend your ladyship to be full as guilty as I am, and therefore that is out of the question—but as to your mamma's taking them off our hands, devil take me if I am not exceedingly obliged to her for it. Your mamma is welcome to take them all, if she pleases.—I only wanted to know what was going to be done with the girl, and now I am most perfectly satisfied;' which he uttered with the most taunting pronunciation in the world.

THERE is nothing so exceedingly provoking as a sneer to people enraged and inflamed with pride. The captain perceived the effect it had, and resolving to pursue his triumph, 'My dear,' added he, 'to be sure the prudent care you are taking to provide for your children is highly commendable, but I am afraid your mamma will debauch the girl with religion.—She'll teach her perhaps to whine, and cant, and say her prayers under the godly Mr. *Whitefield*.'

LADY *Betty* had never in her life shewn the least regard for her mother. She had married in direct opposition to her will, and partly out of revenge, because she happened at that time to have a quarrel with her, and knew her disinclination to the match: but now so much was she galled with the captain's raillery, that she gladly seized on any thing which offered as a handle of reproach. With rage therefore sparkling in her eyes, and indignation glowing all over her face, she cried out, 'How dare you ridicule my mamma? If mamma has a mind to be an old doting idiot, and change her religion, does it become you of all people to reproach her with it? You have the greatest obligations to her, sir, and you may be ashamed to give yourself such airs. You ridicule my mamma!— You of all people in the world!—'Twould have been well for me, I am sure, if I had taken mamma's advice, and never *had you*; for you know you *brought* nothing but your little beggarly commission, and what is the income of a little beggarly commission? 'tis not sufficient to furnish one's pin-cushion with pins. And who pray *was you*, when I *had you*? You know you was *no blood* or *family*; and yet you pretend to ridicule my mamma! you of all people! you!—if it was not for mamma now, you would starve, you and all your brats would starve with want.'

WHEN a dispute is grown to the highest, especially if it be a matrimonial one, all sober argument and cool reply are nothing better than words spoken against the wind. The judicious captain therefore, instead of answering this invective of his spouse, very wisely, in my opinion, fell a singing; which so exasperated the fair lady, and so utterly over-set her patience, that she started from her chair, swept down two or three bottles and glasses with her hoop-petticoat, flounced out of the room, and rushed up stairs ready to burst with spite and indignation.

ALL the while this dispute was passing in the parlour, our hero was the subject of as fierce a one among his little owners, or rather tormentors, in another room. For as the eldest girl was going into a different family, it was necessary they should make a separation of their playthings; and our hero being incapable of division, unless they had carved him out into shares, a warm debate arose concerning him, both sides obstinately refusing to wave their pretensions. This perhaps may seem a little wonderful to the reader; but let him consider the tempers of this little family, begotten in spleen, peevishness, and pride, and I believe he will not think it unnatural, after the recent example he has seen of their parents, that a spirit of opposition should make them contend with the greatest vehemence for a matter of the most absolute indifference to them. This was in reality the cause of their contention, and they would soon have gone together by the ears, had not their mamma appeared to decide the question in favour of her eldest girl.

LADY *Betty* was hardly yet recovered from her passion, but being now told that lady *Harridan's* coach was waiting for her at the door, she composed her face as well as she could, and mounted into it, attended by her daughter and the hero of this history.

CHAPTER XIII

[*A stroke at the methodists.*]

THEY arrived at lady *Harridan's*[1] about seven o-clock in the evening, and were immediately conducted up-stairs into the lady's dining-room, where they found a large company of women assembled. On the first sight of so many ladies, I believe our hero concluded, he was got into some rout or drum, such as he had often seen at Lady *Tempest's*; yet on the other hand he knew not well how to reconcile many appearances with such a supposition. He saw no cards, he heard no laughing— the solemn faces of the servants, who now and then appeared, the sober looks of the company, every thing seemed to inform him, that pleasure never could be the cause of this assembly. It was indeed a sisterhood of the godly, met together to bewail the vanities of human life, and congratulate one another on their common good-luck, in breaking away from the enchantments of a sinful world.

THE causes, which had converted them to methodism, were almost as various as the several characters of the converts. Some the ill-success of their charms had driven to despair; others a consciousness of too great success had touched with repentance; and both these terminated in superstitious melancholy. Disappointed love and criminal amour, tho' opposite in nature, here wrought the same effects: thunder and lightning, ill-omened dreams, earthquakes, vapors, small-pox, all had their converts[1] in this religious collection: but far the most part of them, like the noble president, were women fatigued and worn out in the vanities of life, the battered and super-annuated jades of pleasure, who being grown sick of themselves, and weary of the world, were now fled to methodism, merely as the newest sort of folly, that had lately been invented.

—— *Species non omnibus una,*
Nec diversa tamen; qualem decet esse sororum.[2]

T H E appearance of lady *Betty* in such a company as this, was like a wasp's invading a nest of drones. She was too spirited, too much drest, too worldly to be agreeable to them, and they in return gave as little pleasure to her. In short, she very soon found herself out of her element, and after sitting a few minutes only, rose up and began to make her departing curtsies.

'W H Y sure you are not going, lady *Betty*,' cried the mother—'I presumed upon your staying the evening with us.'

'No thank you,' replied the daughter; 'another time, if you please, mamma; but you seem to be all too religious abundantly for me at present. I can't afford to say my prayers above once a week, mamma, and 'tis not Sunday to-day according to my calculation.'

'F O R shame, for shame, my dear, don't indulge such levity of discourse,' said lady *Harridan*; 'let me prevail on you to stay, lady *Betty*, and I am sure we shall make a convert of you. There is that tranquillity, my dear, that composure, that serenity of mind attending methodism, that I am sure no person who judges fairly, can refuse to embrace it. Pleasure, my dear, is all vanity and folly, an unquiet, empty, transient delusion—believe me, child, I have experienced it, I have proved the vanity of it, and depend upon't, sooner or later you will come to the same way of thinking.'

'VERY likely I may,' replied lady *Betty*; 'but you'll give me leave to grow a little wickeder first, won't you, mamma? I have not sins enough at present, I am not quite wicked enough as yet to turn methodist.'

'FIE! fie! don't encourage that licentiousness of conversation,' cries the old lady; 'you shock me, my dear, beyond measure, you make my blood run cold again to hear you—but let me beseech you to stay, and you'll have the pleasure of hearing the dear *Whitefield* talk on this subject—we expect him every minute.'

'Do you?' says lady *Betty*; 'then upon my honour I'll hie me away this moment, for I'll promise you, mamma, I have not the least desire or curiosity to hear the dear *Whitefield*—and so your servant, ladies, your servant.' Having said this, she brushed down stairs, and left the company astonished at her prophaneness.

As lady *Betty* went out, the dear *Whitefield* and his brother apostle entered, who were the only people wanting to compleat this religious collection. On their appearance the mysteries began, and they all fell to lamenting the wickedness of their former lives. The great guilt of loving cards, the exceeding sinfulness of having been fond of dancing in their youthful days, were enumerated as sins of the most atrocious quality; whilst other crimes, of a nature perhaps not inferior to these, were very prudently kept out of sight. Then Mr. *Whitefield* began to preach the history of his life, and related the many combats and desperate encounters he has had with the devil; how Satan confined him to his chamber once at college, and permitted him not to eat for several days together; with ten thousand other malicious pranks play'd by the prince of darkness on the body of that unfortunate adventurer, if we may believe his own journals. He proceeded in the next place to describe the many miracles, which heaven has wrought in his favour; how it ceased to rain once, and the sun broke out on a sudden, just as he was beginning to preach on *Kennington-Common*;[1] with a million more equally stupendous prodigies, which shew how great an interest heaven takes in all the actions of that religious mountebank. When the company had enjoyed enough of this spiritual and suspirious[2] conversation, they proceeded in the last place to singing of psalms, and this concluded the superstition of the evening.

ALL the former part of the time, our hero sat very composed and quietly before the fire; but when they began to chant their hymns, surprized and astonished with the novelty of this proceeding, he fell to howling with the most sonorous accent, and in a key much higher than any of the screaming sisters. Nor was this all; for presently afterwards, Mr. *Whitefield* attempting to stroke him, he snarled and bit his finger: which being the self-same indignity that *Lucian* formerly offered to the hand of a similar impostor,[3] we thought it not beneath the dignity of this history to relate it. To say the truth, I believe he had taken some disgust to that exceeding pious gentleman; for besides these two instances of ill-behaviour, he was guilty of a much greater rudeness the next day to his works.

LADY *Harridan*, as soon as she arose the next morning, sent for her little grand-daughter immediately into her closet, and made her repeat some long methodistical prayers; after which she heard her read several pages out

of the apostle's journal, and then they went to breakfast;
but by mistake left poor *Pompey* shut up in the closet.
The little prisoner scratched very impatiently to be
released, and made various attempts to open the door;
but not having the good fortune to succeed, he leaped
upon the table, and wantonly did his occasions on the
field-preacher's memoirs, which lay open upon it. Whether
this was done to express his contempt of the book, or
merely from an incapacity of suppressing his needs, is
hardly possible for us to determine; tho' we are sensible
how much it would exalt him in the reader's esteem, to
ascribe it to the former motive; and indeed it must be
confessed, that his chusing to drop his superfluities on so
particular a spot, may very well countenance such a
suspicion; but unless we had the talents of *Æsop*, to
interpret the sentiments of brutes, it will for ever be
impossible to come at the truth of this important affair.

HOWEVER that be, lady *Harridan* unfortunately
returned to her closet soon afterwards, and saw the crime
he had been guilty of. Rage and indignation sparkled
in her eyes; she rang her bell instantly with the greatest
fury, and on the appearance of a footman, ordered him
immediately to be hanged. His young mistress, whose
love for him had long since cooled, and who besides
feared her grand-mamma's resentment, did not think
proper to oppose the sentence. He was had away therefore that moment to execution; which I dare say, courteous
reader, thou art extremely glad to hear, as it would put
a period to his history, and prevent thee from misspending
any more of thy precious time. But alas! thy hopes are
vain—thy labours are not yet at an end. The footman,
who happened to have some few grains of compassion in
his nature, instead of obeying his lady's orders, sold him
that day for a pint of porter to an ale-house keeper's
daughter in *Tyburn-Road*. Here then, gentle friend, if
thou art tired, let me advise thee to desist and fall asleep;

or if perchance thy spirits are fresh, and thou dost not yet begin to yawn, proceed on courageously, and thou wilt in good time arrive at the end of thy journey.

CHAPTER XIV

The History of a modish Marriage; the Description of a Coffee-house, and a very grave political Debate on the Good of the Nation.

POMPEY was sold, as we have just observed, to an Alehouse-Keeper's Daughter, for the valuable Consideration of a Pint of Porter. This amiable young Lady was then on the Point of Marriage with a Hackney-Coachman, and soon afterwards the Nuptials were consummated to the great Joy of the two ancient Families, who were by this Means sure of not being extinct. As soon as the Ceremony was over at the *Fleet*, the new-married Couple set out to celebrate their Wedding at the *Old blue Boar* in *Tyburn* Road, and the Bride was conducted home at Night dead-drunk to her new Apartments in a Garret in *Smithfield*.[1]

THIS fashionable Pair had scarce been married three Days before they began to quarrel on a very fashionable Subject: For the civil well-bred Husband coming home one Night from his Station, and expecting the Cow-heels to have been ready for his Supper, found his Lodgings empty, and his darling Spouse abroad. At about eleven o'Clock she came flouncing into the Room, and telling him, with great *gaitè de cœur*, that she had been at the Play, began to describe the several Scenes of *Hamlet* Prince of *Denmark*. Judge if this was not Provocation too great for a Hackney-Coachman's Temper. He fell to exercising his Whip in a most outrageous Manner, and she applying herself no less readily to more desperate

Weapons, a most bloody Fray ensued between them; in which *Automedon*[1] had like to have been stabbed with a Penknife, and his fair Spouse was obliged to keep her Bed near a Month with the Bruises she received in this horrid Rencounter.

LITTLE *Pompey* now most sensibly felt the ill Effects of his former Luxury, which served only to aggravate the Miseries of his present Condition. The coarse Fare he met with in roofless Garrets, or Cellars under Ground, were but indelicate Morsels to one who had formerly lived on *Ragouts* and *Fricassees*; and he found it very difficult to sleep on hard and naked Floors, who had been used to have his Limbs cushioned up on *Sopha*'s and Couches. But luckily for him, his Favour with his Mistress procured him the Hatred of his Master, who sold him a second Time to a Nymph of *Billingsgate* for a Pennyworth of Oysters.

HIS Situation indeed was not mended for the present by this Means, but it put him in a Way to be released the sooner from a Course of Life so ill suited to his Constitution or his Temper. For this delicate Fisherwoman, as she went her Rounds, carried him one Evening to a certain Coffee-house near the *Temple*, where the Lady behind the Bar was immediately struck with his Beauty, and with no great Difficulty prevailed on the gentle Water-Nymph to surrender him for a Dram of Brandy.

HIS Fortunes now began to wear a little better Aspect, and he spent his Time here agreeably enough in listening to the Conversations and Disputes that arose in the Coffee-Room among People of all Denominations; for here assembled Wits, Critics, Templars, Politicians, Poets, Country Squires, grave Tradesmen, and sapient Physicians.

THE little Consistories of Wit claimed his first Attention, being a Dog of a natural Turn for Humour, and he took a Pleasure to hear young *Templars* criticise the Works of *Shakespear*, call Mr. *Garrick* to Account every Evening for his Action, extol the Beauty of Actresses, and the Reputation of Whores. Here the illustrious Mr. *F——t* (before he was yet exalted to the Dignity of keeping a Chariot and Bay-horses, which perhaps may not be *the highest Exaltation*[1] he has yet to undergo) used to harangue to a Club of his Admirers, and like a great Professor of Impudence, teach them the Principles of that immortal Science. Here he conceived the first Thought of *giving Tea*, and *milling Chocolate*;[2] and here he laid the Plan of all those mighty Operations he has since atchieved. The Master of the Coffee-house himself is a great Adept in modern Literature, and, I believe reads Lectures of Wit to young *Templars* on their first Appearance in Town.

POMPEY, when he was tired of the Clubs of Humour, would betake himself to another Table, and listen to a Junto of Politicians, who used to assemble here in an Evening with the most public-spirited Views; namely, to settle the Affairs of the Nation, and point out the Errors of the Ministry. Here he has heard the Government arraigned in the most abusive manner, for what the Government never performed or thought of; and the lowest Ribaldry of a dirty News-paper cried up as the highest Touches of Attic Irony. He has heard Sea-fights condemned by People who never saw the Sea even thro' a Telescope; and the General of an Army called to Account for his Disposition of a Battle, by Men whose Knowledge of War never reached beyond a Cock-match.

A CURIOUS Conversation of this kind happened one Day in his hearing, which I shall beg leave to relate as a little Specimen of Coffee-house Oratory. It happened at the End of the late Rebellion;[3] and the chief Orator of the Club began as usual with asserting, that the Rebellion was promoted by the Ministry for some private Ends of their own. 'What was the Reason, said he, of its being disbelieved so long? Why was our Army absent at

such a critical Conjuncture? let any Man tell me that. I
should be glad to hear any Man answer me these Questions.
D—mn it, they may think perhaps they are acting all this
while in secret, and applaud themselves for their Cunning;
but I believe I know more than they would wish me to
know. Thank God I can see a little, if I please to open
my Eyes; and if I was in the House of Commons——
'Zounds, old *Walpole* is behind the Curtain still, notwithstanding his Resignation, and the old Game is
playing over again, whatever they may pretend——
There was a Correspondence between *Walpole* and *Fleury*,[1]
to my Knowledge, and they projected between them all
the Evils that have since happened to the Nation.'

THE Company all seemed to agree with this eloquent
Gentleman's Sentiments; and one of them ventured to
say, he believed the Army was sent into *Flanders*, on
purpose to be out of the Way at the Time of the In-
surrection. ''Zounds, says the Orator, I believe you are
in the right, and the Wind blew them over against their
Inclinations. Pox! What made *What-d'ye-callum's* Army
disperse as it did? let any body answer me that, if they are
able. Don't you think they had Orders from above to
run away?—By-G—d I do, if you don't, and I believe
I could prove it too, if I was to set about it. Besides, if
they have any Desire of preventing future Invasions
from *France*, why don't they send out and burn all their
Shipping? Why don't they send out *V-rn-n*[2] with a
strong Fleet, and let him burn all their Shipping? I
warrant him, if he had a proper Commission in his
Pocket, he would not leave a Harbour or a Ship in
France——but they know they don't dare do it for fear
of Discoveries; they are in League with the *French*
Ministry; or else, damme, can any thing be so easy as
to take and burn all the Shipping in *France*?'

A GENTLEMAN, who had hitherto sat silent at the
Table, replied, with a Sneer on his Countenance, 'No,

Sir, nothing in the World can be so easy, except talking about it.' This drew the Eyes of the Company upon him, and every one began to wink at his Neighbour, when the Orator resumed the Discourse in the following manner. 'Talk, Sir? No, by G—d, we are come to that pass, that we don't dare talk now-a-days; things are come to such a pass, that we don't dare open our Mouths.' 'Sir, said the Gentleman, I think you have been talking already with great Licentiousness; and let me add too, with great Indecency on a very serious Subject.' ''Zounds, Sir, said the Orator, may not I have the liberty of speaking my Mind freely upon any Subject that I please? why, we don't live in *France*, Sir; you forget, surely——This is *England*, this is honest *Old England*, Sir, and not a *Mahometan* Empire; tho' God knows how long we shall continue so in the Way we are going on——and yet, forsooth, we must not talk; our Mouths are to be sewed up, as well as our Purses taken from us——Here we are paying four Shillings in the Pound, and yet we must not speak our Minds freely.' 'Sir, said the Gentleman, undoubtedly you may speak your Mind freely; but the Laws of your Country oblige you not to speak Treason, and the Laws of Good manners should dispose you to speak with Decency and Respect of your Governors. You say, Sir, we are come to that pass, that we dare not talk——I protest, that is very extraordinary; and if I was called upon to answer this Declaration, I would rather say we are come to that pass now-a-days, that we talk with more Virulence and Ill-language than ever——we talk upon Subjects, which it is impossible we should understand, and advance Assertions, which we know to be false. Bold Affirmations against the Government are believed merely from the Dint of Assurance with which they are spoken, and the idlest Jargon often passes for the soundest Reasoning. Give me leave to say, You, Sir, are a living Example of the Lenity of that Government, which you are abusing for want of Lenity, and your own Practice in the strongest manner confuses your own Assertions—but I beg we may call another Subject.'

HERE the Orator having nothing more to reply, was resolved to retire from a Place where he could no longer make a Figure. Wherefore, flinging down his Reckoning, and putting on his Hat with great Vehemence, he walked away muttering surlily to himself, *Things are come to a fine pass truly, if People may not have the liberty of Talking.* The rest of the Company separated soon afterwards, all of them harbouring no very favourable Opinion of the Gentleman, who had taken the Courage to stand up in Defence of the Government. Some imagined he was a Spy, others concluded he was a Writer of the Gazettes, and the most part were contented with only thinking him a Fool.

THE angry Orator was no sooner got home to his Family, and seated in his Elbow-chair at Supper, than he began to give vent to the Indignation he had been collecting; ''Zounds, said he, I have been called to account for my Words to-night. I have been told by a Jack-a-napes at the Coffee-house, that I must not say what I please against the Government. *Talk with Decency indeed!* a Fart of Decency!—let them act with Decency, if they have a mind to stop People's Mouths—Talk with Decency! d—mn 'em all, I'll talk what I please, and no King or Minister on Earth shall controul me. Let 'em behead me, if they have a mind, as they did *Balmerino*, and t'other Fellow, that died like a Coward.[1] Must I be catechized by a little Sycophant that kisses the A—e of a Minister? What is an *Englishman*, that dares not utter his Sentiments freely?—Talk with Decency! I wish I had kicked the Rascal out of the Coffee-house, and I will, if ever I meet him again, damme——Pox! we are come to a fine pass, if every little prating, pragmatical Jack-a-napes is to contradict a true-born *Englishman*.'

WHILE his Wife and Daughters sat trembling at the Vehemence of his Speeches, yet not daring to speak, for fear of drawing his Rage on themselves, he began to curse them for their Silence; and addressing himself to his Wife, 'Why do'st not speak, cries he? what, I suppose, I shall have you telling me by-and-by too, that I must talk with Decency?' 'My dear, said the Wife, with great Humility, I know nothing at all of the Matter.' 'No, cries he, I believe not; but you might know to dress a Supper, tho', and be d-mn'd to you——Here's nothing that I can eat, according to Custom. Pox, a Man may starve with such a Wife at the Head of his Family.'

WHEN the Cloth was removed, and he was preparing to fill his Pipe, unfortunately he could not find his Tobacco-stopper,[1] which again set his Choler at work. 'Go up Stairs, *Moll*! said he to one of his Daughters, and feel in my old Breeches Pocket——Damme, I believe that Scoundrel at the Coffee-house has robbed me *with his Decency*——Why do'st not stir, Girl? what, hast got the Cramp in thy Toes? Why, Papa, said the Girl flippantly, I am going as fast as I can.'——Upon which, immediately he threw a Bottle at her Head, and proceding from Invectives to Blows, he beat his Wife, kicked his Daughters, swore at his Servants; and after all this, went reeling up to Bed with Curses in his Mouth against the Tyranny of the Government.

NOTHING can be more common than Examples in this way of People, who preside over their Families with the most arbitrary brutal Severity, and yet are ready on all Occasions to abuse the Government for the smallest Exertion of its Power. To say the Truth, I scarce know a Man, who is not a *Tyrant in miniature*, over the Circle of his own Dependents; and I have observed those in particular to exercise the greatest Lordship over their Inferiors, who are most forward to complain of Oppression from their Superiors. Happy is it for the World, that this

Coffee-house Statesman was not born a King, for one may very justly apply to him the Line of *Martial*.

Hei mihi! si fueris tu Leo, qualis eris?[1]

CHAPTER XV

A Description of Counsellor Tanturian.

B UT among the many People, who frequented this Coffee-House, *Pompey* was delighted with no-body more than with the Person of Counsellor *Tanturian*; who used to crawl out once a Week, to read all the public Papers from *Monday* to *Monday*, at the moderate Price of a Penny. His Dress and Character were both so extraordinary, as will excuse a short Digression upon them.

H E set out originally with a very humble Fortune at the *Temple*, not without Hopes, however, of arriving, some Time or other, at the Chancellor's Seat: But having tried his Abilities once or twice at the Bar, to little Purpose, Nature soon whispered in his Ear, that he was never designed for an Orator. He attended the Judges indeed, after this, through two or three Circuits, but finding his Gains by no means equivalent to his Expences, he thought it most prudent to decline the noisy *Forum*, and content himself with giving Advice to Clients in a Chamber. Either his Talents here also were deficient, or Fame had not sufficiently divulged his Merit, but his Chamber was seldom disturbed with Visiters, and he had few Occasions to envy the Tranquillity of a Country Life, according to the Lawyer in *Horace*;

> *Agricolam laudat juris legumque peritus,*
> *Sub Galli cantum consultor ubi ostia pulsat.*[2]

His Temper grew soured and unsocial by Miscarriages, and the Narrowness of his Fortune obliging him to a

strict Frugality, he soon degenerated into Avarice. The
Rust of Money is very apt to infect the Soul; and People,
whose Circumstances condemn them to Œconomy, in
Time grow Misers from very Habit. This was the Case
with Counsellor *Tanturian*, who having quite discarded
the Relish of Pleasure, and finding his little Pittance, by
that Means, more than adequate to his Expences, resolved
to apply the Overplus to the laudable Purposes of Usury.
This noble Occupation he had followed a long Time,
and by it accumulated a Sum of Ten Thousand Pounds,
which his Heart would not suffer him to enjoy, tho' he
had neither Relation or Friend to leave it to at his Death.
He lived almost constantly alone in a dirty Chamber,
denying himself every Comfort of Life, and half-starved
for want of Sustenance. Neither Love, nor Ambition, nor
Joy, disturbed his Repose; his Passions all centered in
Money, and he was a kind of Savage within Doors.

THE Furniture of his Person was not less curious than
his Character. At home indeed he wore nothing but a
greasy Flannel Cap about his Head, and a dingy Night-
gown about his Body; but when he went abroad, he
arrayed himself in a Suit of Black, of full Twenty Years
standing, and very like in Colour to what is worn by
Undertakers at a Funeral. His Peruke, which had once
adorned the Head of a Judge in the Reign of Queen *Anne*,
spread copiously over his Back, and down his Shoulders.
By his Side hung an aged Sword, long rusted in its
Scabbard; and his black Silk Stockings had been so
often darned with a different Material, that, like Sir
John Cutler's,[1] they were now metamorphosed into black
Worsted Stockings.

SUCH was Counsellor *Tanturian*, who once a Week
came to read the News-Papers at the Coffee-house, where
Pompey lived. A Dog of any Talents for Humour could
not help being diverted with his Appearance, and our
Hero found great Pleasure in playing him Tricks, in

which he was secretly encouraged by every Body in the
Coffee-room. At first indeed, he never saw him without
barking at him, as at a Monster just dropped out of the
Moon; but when Time had a little reconciled him to his
Figure, he entertained the Company every Time he
came with some new Prank, at the Counsellor's Expence.
Once he ran away with his Spectacles; at another Time,
he laid violent Teeth on his Shirt, which hung out of his
Breeches, and shook it, to the great Diversion of all
Beholders: But what occasioned more Laughter than
any Thing, was a Trick that follows.

TANTURIAN had been tempted one Day, by two old
Acquaintance, to indulge his Genius at a Tavern; where
he complain'd highly of the Expensiveness of the Dinner,
tho' it consisted only of a Beef-steak and two Fowls.
That nothing might be lost, he took an Opportunity,
unobserved by the Company, to slip the Leg of a Pullet
into his Pocket; intending to carry it home for his Supper
at Night. In his Way he called at the Coffee-house, and
little *Pompey* playing about him as usual, unfortunately
happened to scent the Provision in the Counsellor's
Pocket. *Tanturian*, mean Time, was deeply engaged in
his News-paper, and *Pompey* getting slily behind him,
thrust his Head into the Pocket, and boldly seizing the
Spoils, displayed them in Triumph to the Sight of the
whole Room. The poor Counsellor could not stand the
Laugh, but retired home in a melancholly Mood, vexed
at the Discovery, and more vexed at the Loss of his
Supper.

BUT these Diversions were soon interrupted by a most
unlucky Accident, and our Hero, unfortunate as he has
hitherto been, is now going to suffer a Turn of Fate more
grievous than any he yet has known. Following the Maid
one Evening into the Streets, he unluckily missed her at
the Turning of an Alley, and happening to take a wrong
Way, prowled out of his Knowledge before he was aware.

He wandered about the Streets for many Hours, in vain endeavouring to explore his Way Home; in which Distress, his Memory brought back the cruel Chance that had separated him from his best Mistress Lady *Tempest*, and this Reflection aggravated his Misery beyond Description. At last, a Watchman picked him up, and carried him to the Watch-house. There he spent his Night in all the Agonies of Horror and Despair. 'How deplorable, thought he, is my Condition, and what is Fortune preparing to do with me? Have I not already gone through Scenes of Wretchedness enough, and must I again be turned adrift to the Mercy of Fate? What unrelenting Tyrant shall next be my Master? Or what future Oyster-woman shall next torture me with her Caresses? Cruel, cruel Fortune! when will thy Persecutions end?'

CHAPTER XVI

A short Chapter, containing all the Wit, and all the Spirit, and all the Pleasure of modern young Gentlemen.

As he was thus abandoning himself to Lamentation and Despair, some other Watchmen brought in two fresh Prisoners to bear him Company in his Confinement, who, I am sorry to say it, were two young Lords. They were extremely disordered, both in their Dress, and their Understanding; and Champaigne was not the only Enemy they had encountered that Evening. One of them had lost his Coat and Waist-coat; the other his Bag and Peruke,[1] all but a little circular Lock of Hair, which grew to his Forehead, and now hanging over his Eyes, added not a little to the Drollery of his Figure.

THE generous God of the Grape had cast such a Mist over their Understandings, that they were insensible at first of the Place they were promoted to; but at length,

one of them a little recovering his Wits, cried out, 'What
the Devil Place is this? A Bawdy-house, or a Presbyterian
Meeting-house?' 'Neither, Sir, answered a Watchman,
but the Round-house.' 'O P—x, said his Lordship, I
thought you had been a dissenting Parson, old Grey-
beard, and was going to preach against Wh—ring, for
you must know, old Fellow, I am confoundedly *in for it*—
But what Privilege have you, Sir, to carry a Man of
Honour to the Round-house?' 'Ay, said the other, what
Right has such an old Fornicator as thou art, to interrupt
the Pleasures of Men of Quality? May not a Nobleman
get drunk, without being disturbed by a Pack of Rascals
in the Streets?' 'Gentlemen, answered the Watch, we
are no Rascals, but Servants of His Majesty King *George*,
and His Majesty requires us to take up all People that
commit disorderly Riots in His Majesty's Streets.' 'You
lie, you Scoundrels, said one of their Lordships, 'tis the
Prerogative of Men of Fashion to do what they please,
and I'll prosecute you for a Breach of Privilege——
D—mn you, my Lord, I'll hold you Fifty Pound, that
old Prig there, in the great Coat, is a Cuckold, and he
shall be Judge himself.—How many Eyes has your Wife
got, old Fellow? one or two?' 'Well, well, said the Watchman, your Honours may abuse us as much as you please;
but we know we are doing our Duty, and we will perform
it in the King's Name.' 'Your Duty, you Rascal, cried
one of these Men of Honour, is immediately to fetch us a
Girl, and a Dozen of Champagne; if you'll perform that,
I'll say you are as honest an old Son of a Whore, as ever
lay with an Oyster-woman. My dear *Fanny!* if I had but
you here, and a Dozen of *Ryan*'s Claret, I should esteem
this Round-house a Palace—Curse me, if I don't love to
sleep in a Round-house sometimes; it gives a Variety to
Life, and relieves one from the Insipidness of a soft Bed.'
'Well-said, my Hero, answered his Companion, and
these old Scoundrels shall carry us before my Lord Mayor

To-morrow, for the Humour of the Thing. Pox take him, I buy all my Tallow-candles of his Lordship, and therefore I am sure he'll use me like a Man of Honour.'

IN such kind of gay modish Conversation did these illustrious Persons consume their Night, and principally in laying Wagers, which at present is the highest Article of modern Pleasure. Every Particular of human Life is reduced by the great Calculators of Chances to the Condition of a *Bet*; but nothing is esteemed a more laudable Topic of *Wagering*, than the Lives of eminent Men; which, in the elegant Language of *Newmarket*, is called *running Lives*;[1] that is to say, a Bishop against an Alderman, a Judge against a Keeper of a Tavern, a Member of Parliament against a famous Boxer; and in this Manner all People's Lives are wager'd out, with proper Allowances for their Ages, Infirmities, and Distempers. Happy the Nation that can produce such ingenious, accomplished Spirits!

THESE two honourable Peers had been spending their Evening at a Tavern, with many others, and when the rational Particle was thoroughly drowned in Claret, one of the Company leaping from his Chair, cried out, *Who will do any Thing?* upon which, a Resolution was immediately taken, to make a Sally into the Streets, and drink Champagne upon the Horse at *Charing-Cross*.[2] This was no sooner projected than executed, and they performed a great Number of heroical Exploits, too long to be mentioned in this Work, but we hope some future Historian will arise to immortalize them for the sake of Posterity. After this was over, they resolved to scour the Streets, and perceiving a Light in a Cellar under Ground, our two Heroes magnanimously descended into that subterranean Cave, in quest of Adventures. There they found some Hackney Coachmen enjoying themselves with Porter and Tobacco, whom they immediately attacked, and offered to box the two sturdiest Champions

of the Company. The Challenge was accepted in a
Moment, and whilst our Heroes were engaged, the rest
of the Coachmen chose to make off with their Cloaths,
which they thought no inconsiderable Booty. In short,
these Gentlemen of Pleasure and High-life were heartily
drubbed, and obliged to retreat with Shame from the
Cellar of Battle, leaving their Cloaths behind them, as
Spoils, at the Mercy of the Enemy. Soon afterwards, they
were taken by the Watch, being too feeble to make
Resistance, and conducted to the Round-house; where
they spent their Night in the Manner already described.
The next Morning, they returned Home in Chairs,
new-dressed themselves, and then took their Seats in
Parliament, to enact Laws for the Good of their Country.

CHAPTER XVII

Our Hero falls into great Misfortunes.

WHEN the Watchman had discharged himself in the
Morning of these honourable Prisoners, he next
bethought himself of little *Pompey*, who had fallen into
his Hands in a more inoffensive manner. Him he presented that Day to a blind Beggar of his Acquaintance,
who had lately lost his Dog, and wanted a new Guide to
conduct him about the Streets. Here *Pompey* again fell
into the most desponding Meditations. 'And was this
Misery, thought he, reserved in store to compleat the
Series of my Misfortunes? Am I destined to lead about
the dark Footsteps of a blind, decrepit, unworthy Beggar?
Must I go daggled thro' the Streets with a Rope about
my Neck, linking me to a Wretch that is the Scorn of
human Nature? O that a Rope were fixed about my
Neck indeed for a nobler Purpose, and that I were here
to end a dreadful, tormenting Existence! Can I bear to

hear the Sound of, *Pray remember the poor blind Beggar?*
I who have conversed with Lords and Ladies; who have
slept in the Arms of the fairest Beauties, and lived on the
choicest Dainties this habitable Globe can afford! Cruel,
cruel Fortune! when will thy Persecutions end?'

BUT when the first Emotions of his Grief were a little
calmed, he began to call in the Aids of Philosophy; the
many useful Lessons he had learnt from the sage *Mopsa*,
inspired him with Resolution; and he fortified himself
besides, with remembering a Speech in *King Lear*,[1] which
he had formerly heard at *Drury-Lane* Play-house.——

> *To be worst,*
> *The lowest, most dejected thing of Fortune,*
> *Stands still in Esperance, lives not in Fear;*
> *The lamentable Change is from the best,*
> *The worst returns to Laughter. Welcome then*
> *Thou unsubstanstial Air, which I embrace;*
> *The Wretch, that thou hast blown unto the worst,*
> *Owes nothing to thy Blasts.*

TO say the Truth, his Condition was not so deplorable
upon Trial, as it appeared in Prospect: For tho' he was
condemned to travel thro' dirty Streets all Day long in
quest of Charity, yet at Night, both he and his Master
fared sumptuously enough on their Gains; and many a
lean Projector,[2] or starving Poet might envy the Suppers
of this blind Beggar. He seldom failed to collect four
Shillings a Day, and used to sit down to his hot Meals
with as much Stateliness, as a Peer could do to a regular
Entertainment and Dessert.

THERE is a Story I have often heard of a crippled
Beggar, who used constantly to apply for Alms at *Hyde-
Park* Corner; where a Gentleman, who was then just
recovered from a dangerous Fit of Illness, never failed to
give him Six-pence every Morning, as he passed by in his
Chariot for the Air. A Servant of this Gentleman's going

by chance one Day into an Alehouse, discovered this same
Beggar sitting down to a Breast of Veal with some more
of the Fraternity, and heard him raving at the Landlord,
because the Bur[1] was gone, and he had no Lemon ready
to squeeze over it; adding many Threats of leaving the
House, if their Dinners were not served up for the future
with more Regularity and Respect. The Servant informed
his Master of this extraordinary Circumstance, and next
Morning when the pampered Hypocrite applied for his
Charity as usual, in the old lamentable Voice, the
Gentleman put his Head out of the Chariot, and told him,
with a Sarcasm, *No, Sir, I can eat Veal without Lemon.*

THE Reader, I hope, will be contented to pass over
many of the Miseries which *Pompey* suffered in this wretched
Service; for as we have a great Regard for his Memory,
we cannot be supposed to dwell with any Pleasure on his
Misfortunes. After he had lived some Months in *London*,
his blind Master set out for *Bath*; whither he always
resorted in the public Seasons; not for the sake of playing
at EO, it may be imagined, nor yet for the Pleasure of
being taken out by the accomplish'd Mr. *Nash*,[2] to dance
a Minuet at a Ball; but with the hopes of a plentiful
Harvest among infirm People, whom Ill-health disposes
to Charity. The Science of Begging is reduced to certain
Principles of Art, as well as all other Professions; and as
Sickness is generally a Motive to Compassion, the Objects
of Charity flock thither in great Numbers; for wherever
the Carrion is, there will the Crows be also.

[. . . .]

[THE many adventures that befel them on their
journey; how terribly our hero was fatigued with travelling thro' miry highways, who had been used to ride in
coaches and six; and how often he wished his blind tyrant
would drop dead with an apoplexy, shall all be left to the
reader's imagination. Suffice it to say, that in about
three weeks or a month's time, they arrived at the end

of their journey, and the beggar readily groped out his way to a certain alehouse, which he always favoured with his company; where the landlord received him with great respect, professing much satisfaction to find *his honour* so well in health. By this the reader will perceive that he was a beggar of some distinction.

IF our hero made any reflexion, he could not help being surprized at such civility, paid to such a person in such a place; but how much greater reason had he for astonishment, when on the evening of their arrival, he saw a well-drest woman enter the room, and accost his master in the following terms, 'Papa, how do you do? you are welcome to *Bath*.' The beggar no sooner heard her voice, than he started from his chair, and gave her a paternal kiss; which the fair lady received with an air of scorn and indifference, telling him, 'he had poisoned her with his bushy beard.' When this ceremony was over, she threw herself into an arm-chair, and began to harangue in the following manner——'Well, papa, so you are come to *Bath* at last; I thought we should not have seen you this season, and I have immediate necessity for a sum of money. Sure no mortal ever had such luck at cards, as I have had. You must let me have five or ten pound directly.' 'Five or ten pound!' cries the beggar in amaze; 'how in the devil's name should I come by five or ten pound?' 'Come, come, no words,' cried the daughter, 'for I absolutely must and will have it in spite of your teeth. I know you are worth above a hundred pounds, and what can you do with your money better, than give it me to make a figure in life with? Deuce take the men, they are grown so plaguy modest, or so plaguy stingy, that really 'tis hardly worth coming to *Bath* now in the seasons. Hang me if I have had a cull this twelve-month— but do you know, old dad, that brother *Jack's* at the *Bath?*'

'OH!' cries the beggar, 'there's another of my plagues—

I shall have him dunning me for money too very soon I suppose, for the devil can't answer the extravagancies of that fellow. Well, he'll certainly come to be hanged at last, that's my comfort, and I think the sooner he swings, the better it will be for his poor father, and the whole kingdom.'

'HANGED!' replied the lady; 'no, no, *Jack* is in no danger of hanging at present, I assure you; he is now the most accomplished, modish, admired young fellow at the *Bath*; the peculiar favourite of all the ladies; and in a fair way of running off with a young heiress of considerable fortune. Let me see, old dad—If you'll bespeak a private room, and have a little elegant supper ready at eleven o'clock to morrow night (for *Jack* won't be able to get away from the rooms sooner than eleven) I'll bring him to sup with you, and you shall hear his history from his own mouth.' To this the old hypocrite her father readily consented, and promised to provide something decent for them; after which, starting from her chair, 'well, papa,' said she, 'you must excuse me at present, for I expect company at my lodgings, and so can't afford to waste any more time with you in this miserable dog-hole of an ale-house.' Having made this polite apology, she flew to her chair, which waited at the door, and was conducted home with as much importance, as if she had been a princess of the blood.

THE next day, the blind imposter, attended by our hero, went out on his pilgrimage, and continued whining for charity, and profaning the name of G—d till night; after which, he returned to his ale-house, put on a better coat, and got himself in readiness for the reception of his son and daughter. At the hour appointed, these illustrious personages entered the room, and the conversation was opened by the son in the following easy strain. 'Old boy!' (cries he, seizing his father by the hand) 'I am glad to see thee with all my heart. Well, old fellow, how does your crutch and blind eyes do? what, you continue still in the old canting hypocritical way, I perceive—Pox take you, I saw you hobbling through the streets to-day, old miserable, but you know I am ashamed to take notice of you in public—tho' I think I have thrown you down many a tester at the corner of a street, without your knowing whom you are obliged to for such a piece of generosity.'

'SIR, I honour your generosity,' replied the beggar; 'but, prythee *Jack*, they tell me you are going to be married to an heiress of great fortune, is there any truth in the story?'

HERE the beau-sharper took a *French* snuff-box out of his pocket, and having entertained his nose with a pinch of rappee,[1] replied as follows. 'Yes, sir, my unaccountable somewhat has had the good luck to make conquest of a little amorous tit, with an easy moderate fortune of about fifteen thousand pounds, who does me the honour to doat on this person of mine to distraction. But prythee, old blue-beard, how didst thou come by this piece of intelligence?' 'From that fine lady your sister, sir,' replied the beggar. 'O pox! I thought so,' cries the beau. '—*Bess* can never keep any thing in her but her teeth, nor them neither, can you *Bess?* you understand me—but as I was saying, concerning this match; yes, sir, I have the honour at present to be principal favourite of all the women at *Bath*; they are all dying with love of me, and I may do what I please with any of them; but I, sir, neglecting the rest, have singled out a little amorous wanton, with a trifling fortune of fifteen or twenty thousand pounds only, whom I shall very soon whip into a chariot, I believe, and drive away to a parson.'

'LORD!' cries the father, 'if she did but know what a thief she is going to marry!'

'WHY, what then? you old curmudgeon! she would be the more extravagantly fond of me on that account.

'Tis very fashionable, sir, for ladies to fall in love with highwaymen now-a-days. They think it discovers a soul, a genius, a spirit in them, above the little prejudices of education; and I believe I could not do better than let her know that I have returned from transportation.—But prythee, old dim, what hast got for supper to night?' 'Nothing I am afraid that a gentleman of your fashion can condescend to eat,' replied the beggar; 'for I have only ordered a dish of veal cutlets, and a couple of roasted fowls.' 'Come, come, prythee don't pretend to droll, old blinker!' cries the son, 'but produce your musty supper as fast as you can, and then I'll treat you with a bottle of *French* claret. Come, let us be merry, and set in for a jovial evening. Pox! I have some little kind of sneaking regard for thee, for begetting me, notwithstanding your crutch and blind eyes, and I think I am not altogether sorry to see thee.—Here, drawer, landlord, bring up supper directly, you dog, or I'll set fire to your house.'

THIS extraordinary summons had the desired effect, and supper being placed on the table, the three worthy guests sat down to it with great importance. The lady took upon her to manage the ceremonies, and asked her papa in the first place, if she should help him to some veal cutlets? to which the answer was, 'if you please madam!' When she had served her father, she then performed the same office to herself; after which, twirling the dish round with a familiar air, 'I'll leave you,' said she, 'to take care of yourself, *Jack!*' Much mirth and pleasantry reigned at this peculiar meal, to the utter astonishment of the master of the house, who had never seen the like before. When supper was over, and they began to feel the inspiration of the claret, '*Jack!*' says the father, 'I think I know nothing of your history, since you returned from transportation—Suppose you should begin and entertain us with an account of your exploits.' 'With all my heart,' cries the son; 'I believe I shall publish my life one of these days, if ever I am driven to necessity, for I fancy it will make a very pretty neat *duodecimo*; and 'tis the fashion, you know, now-a-days for all whores and rogues to entertain the world with their memoirs.— Come, let us take another glass round to the health of my dear little charmer, and then I'll begin my adventures.' Having so said, he filled out three bumpers, drank his toast on his knees,[1] and then commenced his narration in the following manner.]

CHAPTER XVIII

[*The history of a highwayman.*]

I THINK you have often told me, old father hypocrite, that you begat me under a hedge near *Newberry* in *Berkshire*. This, I confess, is not the most honourable way of coming into the world, but no man is answerable for his birth, and therefore what signifies prevarication? *Alexander* I have heard was the son of a flying dragon, and *Romulus* was suckled by a plaguy confounded wolf, as I have read in *Hooke's Roman* history,[2] and yet in time he grew to be a very pretty young fellow, and a king— but you are ignorant of these matters, both of you, and therefore I only play the fool to talk about them in such company.

'WELL, sir, as soon as I was born, my mother, I suppose, wrapped me up in the dirty rags of an old rotten petticoat, and lugged me about behind her shoulders, as an object to move compassion. In this agreeable situation, nuzzling behind the back of a lousy drab—excuse me, old fellow, for making so free with your consort—in this situation, I suppose, I visited all the towns in *England*, and 'tis amazing I was not crippled with having my feet and limbs bundled up in such close confinement. But I kicked hard for liberty, and at length came out that easy, *degagé*, jaunty young fellow of fashion, which you now behold me.

'MY genius very early began to shew itself, and before I was twelve years old, you know I had acquired a great reputation for sleight of hand: which being reported to a great master of that science, he immediately took me under his care, and promised to initiate me into all the mysteries of the art. Thus I bade adieu to the dirty employment of begging, left father and mother, and struck into a higher sphere in life.

'AT first indeed I meddled only with petty larceny, and was sent out to try my hand on execution-days at *Tyburn*; where having acquitted myself with honour, I was quickly promoted to better business, and by the time I was fifteen, began to make a great figure in the passages about the theatres. Many a gentleman's fob have I eased of the trouble of carrying a watch; and tho' it may look like vanity to say so, I believe I furnished more brokers shops and pedlars boxes, than half the pickpockets in *London* besides. None of them all had so great a levee of travelling *Jews* to traffick for buckles, seals, watches, tweezar-cases, and the like, as I had. But my chief dexterity was in robbing the ladies—there is a particular art, a peculiar delicacy required in whipping one's hand up a lady's petticoats, and carrying off her pockets, which few of them ever attain to with any success. That now was my glory—that was my delight— I performed it to admiration, and out-did them all in this branch of the craft.

'I REMEMBER once a chambermaid of my acquaintance, a flame of mine, gave me notice that her young lady would be at the play such a night, with a pair of diamond buckles in her shoes. You may be sure I watched her into her coach, marked her into her box, and waited for her coming out, with some more of the fraternity to assist me. At last, as soon as the play was over, out she came tittering and laughing with her companions, who by good luck happened to be all of her own sex. This now was my time; I had her up in my arms in a moment, while one of my comrades whipped off her shoes with prodigious expedition: but my reason for telling the story is this—while I had her in my arms, let me die if I could help giving her a kiss, which hang me, if the little trembler did not seem to return, with her heart panting, and breasts heaving—Deuce take me, if I was not almost sorry afterwards to see her walking to her coach, without any shoes upon her feet.

'WELL, sir, this was my course of life for a few years. But ambition, you know, is a thing never to be satisfied, and having gained all the glory I could in this way, my next step of promotion was to the gaming-tables. Here I played with great success a long while, and shared in the fleecing many raw young cullies, who had more money than wit. But one unfortunate night, the devil or my evil genius carried me to a masquerade, and there in the ill-omen'd habit of a fryer, being fool enough to play upon an honourable footing, I lost all I had to a few shillings. This was a confounded stroke, this was a stunning blow to me—I lay a bed all the next day, raving at my ill-fortune, and beating my brains, to think I could be such an ass as to play upon the square. At last in a fit of despair, I started out of bed about nine or ten o'clock at night, borrowed a friend's horse, bought a second-hand pair of poppers,[1] with the little silver that was left me, and away I rode full gallop, night and rainy as it was, for *Hounslow Heath*. There I wandered about half-dead with cold and fear till morning, and to say the truth, began to grow devilish sick of my business. When day broke, the first object that presented itself to my eyes, I remember, was a gallows within a hundred yards of me; this seemed

plaguy ominous, and I was very near riding back to
London without striking a stroke. At last, while I was
wavering in this state of uncertainty, behold, a stage-
coach comes gently, softly ambling over the *Heath*.
Courage, my heart, cries I, there can be no fear of resistance here; a stage-coach is the most lucky thing in
the world for a young adventurer; and so saying, I clapt
on my mask, (the same I had worn the night before at
the *Hay-Market*) set spurs to my horse, and presented my
pistol at the coach-window. How the passengers behaved,
I know not. For my own part, I was more than half
blind with fear, and taking what they gave me without
any expostulation, away I rode, exceedingly well satisfied
to have escaped without resistance. Taking courage
however at this success, I attacked another stage-coach
with greater bravery, and afterwards a third with so
much magnanimity, that I even ventured to search some
of the passengers, who I thought defrauded me of my due.
Here now I should have left off, and all had been well—
but that devil avarice prompting me to get a little more,
I attacked a single horseman, and plundered him of a
watch and about thirty guineas. The scoundrel seemed to
pursue his journey quietly enough, but meeting afterwards with some of his friends on the road, and relating
his case to them, they all agreed to pursue me. Meanwhile,
sir, I was jogging on contentedly at my ease, when turning
round on a sudden, I saw this tremendous grazier, and
two or three more bloody-minded fellows, that seemed
each as big as a giant, in full pursuit of me. Away I
dashed thro' thick and thin, as if the devil drove; but
being wretchedly mounted, I was surrounded, appre-
hended, carried before that infernal Sir *Thomas Deveil*,[1]
and he committed me.

'N o w I was in a sweet condition. This was a charming
revolution in my life. *Newgate* and the prospect of a
gallows, furnish a man with very agreeable reflexions.

O that cursed *Old-Baily!* I shall never forget the sentence which the hum-drum son of a whore of a judge passed upon me—*You shall hang till you are dead, dead, dead*—faith I was more than half-dead with hearing it, and in that plight I was dragged back to my prison.

'EXCELLENT lodging in the condemned hole!——pretty music the death warrant rings in a man's ears!——but as good luck would have it, while I was expecting every hour to be tucked up, his majesty (G—d bless him) took pity on me the very day before execution, and sent me a reprieve for transportation. To describe the transport I felt at this moment, would be impossible; I was half-mad with joy, and instead of reflecting that I was going to slavery, fancied myself going to heaven. The being shipped off for *Jamaica* was so much better a voyage, I thought, than ferrying over that same river *Styx* with old gaffar *Charon*, that I never once troubled myself about what I was to suffer, when I got thither.

'NOT to be tedious, (for I hate a long story) to *Jamaica* I went, with a full resolution of making my escape by the first opportunity, which I very soon accomplished. After leading the life of a dog for about a year and a half, I got on board a ship which was coming for *England*, and arrived safe and sound on the coast of *Cornwal*. My dear native country! how it revived my heart to see thee again! O *London, London!* no woman of quality, after suffering the vapours for a whole summer in the country, ever sighed after thee with greater desire than I did. But as I landed without a farthing of money in my pocket, I was obliged to beg my way up to town in the habit of a sailor, telling all the way the confoundedst lies—how I had been taken by pirates, and fought with the *Moors*, who were going to eat me alive, and twenty other unaccountable stories, to chouse[1] silly women of a few half-pence.

'WELL, at last I entered the dear old metropolis, and went immediately in quest of a gang of sharpers, which I formerly frequented. These jovial blades were just then setting out for *New-Market* races, and very generously took me into their party. They supplied me with cloaths, lent me a little money to begin with, and in short set me up again in the world. There is nothing like courage— 'tis the life, the soul of business—Accordingly on the very first day's sport, having marked out the horse that I saw was the favourite of the knowing-ones, I offered great odds, made as many bets as I could, and trusted myself to fortune; resolving to scamper off the course as hard as I could drive, if I saw her likely to declare against me. But as it happened to make amends for her former ill-usage, the jade now decided in my favour; 'twas quite *a hollow thing*;[1] *Goliah* won the day, and I pocketted up about three-score guineas. Of this I made excellent use at the gaming-tables, and in short when the week was over, carried away from *New-Market* a cool three hundred. Now, my dear *Bess*, I was a man again; I returned immediately to *London*, equipped myself with lace-cloaths, rattled down to *Bath* in a post-chaise, gave myself out for the eldest son of Sir *Jeremy Griskin* of the kingdom of *Ireland*, and struck at once into all the joys of high-life. This is a little epitome of my history—Having been a pick-pocket, a sharper, a slave, and a highwayman, I am now the peculiar favourite of all the ladies at *Bath*.'

HERE the beau finished his story, and sat expecting the applauses of his company, which he very soon received on the part of his sister: but as to that worthy gentleman his father, he had been fast asleep for several minutes, and did not hear the conclusion of this wonderful history. Being now waked by silence, and the cessation of his son's voice, as he had been before lulled to sleep by his talking, he cried out from the midst of a doze——'So, she's a very fine girl, is she, *Jack?*—a very fine girl?'

'WHO is a very fine girl?' cries the sharper, slapping him over the shoulder; 'why, zounds thou art asleep, old miserable, and dost not know a syllable of what has been said.'

'YES, sir, I do know what has been said,' returned the father, 'and therefore you need not beat one so, *Jack!*—You was telling about going to be married—and going to *Jamaica.*'

'GOING to *Jamaica!* pox take thee, thou wantest to be going to bed. Why was there ever such a wretched old dotard? I have not seen thee these seven or eight years, and perhaps may never see thee again, for thou'lt be rotten in a year or two more, and yet canst not put a little life into thyself for one evening. Come *Bess*,' added he, 'let us take another bumper, and then bid old drowsy good night——*Silenus*[1] will snore, do what one can to prevent him. Here my girl! here's prosperity to love, and may all sleepers go to the devil.'

'NAY, nay,' cries the father; 'consider *Jack*, 'tis past my bed-time many hours ago. You fine gentlemen of the world are able to bear these fashionable hours, but I have been used to live by the light of the sun. Besides, if you had been drudging about after charity, as I have all day long, I fancy you would not be in a much better condition than your poor father; but really you sharpers don't consider the toil and trouble of earning one's bread in an honest way. Why now I have not gathered above six or seven shillings this whole day, and that won't half pay for our supper to night.'

HERE the beau bestowed several curses on him for his stinginess, and contemptuously bidding him hoard up his miserable pelf, generously undertook to pay the whole. The bill was then called for, the reckoning discharged, and the company separated, having first however made an agreement to meet there the succeeding evening. And thus ended this illustrious compotation.

CHAPTER XIX

[*Adventures at the* Bath.]

NEXT morning the blind beggar, conducted by our hero, went out as usual, and presented himself before the beau-monde on the parade. Some few people, afflicted with very ill health, were generous enough to throw him down a few sixpences; others only commended the beauty of his pretty dog; and far the greater number walked on without casting their eyes upon him.

As he was here howling forth the miseries of his condition in a most lamentable tone of voice, who should happen to pass by but his own accomplished son, in company with two ladies of figure, to whom he was talking with the greatest familiarity and ease? The gaiety of his laugh, the vivacity of his conversation, made him universally observed, and all the women on the parade seemed to envy the happiness of the two ladies with whom he was engaged.

As the party came very near the place, where the old hypocrite was stationed, he could not escape their notice; and the youngest of the ladies being struck with compassion at the sight of him, 'bless me,' says she, 'I am sure that poor old man is an object of charity. Do stay a moment, lady *Marmazet*, I am resolved to give him something.' 'Pshaw, my dear! come along, child,' cries her ladyship; 'how can you be so ridiculous, miss *Newcome*? who gives any money to charity now a-days?' 'True, madam, your ladyship is perfectly in the right,' replied the beau, (who now discovered his own father) 'nothing can be more idle, I think, than throwing one's money away upon a set of thievish tatterdemallion wretches, who are the burthen of the nation, and ought to be exterminated from the face of the earth.' 'Well, well, you may say what you please, both of you,' says miss *Newcome*, 'but I am resolved to be generous this morning, and therefore it does not signify laughing at me. Here, master, gaffar——, here's sixpence for you.'

ALL this while Mr. *Griskin* was in extreme pain, for tho' he had no reason to fear any discovery, yet the consciousness that this deplorable object was his own father, hurt the gentleman's pride in the presence of his mistress, and greatly checked his vivacity. He endeavoured therefore all he could to hurry the young lady away from so unpleasant a scene; in which he was seconded by lady *Marmazet*, who kept crying out; 'How can you be so monstrously preposterous, miss *Newcome?* come along girl! as I hope to be saved I am ashamed of you—we shall have all the eyes of the company upon us in a few minutes.' 'I don't care a farthing for the company,' replied the young lady; 'I am resolved to ask the old man some questions, and therefore hold your tongue——What? are you quite blind, gaffar?'

BY this time 'squire *Griskin* was recovered from his first surprize, and perceiving no bad consequences likely to happen, thought he might venture to shine a little upon the occasion. 'Sirrah,' cries he, 'you miserable old dog! what do you mean by shocking people of quality here with a sight of your detestable physiognomy? whence do you come? what do you do out of your own parish? I'll have you whipt from constable to constable back to your own settlement.'

'No, please your noble honour,' cries the beggar, 'I hope your noble honour won't be so cruel to a poor blind man—a poor blind man, struck blind with lightning. Heaven preserve your honour from such calamities! I have very good friends down in *Cumberland*, please your royal worship, and I am travelling homeward as fast as I can, but it pleased heaven to strike me blind with a flash of lightning a long way from my relations, and I am reduced to beg for a little sustenance.'

'MERCY upon me!' cries miss *Newcome*——'why, what a vast way the miserable wretch has to travel, Mr. *Griskin!* how will he ever be able to get home?'

'OH, curse him, all a confounded lie from beginning to end, depend upon't madam! the dog has no relations or friends in the world, I'll answer for him,' cries the beau. Then turning to his father, 'here you old rascal,' added he, 'here's a shilling for you, and do you hear me, take yourself off this moment—If ever I see you upon the parade again, I'll have you laid by the heels, and sent to the house of correction.' The blind wretch then hobbled away, pouring forth a thousand benedictions upon them, while lady *Marmazet* and the sharper rallied miss *Newcome* for her unfashionable generosity.

LEAVING the reader to make his own remarks on this extraordinary occurrence; I shall pass over the intermediate space of time, in which nothing happened material to this history, and rejoin the three illustrious guests at their ale-house in the evening. The lady was the first that came, to whom her father related the adventure of the morning, which greatly delighted her: While she was laughing at this story, that sprightly knight her brother also came singing into the room, and throwing himself negligently into a chair, picked his teeth for a moment or two in silence. Then addressing himself to his father, 'old fellow,' cries he, 'I was obliged to use you a little roughly this morning, but you'll excuse me——There was a necessity you know of treating you like a scoundrel and an impostor, to prevent any suspicion of our relationship.' 'Well, well *Jack!*' replied the father, 'I forgive you, I forgive you with all my heart; for I suppose one of the ladies was your sweetheart, and to be sure 'twas as well not to let her know you was my son, for fear of the worst that might happen, tho'f you tell me women are so fond of marrying highwaymen now-a-days. Adad *Jack!* I wished for my eyes again, just to have had one little peep at her—what, is she a deadly fine girl?'

'A DIVINE creature, sir,' replied the beau; 'young, melting, amorous and beautiful; innocent as an angel, and yet wanton as the month of *May*; and then—she doats on me to distraction. Did you mind how tenderly the little fool interested herself about your blind eyes, and pitied you for the confounded lies you told her?'

'WHY yes, there was something very pretty I must confess,' said the father, 'very pretty indeed, in her manner of talking. How the deuce do you get acquainted with these great ladies?'

'O LET me alone for that,' returned Mr. *Griskin*; 'I am made for the women, sir! I have the *toujours gay*, which is so dear to them; I am blest with that agreeable impudence, that easy familiar way of talking nonsense, that happy insensibility of shame, which they all adore in men. And then, consider my figure, my shape, my air, my legs—all together, I find I am irresistible. How in the name of wonder, old fellow, could you and your trull strike out such a lucky hit under a country hedge?'

HERE the fair lady was in raptures at her brother's wit, and asked her father, if he did not think him a most delightful, charming young fellow? to which the beggar replied with a groan, 'O *Jack, Jack!* thou wilt certainly come to be hanged in the end; I see it as plain as can be; so much wit and impudence will certainly bring thee to the gallows at last.'

MUCH more of this sort of ribaldry and licentious conversation passed between them; and as the father was more wakeful this night, than he had been the preceding one, they protracted their cups till very late: they roared, they sung, they danced, and practised all sorts of unruly, drunken mirth. At last however, they separated once more to their several beds, and fate had destined that they should never meet again in joy and friendship, at this or any other ale-house; the cause whereof will be seen in the following chapter.

CHAPTER XX

[*More adventures at* Bath.]

THE father of young *Jeremy Griskin* was so pleased with the advantageous match his son was concluding, that in the joy of his heart, he could not help talking of it to the alehouse-keeper where he lodged; tho' he had imprecated a thousand curses on his head, if ever he revealed it. The alehouse-keeper likewise had bound himself by an equal number of oaths, never to discover what he heard from the beggar; and perhaps at the time he made these vows, he meant to observe them: but being once in possession of a secret, he found it impossible to be long easy with so troublesome a guest in his bosom. With a very mysterious face therefore he whispered to several coachmen and footmen, who frequented his house, 'that a very fine gentleman and lady came privately every night to visit an old blind beggar, who lodged with him; that these fine folks, by what he could learn, were the beggar's son and daughter; and that the fine gentleman lived amongst the quality, and was going to run away with a great fortune.'

THE story having made this progress, could not fail of proceeding farther; for being once communicated to the servants of several families, it was quickly served up to the tables of the great. The valets informed their masters, and the waiting gentlewomen their mistresses, as a new topic of conversation while they were dressing them.

FROM hence the rumour became public, and dispersed itself all over the *Bath*; so that the very next morning after the last rendezvous at the alehouse, when 'squire *Griskin* appeared with lady *Marmazet* and miss *Newcome* as usual in the pump-room, they found themselves stared on with more than common attention by all the company. Several gentlemen laughed aloud as they passed by them; the young ladies all affected to titter under their fans; and the elder dames tossed up their noses with the most insolent air of disdain. As all this could not be done without a meaning, the two ladies his companions were greatly astonished, and even the beau himself, fortified as he was in impudence, could not stifle some unpleasant apprehensions. He affected however to turn it off with an air of raillery, imputed it to the d—mn'd censoriousness of the *Bath*; and expressed his wonder that people could not be allowed to be free and intimate, without drawing on themselves the scandalous observations of a whole public place.

WHILE Mr. *Griskin* was supposed to be a gentleman, the whole tribe of coquettes and beauties looked on miss *Newcome* with eyes of jealousy and indignation, all of them envying her the happiness of engaging so accomplished a lover: but no sooner were they let into the secret of his parentage, than they began to triumph in their turns, and shewed their malice another way. Envy now changed into contempt; a malicious sneer was seen on all their faces, and they huddled together in little parties to feast on so agreeable a discovery. For spite is never so spiteful as among young ladies, who are rivals in love and beauty. 'Really, madam,' said one of them, 'one must be obliged to take care of one's pockets, because you know if sharpers are allowed to come into public places, and appear like gentlemen, one can never be safe a moment.' To which another replied, 'indeed I shall leave my watch at home when I go to the ball to night, for I don't think it safe to carry any thing valuable about one, while *miss Newcome's admirer* continues among us.' Many such speeches were flirted about; for tho' the story hitherto was only a flying suspicion, they were all fully persuaded of its truth, and resolutely bent to believe it, without waiting for any confirmation, and indeed without once troubling themselves to enquire on what authority it was founded.

THE gay sharper manifestly perceived from all this, that some discovery had been made to his disadvantage; but not being willing to resign his hopes till affairs appeared a little more desperate, he very courageously presented himself that evening in the ball-room. He was indeed prudent enough to abstain from minuets, not chusing to encounter the eyes of people in so conspicuous an attitude; but as soon as the company stood up to country-dances, with a face of infinite assurance, he led miss *Newcome* towards the top of the room, and took his station as usual among the foremost files. A buz immediately ran thro' the company, and when they came to dance, most of the ladies refused him their hands. This was a terrible blow to him; he knew not how to revenge the affront, nor yet how to behave under such an interdiction. Lady *Marmazet*, who saw with what scorn he was treated, very resolutely advanced and reprimanded several of her female acquaintance with much warmth for their behaviour, pretending it was an affront to miss *Newcome*, who came to *Bath* under her protection, and whose cause she was obliged to espouse. In reality, I believe there was another reason which quickened her ladyship's resentment, and made her behold with concern the indignities offered to a man, who had found the way of being agreeable to her ladyship, as well as to the young lady her companion. But however that be, 'tis certain her interfering did him little service; and after a thousand taunts and fleers, the unfortunate couple were obliged to sit down in a corner of the room. They stood up again some time afterwards to make a fresh attempt, which proved as unsuccessful as the former: in short, after repeated disgraces, they were obliged to give over all thoughts of dancing for the remaining part of the night; the poor girl trembling and wondering what could be the reason of all this behaviour; and even the beau himself looking very foolish under the consciousness of his own condition.

As it was pretty plain however that his father must have betrayed his secret, the ball no sooner broke up, than he flew with the greatest rage to the ale-house, rushed eagerly into the room, where the miserable wretch was then dozing, and fell upon him with all the bitterness of passion. 'Where is this old rascal?' cries he; 'what is it you mean by this, you detestable miscreant? I have a great mind to murder you, and give your carcase to the hounds!'

'BLESS us! what's the matter now, *Jack?*' said the beggar. 'Matter!' returned he; 'you have been prating, and tattling, and chattering. You have ruined me, you old villain, you have blown me up for ever. Speak, confess that you have discovered my secrets.'

HERE the beggar stammered and endeavoured to excuse himself, but was obliged at last to acknowledge, that he believed he might have mentioned something of the matter to the man of the house. 'And how durst you mention any thing of the matter?' cries the son, seizing his father by the throat; 'how durst you open your lips upon the subject? I have a great inclination to pluck your tongue out, and burn it before your face. You have told him, I suppose, that I am your son—'tis a lie; you stole me, you kidnapped me, 'tis impossible I could be the offspring of such an eyeless, shirtless, toothless ragga-muffin as thou art. Here I have been insulted by every body to-night, I have run the gauntlope thro' the whole ball-room; all my hopes, all my strategems are destroyed, and all is owing to your infamous prating. But mark what

I say to you—set out directly, to-night, or to-morrow morning before sunrise, and budge off as fast as your legs can carry you. If I find you here to-morrow at seven o'clock, by hell I'll cut your throat. You have done mischief enough already—you shall do me no more, and therefore pack up your wallet, and away with you, or prepare to feed the crows.' Having uttered this terrible denunciation of vengeance, he rushed out of the room with as much impetuosity as he came into it, and left the poor offender staring and trembling with amazement.

THE first thing he did after his son had quitted him, was to heave up a prodigious groan, which he accompanied with a moral reflexion on the hard fate of all fathers, who are cursed with rebellious unnatural children. As such usage he thought was sufficient to cancel all paternal affection, he felt in himself a strong desire at first to be revenged, by impeaching, and bringing the villain to justice. But then considering on the other hand, that he could not well do this, without discovering his own hypocrisy and impostures at the same time, he prudently suppressed those thoughts, and resolved to quit the place. 'Twas hard, he said to himself, to obey the orders of such an abandoned profligate, but he comforted himself with the agreeable, and indeed very probable hopes, that he should soon see his son come to the gallows, without his being accessory to such an event.

VERY early then the next morning, he set out with his unfortunate little guide, and made forced marches for *London*. Being willing to escape beyond the reach of his son's resentment as soon as possible, he travelled so very fast, that in little more than a week's time he arrived at *Reading*: from whence, after a day's resting, he again renewed his journey. But sorrow and fatigue so entirely overcame him, that he fell sick on the road, and it was with the greatest difficulty that he crawled up to the gate of a celebrated inn, not used to the entertainment of such guests, where he fainted and dropped down in a fit. Two or three ostlers, who were the first that saw him, conveyed him to an apartment in the stable, where he lay for several days in a most miserable condition. His disorder soon rendered him speechless, and being able to ask for nothing, he was supplied with nothing: for tho' the good landlady of the house would gladly have done any thing in the world to relieve him, had she known his condition; her servants, happening not to have the same spirit of humanity in them, never once informed her, that such an object of charity lay sick in her stable. Finding himself thus neglected and destitute of all comfort, he very prudently gave up the ghost, leaving our hero once more at the disposal of chance.

WHAT future scenes of good or evil are next to open upon him, fate does not yet chuse to divulge, and therefore begging the reader to suspend his curiosity, till we have received a proper commission for gratifying it, we here put an end to this first book of our wonderful history.

End of the FIRST BOOK.

THE HISTORY OF

Pompey the Little.

BOOK II

CHAPTER I

A Dissertation upon Nothing.

THAT great Master of human Nature, the ingenious
Author of *Tom Jones*, who justly styles himself King
of *Biographers*, published an Edict in his last Work,
declaring, that no Person hereafter should presume to
write a Novel, without prefixing a prefatory Chapter to
every Book, under the Penalty of being deemed a Blockhead. This introductory Chapter, he says, is the best
Mark of Genius, and surest Criterion of an Author's
Parts; for by it the most indifferent Reader may be
enabled to distinguish what is true and genuine in this
historic kind of Writing, from what is false and counterfeit:
And he supposes the Authors of the *Spectators* were induced
to prefix *Latin* and *Greek* Mottos to every Paper, from the
same Consideration of guarding against the Pursuit of
Scribblers; because by this Device it became impracticable
for any Man to presume to imitate the *Spectators*, without

understanding at least one Sentence in the learned Languages.

In compliance therefore with the Edict of this royal *Biographer*, I shall beg Leave, in the Entrance of this second Book of our History, to detain the Reader with an introductory Chapter upon *Nothing*; being the most proper Subject I can recollect at present for such an initial Section; which I hope will testify my Loyalty to the great Lawgiver abovementioned, and also dispose the Reader to a favourable Opinion of my historic Abilities.

I DO not recollect any Writer before myself, excepting the great Lord *Rochester*,[1] who has professedly treated this abstruse, learned and comprehensive Subject; which is something wonderful, considering the great Number of Penmen, whose Works shew them to have been excellently qualified for it. But though none have treated it professedly, many and various have indirectly handled it in all Branches of Science, and in all human Probability will continue to do so to the End of the World. For though neither Poet, Philosopher, Divine, or Lawyer have ever been courageous enough to declare the Subject they were writing upon; yet Poems, Systems of Philosophy, Bodies of Divinity, and huge Reports of Law have in all Ages swelled themselves to the greatest Bulk upon *Nothing*.

NOT to recur to those venerable Tomes of Antiquity, which have been delivered down to us from the peaceful Ages of monkish Darkness, modern Examples present themselves in great Abundance to our Choice. What is contained in all the Treatises of Mr. *William Wh——n* on the Trinity? Nothing. What is contained in the mighty and voluminous Epic Poems of Sir *Richard Blackmore*, Knight? absolute Nothing. What again can be collected from that universal Maze of Words, called the Universal History of all Nations, Languages, Customs, Manners, Empires, Governments, Men, Monsters, Land-Fights,

Sea-Fights, and a Million more of inexhaustible Topics?[1]
What, I say, can be comprehended in the tedious Pages
of that ostentatious History? every Reader will be ready
to answer, Nothing. The Works of *Dennis, Descartes*, Lord
Sh—f—ry, and the mighty Mr. *W—rb—n*, all treat of
the same immortal Subject, however the ingenious
Authors, out of pure Modesty, may have been contented
to let them pass under the fictitious Names of Plays,
Systems of Philosophy, miscellaneous Reflections, and
Divine Legations.[2]

THAT Nothing can arise out of Nothing, *ex nihilo nil
fieri*, has long reigned an uncontroverted Maxim of
Philosophy, and been a first Principle of the Schools:
But Novelty, and a modish Love of Paradox carry me to
endeavour its Confutation; and this I hope to do on
the general Testimony and verbal Confession of all
Mankind.

FOR let us attend carefully to what passes around us,
and we shall find *Nothing* to have the greatest Sway in all
human Actions. Does any one ask his Friend or a Stranger,
What is the News at Court to Day? he receives constantly
and universally for answer, *Nothing, Sir,——What was done
yesterday in the House?* Nothing at all, Sir.—*Any News in the
City, or upon Change?*[3] Nothing in the world—*Are our
Armies in Motion, and have they atchieved any thing lately
against the Enemy?* Nothing in nature, Sir, is the sure and
invariable Answer, which may for ever be expected to
all Questions of this kind. Yet notwithstanding this
universal Declaration, if we look abroad, and trust rather
to the Information of our Eyes than our Ears, we shall
really find a great deal done in the World, considering
how People have been employed, and that Mankind are
by no means idle, tho' they are always *doing Nothing*.

LET us first cast our Eyes upon the Court, where tho'
Nothing is said to be done, every thing is in reality performed. There we see Feuds, Animosities, Divisions,

Jealousies, Revolutions, and Rerevolutions; Ministers deposed and again restored; Peace and War decreed, contending Nations reconciled, and the Interests of *Europe* adjusted. Yet all this is Nothing.

FROM the Court let us turn to the Change and City, and there also admire the infinite Productions of *Nothing*. There we see Avarice, Usury, Extortion, Back-biting, Fraud, Hypocrisy, Stock-jobbing, and every Evil that can arise from the Circulation of Money. Thousands were there ruined Yesterday, thousands are ruining To-day, and thousands will be ruined To-morrow: Yet all this *is Nothing*.

AGAIN, let us take a second Survey of it, and we shall see little Politicians hatching Scandal against the Government, and propagating malicious Stories, which they know to be false: We shall see Lies circulating from Coffee-house to Coffee-house, and gathering additional Strength in every Minute of their Conveyance: We shall see the turbulent Offspring of Wealth, restless in Peace, and dissatisfied in War; compelling their Sovereign to take up Arms in one Year, and almost wresting them from his Hands in another: Yet all this is Nothing.

ONCE more let us direct our Views to the Camp, and there again admire the Productions of *Nothing*. For tho' Nothing was said to be done during the late War,[1] and the little Politicians above-mentioned took a Pleasure to talk of the Inactivity of our Armies, yet in reality every thing was performed, that could reasonably be expected from them. 'Tis true, they did not over-run the Kingdom of *France*, besiege its Capital, and take its King Prisoner; all which I believe many People thought easy and practicable; but they kept the most numerous Armies of the most formidable Monarchy in *Europe* at bay, and often contended hard with them for the Victory, in spite of the Treachery of Allies, and the almost infinite Superiority of their Enemies. If any body chuses to call this Nothing, he has my full Consent, because it confirms the Doctrine I want to establish, that Nothing produces every Thing.

LASTLY, let us examine what passes in private Life, and that will likewise furnish us with the same Reflections. Do not Quarrels of all sorts arise from Nothing? Do not matrimonial Jealousies spring from Nothing? What occasions Law-Suits, Dissentions among Neighbours, improbable Suspicions, ill-founded Conjectures, and the like? What is it that fills the Brains of Projectors, exercises the Fancy of Poets, employs the Machinations of Women, and draws the Swords of young coxcomb Officers in the Army, when they are strutting with the first Raptures of sudden Elevation? To all these Interrogations we may answer, *Nothing*. And not to multiply foreign Examples, what is it that I am now writing? undoubtedly the Reader will esteem it Nothing. In short, whatever we see around us,

> *Quicquid agunt homines, votum, timor, ira, voluptas,*
> *Gaudia, discursus.*[1]

All these are the genuine Productions of Nothing.

I WOULD therefore humbly recommend it to the Consideration of the two great Seminaries of *Oxford* and *Cambridge*, whether their Wisdoms shall not think fit to make an Alteration in that old erroneous Maxim of *Ex nihilo nil fit*, and say rather *Ex nihilo omnia fiunt*; which I take to be more consistent with Truth and the Reality of Things.

HAVING thus discharged the Duty imposed upon me, of writing an introductory Chapter, I hope I am now at liberty to pursue the Fortunes of my Hero, without incurring the grievous Imputation of Dullness, denounced on all those, who shall disobey the royal Edict issued out for that Purpose.

CHAPTER II

Fortune grows favourable to our Hero, and restores him to High-life.

THE blind Beggar, to whose Tyranny Fortune had committed our Hero, groaned out his Soul, as the Reader has already seen, in a Stable at a public Inn. *Pompey*, standing by, had the *Pleasure of seeing the Tyrant fall as he deserved*, and exulted over him, like *Cicero* in the Senate-house over the dying *Cæsar*.[1] [This misfortune was first discovered by an ostler, who coming accidentally into the stable, and perceiving the miserable creature stretched out on the straw, began at first to holla in his ear, imagining him to be asleep: but finding him insensible to three or four hearty kicks, which he bestowed upon him, 'odrabbet un,' cries he, 'why sure a can't be dead, can a? by gar he is—pillgarlick[2] is certainly dead.' He then called together two or three of his brethren, to divert themselves with this agreeable spectacle, and many stable jokes passed upon the occasion. When their diversion was over, one of them ran in doors to inform their mistress;] but the good Woman was not immediately at leisure to hear his Intelligence, being taken up in her Civilities to a Coach-and-Six, which was just then arrived, and very busy in conducting the Ladies to their Apartments. However, when Dinner was over, she bethought herself of what had happened, and went into the Stable, attended by two of her Chamber-maids, to survey the Corpse, and give Orders for its Burial. There little *Pompey*, for the first Time, presented himself to her View; but Sorrow and Ill-usage had so impaired his Beauty, and his Coat too was in such a Dishabille of Dirt and Mire, that he bespake no favourable Opinion in his Beholders. We must not therefore think Mrs. *Wilkins* of a cruel Nature, because she ordered him to be hanged, for, in reality, she is a very humane and friendly Woman; but perceiving no Beauty in the Dog to incline her to Compassion, and concluding him to be a Thief, from the Company he was found with, it was natural for her to shew him no Mercy. A Consultation therefore was held in the Yard, and Sentence of Death pronounced upon him; which had been executed as soon as commanded (for the Ostler was instantly preparing a Rope with great Delight) had not one of the Chamber-maids interposed, saying, *She believed he was a sweet pretty Creature, if he was washed,* and desired her Mistress to save him. A Word of this Kind was enough to Mrs. *Wilkins,* who immediately granted him a Reprieve, and ordered him into the Kitchen for a Turn-spit. But when he had gone thro' the Ceremony of Lustration,[1] and was thoroughly cleaned, every Body was struck with his Beauty, and Mrs. *Wilkins* in particular; who now changed her Resolutions, and, instead of condemning him to the Drudgery of a Turn-spit, made him her Companion, and taught him to follow her about the House. He soon grew to be a Favourite with the whole Family, as indeed he always was wherever he came; and the Chamber-maids used to quarrel with one another, who should take him to their Beds at Night. He likewise got acquainted with *Captain,* the great House-dog, who, like *Cerberus,* terrified the Regions round-about with his Barking: yet would he often condescend to be pleased with the Frolicks of little *Pompey,* and vouchsafe now and then to unbend his Majesty with a Game of Play.

AFTER he had lived here near a Fortnight, a Post-chaise stopt one Day at the Door, out of which alighted two Ladies, just arrived from the *Bath.* They ran directly to the Fire, declaring they were almost frozen to Death with Cold; whereupon Mrs. *Wilkins* began to thunder for Wood, and assisted in making up an excellent Fire: After which, she begged the Favour to know what their Ladyships would please to have for Dinner. 'If you please, Madam, said the Eldest, I'll look into your Lardery.' 'With all my Heart, Madam, answered the good Landlady; I have Fish and Fowls of all Kind, and Rabbets and Hares, and Variety of Butcher's Meat—— but your Ladyship says you will be so good to accommodate yourself on the Spot——I am ready to attend your Ladyship, whenever your Ladyship pleases.'

WHILE the Eldest was gone to examine the Lardery, the Youngest of these Ladies, having seized little *Pompey*, who followed his Mistress into the Room, was infinitely charmed with his Beauty, and caressed him during the whole Time of her Sister's Absence. *Pompey*, in return, seemed pleased to be taken Notice of by so fair a Lady; for tho' he had long been disused to the Company of People of Fashion, he had not yet forgot how to behave himself with Complaisance and Good-manners. He felt a kind of Pride returning, which all his Misfortunes had not been able to extinguish, and began to hope the Time was come, which should restore him to the Beau-monde. With these Hopes he continued in the Room all the Time the Ladies were at Dinner, paying great Court to them both, and receiving what they were pleased to bestow upon him with much Fawning, and officious Civility.

As soon as the Ladies had dined, Mrs. *Wilkins* came in to make her Compliments, as usual, hoping the Dinner was dressed to their Ladyships' Minds, and that the Journey had not destroyed their Appetites. She received very courteous Answers to all she said, and after some other Conversation on indifferent Topics, little *Pompey* came at last upon the Carpet. 'Pray Madam, said the youngest of the Ladies, how long have you had this very pretty Dog?' Mrs. *Wilkins*, who never was deficient, when she had an Opportunity of talking, having started so fair a Subject, began to display her Eloquence in the following Manner. 'Madam, says she, the little Creature fell into my Hands by the strangest Accident in Life,

and it is a Mercy he was not hanged—An old blind
Beggar, Ladies, died in my Stable about a Fortnight ago,
and it seems, this little Animal used to lead him about the
Country. 'Tis amazing how they come by the Instinct
they have in them—and such a little Creature too—But
as I was telling you, Ladies, the old blind Beggar was just
returned from *Bath*, as your Ladyships may be now, and
the poor miserable Wretch perished in my Stable. There
he left this little Dog, and, Will you believe it, Ladies?
As I am alive, I ordered him to be hanged, not once
dreaming he was such a Beauty; for indeed he was quite
covered over with Mire and Nastiness, as to be sure he
could not be otherwise, after leading the old blind Man
so long a Journey; but a Maid servant of mine took a
Fancy to the Little Wretch, and begged his Life; and
would you think it, Ladies? I am now grown as fond of
the little Fool, as if he was my own Child.'

THE two Sisters, diverted with Mrs. *Wilkins*'s Oration,
could not help smiling on one another; but disguising
their Laughter as well as they could, 'I do not wonder,
said the youngest, at your Fondness for him, Madam!
he is so remarkably handsome; and that being the Case,
I can't find it in my Heart to rob you of him, otherwise
I was just going to ask if you should be willing to part
with him.' 'Bless me, Madam, said the obliging Hostess,
I am sure there is nothing I would not do to oblige your
Ladyship, and if your Ladyship has such an Affection
for the little Wretch—Not part with him indeed!' 'Nay,
Madam, said the Lady interrupting her, I would willingly
make you any Amends, and if you will please to name
your Price, I'll purchase him of you.' 'Alack-a-day,
Madam, replied the Landlady, I am sorry your Ladyship
suspects me to be of such a mercenary Disposition;
purchase him indeed! he is extremely at your Ladyship's
Service, if you please to accept of him.'—With these
Words she took him up, and delivered him into the Lady's

Arms, who received him with many Acknowledgements of the Favour done her; all which Mrs. *Wilkins* repaid with abundant Interest.

WORD was now brought, that the Chaise was ready, and waited at the Door; whereupon, the two Ladies were obliged to break off their Conversation, and Mrs. *Wilkins* to restrain her Eloquence. She attended them, with a Million of civil Speeches, to their Equipage, and handing little *Pompey* to them, when they were seated in it, took her Leave with a great Profusion of Smiles and Curtsies. The Postilion blew his Horn; the Ladies bowed; and our Hero's Heart exulted with Transport, to think of the Amendment of his Fate.

CHAPTER III

A long Chapter of Characters.

THE Post-chaise stopped in a genteel Street in *London*, and *Pompey* was introduced into decent Lodgings, where every Thing had an Air of Politeness, yet nothing was expensive. The Rooms were hung with *Indian* Paper; the Beds were *Chinese*; and the whole Furniture seemed to shew how elegant Simplicity can be under the Direction of Taste. Tea was immediately ordered, and the two Ladies sat down to refresh themselves after the Fatigue of their Journey, and began to talk over the Adventures they had met with at the *Bath*. They remembered many agreeable Incidents, which had happened in that great Rendezvous of Pleasure, and ventured to laugh at some Follies of their Acquaintance, without Severity, or Ill-nature.

THESE two Ladies were born of a good Family, and had received a genteel Education. Their Father indeed left them no more than Six Thousand Pounds each; but as they united their Fortunes, and managed their Affairs with Frugality, they made a creditable Figure in the World, and lived in Intimacy with People of the greatest Fashion. It will be necessary, for the sake of Distinction, to give thcm Names, and the Reader, if he pleases, may call them *Theodosia* and *Aurora*.

THEODOSIA, the eldest, was advancing towards Forty, an Age when personal Charms begin to fade, and Women grow indifferent at least, who have nothing better to supply the Place of them. But *Theodosia* was largely possessed of all those good Qualities, which render Women agreeable without Beauty: She was affable and easy in her Behaviour; well-bred without Falshood; chearful without Levity; polite and obliging to her Friends, civil and generous to her Domestics. Nature had given her a good Temper, and Education had made it an agreeable one. She had lived much in the World, without growing vain or insolent; improved her Understanding by Books, without any Affectation of Wit or Science, and loved public Places, without being a Slave to Pleasure. Her Conversation was always engaging, and often entertaining. Her long Commerce with the World had supplied her with a Fund of diverting Remarks on Life, and her good Sense enabled her to deliver them with Grace and Propriety.

AURORA, the youngest Sister, was in her Four and Twentieth Year, and Imagination cannot possibly form a finer Figure than she was, in every Respect. Her Beauty, now in its highest Lustre, gave that full Satisfaction to the Eye, which younger Charms rarely inspire. She was tall and full-formed, but with the utmost Elegance and Symmetry in all her Limbs; and a certain Majesty, which resulted from her Shape, was accompanied with a most peculiar Sweetness of Face: For tho' she had all the Charms, she had none of the Insolence of Beauty. As if these uncommon Perfections of Nature were not sufficient to procure her Admirers enough, she had added to them the most winning Accomplishments of Art: She danced and sung, and played like an Angel; her Voice naturally clear, full, and melodious, had been improved under the best *Italian* Masters; and she was ready to oblige People with her Music, on the slightest Intimation, that it would be agreeable, without any Airs of Shyness and unseasonable Modesty. Indeed, Affectation never entered into any one of her Gestures, and whatsoever she did, was with that generous Freedom of Manner, which denotes a good Understanding, as well as an honest Heart. Her Temper was chearful in the highest Degree, and she had a most uncommon Flow of Spirits and Good-humour, which seldom deserted her in any Place, or Company. At a Ball she was extremely joyous and spirited, and the Pleasure she gave to her Beholders, could only be exceeded by that unbounded Happiness with which she inspired her Partner. Yet tho' her Genius led her to be lively, and a little romantic, whoever conversed with her in private, admired her good Sense, and heard Reflexions from her, which plainly shewed she had often exercised her Understanding on the most serious Subjects.

A WOMAN so beautiful in her Person, and excellent in her Accomplishments, could not fail of attracting Lovers in great Abundance; and accordingly she had refused a Variety of Offers from People of all Characters, who could scarcely believe she was in earnest in rejecting them, because she accompanied her Refusals with unusual Politeness and Good-humour. She did not grow vain, or insolent, from the Triumphs of her Beauty, nor long to spit in a Man's Face, because she could not approve his Addresses (which I believe is the Case with many young Ladies) but sweetened her Denials with great Civility, and always asked the Advice of her Sister, of whom she was passionately fond. Such was *Aurora*, the present Mistress of our Hero; and as the Characters of some of her Admirers may, perhaps, not be unentertaining, I will give a Description of two or three out of many.

AND first, let us pay our Compliments to *Count Tag*, who had merited a Title by his Exploits; which perhaps is not the most usual Step to Honour, but always most respectable whenever it happens. 'Tis true, he had no Patent to shew for his Nobility, which depended entirely on the *arbitrium popularis auræ*, the Fickleness of popular Applause;[1] but he seems likely to enjoy it as long as he lives, there being no Probability of any Alteration in his Behaviour. His Father raised a Fortune by a Profession, and from him he inherited a competent Estate of about three hundred Pounds *per annum*. His Education began at *Westminster* School, and was finished at *Oxford*; from whence he transported himself to *London*, on the News of his Father's Death, and made a bold Push, as it is called, to introduce himself *into Life*. He had a strong Ambition of becoming a fine Gentleman, and cultivating an Acquaintance with People of Fashion, which he esteemed the most consummate Character attainable by Man, and to that he resolved to dedicate his Days. As his first Essay therefore, he presented himself every Evening in a Side-box at one of the Play-houses, where he was ready to enter into Conversation with any body that would afford him an Audience, and was particularly assiduous in applying himself to young Noblemen and Men of Fortune, whom he had formerly known at School, or at the University. By degrees he got footing in two or three Families of Quality, where he was sometimes invited to Dinner; and having learnt the fashionable Topics of Discourse, he studied to make himself agreeable, by entertaining them with the current News of the Town. He had the first Intelligence of a Marriage or an Intrigue, knew to a Moment when the Breath went out of a Nobleman's Body, and published the Scandal of a Masquerade, or a Ridotta,[2] sooner by half an Hour at least, than any other public Talker in *London*. He had a copious Fluency of Language, which made him embellish every Subject he undertook, and a certain Art of Talking as minutely and circumstantially on the most trivial Subjects, as on those of the highest Importance. He would describe a Straw, or a Pimple on a Lady's Face, with all the Figures of Rhetoric; by which he persuaded many People to believe him a Man of great Parts; and surely no Man's Impertinence ever turned to better Account. As he constantly attended *Bath* and *Tunbridge*, and all the public Places, he got easier Access to the Tables of the Great, and by degrees insinuated himself into all the Parties of the Ladies; among whom he began to be received as a considerable Genius, and quickly became necessary in all their Drums and Assemblies.

FINDING his Schemes thus succeed almost beyond his Hopes, he now assumed a higher Behaviour, and began to fancy himself a Man of Quality from the Company he kept. With this View he thought proper to forget all his old Acquaintance, whose low Geniusses left them groveling in Obscurity, while his superior Talents had raised him to a Familiarity with Lords and Ladies. If therefore any old Friend, presuming on their former Intimacy, ventured to accost him in the Park, he made a formal Bow, and begged Pardon for leaving him; *but really*, *Lady* Betty, *or Lady* Mary *was just entering the Mall*. In short, he always proportioned his Respect to the Rank and Fortunes of his Company; he would desert a Commoner for a Lord, a Lord for an Earl, an Earl for a Marquiss, and a Marquiss for a Duke. Having thus enrolled himself in his own Imagination among the Nobility, it was not without Reason that People gave him the Style and Title of *Count Tag*, thinking it a Pity that such a Genius should be called by the ordinary Name of his Family.

[To say this gentleman was in love, would be too great an abuse of language, for he was in reality incapable of loving any body but himself. But vanity and the mode, often made him affect attachments to women of celebrated beauty, from whose acquaintance he thought he could derive a credit to himself. This was his motive for appearing one of the admirers of *Aurora*, whose charms were conspicuous enough to excite his pride, and that was the only passion which the count ever thought of gratifying. He knew how to counterfeit raptures which he never felt, and had all the *language* of love, without any of its *sentiment*.]

THE second Cavalier, who made his Addresses in the same Place, was an old Gentleman turned of Seventy, whose Chearfulness and Vivacity might have tempted People to forget his Age, if he had not recalled it to their Remembrance, by unseasonable Attempts of Gallantry. The Passions of Youth are always ridiculous in old Age; and tho' many fine Women have sacrificed their Charms to superannuated Husbands, the Union is so unnatural, that we must suppose their Affections were fixed on Title or Estate, or something else besides the Persons of their Lovers. This old Gentleman had led a Life of constant Gallantry almost from his Cradle, and now could not divest himself of the Passion of Love, tho' he was deserted by the Abilities of it. He had already buried three Wives, and was ambitious of a fourth; tho' his Constitution was extremely shattered by Debauchery and high-living, and it seemed as if a Fit of Coughing would at any time have shook him to Pieces. Besides this, he kept several Mistresses, and all the Villages round his Country-seat were in a manner peopled with the Fruits of his stolen Embraces.

AT his first Entrance into Life, he was a younger Brother, and married an ugly old Woman of Fortune for the sake of her Money, who quickly departed to his Wishes, and left him possessed of the only desireable thing belonging to her. Soon afterwards, his elder Brother also went the same Road to Mortality, and left him Heir of three thousand Pounds a Year; which enabled his Genius to display itself, and supplied him with all the Essentials of Pleasure. From this Moment he began his Career, and being a gay young Fellow, handsome in his Person, and genteel in his Address, he resolved to indulge himself in every Gratification that Money could purchase, or Luxury invent. He set up all Nights in Taverns, where he was the Wit and Genius of the Company; travelled and intrigued with Women of all Nations and Languages; made a Figure at the Gaming-Tables, and was not silent in Parliament. In short, whatever Character he undertook to appear in, he supported it always with a Spirit and Vivacity peculiar to himself. His Health of course received many Shocks from his dissolute Course of Life, but he trusted to the Vigour of a good Constitution, and despised all the distant Consequences of Pleasure, as the dull Apprehensions of Cowards in Luxury. As to Marriage, he resolved never more to wear the Fetters of that Slavery, while his Passions had so free a Range in a way more agreeable to his Inclinations: But having a long while sollicited a fine Woman of but slender Fortune to comply with his Desires, and finding her deaf to any but honourable Offers, he was drawn in before he was aware, and married a second time with no other view than to have the present Possession of a Mistress. Yet he discharged the matrimonial Duties for a time with tolerable Decency, and contrived to keep his Amours as secret from his Wife as possible. But the Eyes of Jealousy could not long be deceived; and the Moment she began to expostulate with him on his Behaviour, he grew more bare-faced in his Pleasures, and less careful to conceal them from her Observation. The Lady, disappointed in her Views of Happiness, had Recourse to the common Consolation of Female Sorrows, and tried to drown them in Citron Waters;[1] which pernicious Custom grew upon her so much by Habit and Indulgence, that she often came down exceedingly disordered to Dinner, and sometimes was disqualified from performing the Offices of her Table. This extremely piqued the Pride of her Husband, who could not bear to see the Mistress of his Family in such disgraceful Circumstances, and began to wish her fairly in the other World. Enquiring how she came supplied with these cordial Draughts of Sorrow, he found they were secretly conveyed to her by a Mantua-maker, who attended her three or four times a Week, pretending to bring Caps and Gowns. This again piqued his Pride, to think she should expose her foible to the Knowledge of her Inferiors, and resolving to supply her Wishes at an easier Rate, he ordered his Butler to carry up a certain Number of Bottles every Week into her Dressing-Room. The Stratagem took Effect; and the good Lady having frequent Recourse to the fatal Opiate, in a short time bade adieu to the World and all its Cares.

HE was now again left to the unrestrained Indulgence of his Pleasures, and had Mistresses of all Characters, from the Woman of Quality down to the Farmer's Daughter and Milk-maid. But as he advanced in Years, a Fit of Dotage insensibly stole upon him; and in an unlucky Moment he married a vain spirited young Girl of twenty, who seemed born to punish him for his Sins. Full of herself and Family, she took Possession of his House with a certain conscious Authority, and began to shew the Pleasure she found in Government and Sway. She regarded her Husband only as an Object that was to give her Command of Servants, Equipage, and the like; and her Head was giddy with Notions of domineering and Power. Her Insolence soon became intolerable to a young Lady in the Family, Daughter of his former Wife, who could not endure to be governed by a Mother of her own Age, and therefore with great Spirit left her Father's House. In short, the old Gentleman himself began to curse the Choice he had made, finding himself in a manner quite disregarded by his accomplished Spouse, whose Thoughts ran wholly after Drums, Assemblies, Operas, Masquerades, Ridottas, and the like; all which she pursued with the most ardent Assiduity, and seldom could find one quarter of an Hour's leisure to converse with her Husband. He found her besides, more cold in her Constitution, and less sensible of his Embraces, than he had imagined; for indeed, she was a Thing purely made up of Vanity, and provided she *made a Figure in Life*, she cared not who *enjoyed its Pleasure*. The old Gentleman groan'd severely under this Scourge of his Iniquities, and I question whether he would not have died himself of pure Spite, had not his obliging Wife saved him that Necessity, by kindly dying in his stead. She caught cold one Night in *Vauxhall* Gardens,[1] and after a short Illness of a Week or ten Days, retired to the peaceable Mansions of her Predecessors.

ONE would think he should now have been tired of Matrimonial Blessings; yet notwithstanding the Ill-luck he had hitherto met with, notwithstanding the natural Decay arising from his Age, and the acquired Infirmities of Intemperance, he was once more engaged in Courtship, and made one of the most gallant Admirers of *Aurora*.

SHE had many other Lovers, but I shall forbear the mention of them at present, to give a Description of one, who was every way worthy of her Affections, and to whom, in Reality, she had devoted her Heart. Neither *Count Tag*, nor the aged Gallant last described, had any Share in her Regard; for tho' she received them with Civility, she gave them little Encouragement to hope for Success.

THE fortunate Lover was a young Nobleman, about her own Age, who conducted himself by Rules so very different from the Generality of the Nobility, that it will be a kind of Justice to his Memory to preserve his Character. He had an excellent Understanding, improved by competent Reading; and the most uncommon Uprightness of Heart, joined with the greatest Candour and Benevolence of Temper. His Soul was passionately devoted to the Love of Truth, and he never spoke or acted but with the clearest Sincerity and Ingenuity of Mind. Falshood of any Kind, even in the common Forms of Intercourse and Civility, wherein Custom licenses some Degrees of Dissimulation, he held to be a Crime; and if ever he made a Promise, there was not the least Room to doubt of his performing it. Tho' he frequently mixed in Parties of Diversion, made by other young Noblemen of his Acquaintance, yet he never joined in the Riots, that falsely challenge to themselves the Name of Pleasure, and superior Enjoyment of Life. He did not spend his Mornings in Levity, or his Nights at a Gaming-table. Nor was he ashamed of the Religion of his Country, or deterred from the Worship of his Maker, by the idle Sneers of Infidelity, and the ridiculous Laughter of profane Wits: but, on the contrary, gloried in the Profession of Christianity, and always reprimanded the wanton Sallies of those, who tried to be witty at the Expence of their Conscience. Added to these excellent Endowments, he had the greatest filial Obedience to his Father, the sincerest Loyalty to his Prince, the truest Respect for his Relations, and the most charitable Liberality to all those, whom Poverty, or Distress of any kind, recommended as Objects of Compassion. In short, whoever has read Lord *Clarendon*'s celebrated Character of Lord Viscount *Falkland*,[1] cannot be at a Loss to form an Idea of this amiable young Nobleman; who resembled him exactly in the private social Duties of Life; and we may conclude, he would have acted the same Part in publick, had he been engaged in similar Circumstances.

BEING inspired with a Passion for an agreeable

Woman, he was neither ashamed to own it, nor yet did he use the ridiculous Elogiums, with which Coxcombs talk of their Mistresses, when their Imaginations are heated with Wine. He did not compare her to the *Venus of Medicis*, or run into any of those artificial Raptures, which are almost always counterfeited: But whenever he mentioned her Name, he spoke the Language of his Heart, and spoke of her always with a Manliness, that testified the Reality and Sincerity of his Passion. It was impossible for a Woman not to return the Affections of so deserving a Lover: *Aurora* was happy to be the Object of his Addresses, and met them with becoming Zeal.

CHAPTER IV

*[The characters of the foregoing chapter exemplified.
An irreparable misfortune befals our hero.]*

THE two sisters had lain longer a-bed than usual the morning after their arrival in town, which was owing to the fatigue of their journey. They had but just finished their breakfast by twelve o'clock; *Aurora* was then sitting down to her harpsichord, and *Theodosia* reading the play-bills for the evening; when the door opened, and *Count Tag* was ushered by a servant into the room.

WHEN the first ceremonies were a little over, and the count had expressed the *prodigious satisfaction* he felt in seeing them returned to town; he began to enquire what kind of season they had had at *Bath?* 'Why really,' said *Theodosia*, 'a very good one upon the whole; there were many agreeable people there, and all of them easy and sociable; which made our time pass away chearfully and pleasantly enough.' 'You amaze me,' cries the *Count*; 'impossible, madam! how can it be, ladies?—I had letters from lord *Marmazet*, and lady *Betty Scornful*, assuring me, that, except you and themselves, there were not three human creatures in the place.——Let me see, I have lady *Betty*'s letter in my pocket, I believe, at this moment—Oh no, upon recollection, I put it this morning into my cabinet, where I preserve all my letters of quality.'

AURORA, smothering a laugh as well as she could, said she was extremely obliged to lord *Marmazet*, and lady *Betty*, for vouchsafing to rank her and her sister in the catalogue of human beings; 'but surely,' added she, 'they must have been asleep both of them, when they wrote their letters, for the *Bath* was extremely full.' 'Full!' cries the *Count*, interrupting her; 'oh, madam, that is very possible, and yet there might be no company—that is, none of us; no-body that one knows—for as to all the tramontanes[1] that come by the cross post, we never reckon them as any thing but monsters in human shape, that serve to fill up the stage of life, like cyphers in a play. For instance, you often see an awkard girl, who has sewed a tail to a gown, and pinned two lappets to a night-cap, run headlong into the rooms with a wild frosty face, as if she was just come from feeding poultry in her father's chicken-yard—Or you see a booby 'squire, with a head resembling a stone-ball over a gate-post.—Now it would be the most ridiculous thing in life, to call such people company. 'Tis the want of titles, and not the want of faces, that makes a place empty; for if there is no-body one knows—if there are *none of us* in a place, we esteem all the rest as mob and rabble.'

HERE it was impossible for the two ladies any longer to contain their laughter. 'Hold, hold, for heaven's sake,' said *Theodosia*, interrupting him, 'have a little mercy, *Count*, on us poor mortals who are born without titles, and don't banish us quite from all public places. Consider, sir, tho' you have been so happy as to acquire a title, all of us have not the same good fortune, and must we then be reckoned among the mob and rabble of life?'

'OH, by no means,' cries the *Count*, 'you misunderstand me entirely—you are in the polite circle, ladies; we reckon you among the quality. Whoever belongs to the polite circle, is of the quality. I was only talking of the wretched figures, who know nobody, and are known of nobody; they are the mob and rabble I was speaking of. —You indeed! no, pardon me—but pray ladies, who was this miss *Newcome*, this great beauty, that made such a figure among you at *Bath?* Was she ever in any of our drums or assemblies?'

'NO, sir,' replied *Theodosia*; 'it was the first time of her appearing, I believe, in any public place; she came under the protection of lady *Marmazet*. She is a very agreeable girl, and really exceedingly pretty. I often conversed with her, and indeed she promises to make a very fine woman, if she does not play the fool, and throw herself away upon that odious, detestable *Griskin*.'

'AY, that *Griskin* too!' cries the *Count*, 'who is that detestable *Griskin?* I think I am acquainted with all the families of any note in *England*, and yet in my days I never heard of Sir *Jeremy Griskin*.'

'NO, sir,' said *Aurora*, with a smile, ''tis impossible you should know any such *English* family, for he gave out that he came from *Ireland*; and even there, I fancy, one should be pretty much puzzled to find it; for I am very apt to suspect that Mr. *Griskin* is nothing better than a notorious sharper. We had a report at *Bath*, that he was the son of a blind beggar. The truth of this indeed never came perfectly to light, but sure lady *Marmazet*, if she has any friendship for the girl, must be mad to encourage such a match.'

'ABSOLUTELY distracted,' cries the *Count*; 'I can't imagine what she means by it; and indeed when she comes to town, I shall railly her ladyship for having such a beauty in *petto*,[1] without letting me know any thing of the matter.'

WHILE the *Count* was thus displaying his own merit and acquaintance with the *grand monde*, the door opened on a sudden, and the young lord appeared, whose character concluded the preceding chapter. He approached the ladies with a respectful bow, and enquired tenderly concerning their health, but addressed himself rather in a more particular manner to *Aurora*. Her face immediately changed on his entering the room, and a certain air of affectionate languor took possession of her features, which before were a little expressive of scorn and ridicule: in short, she received him with something more than complaisance, and a tone of voice only calculated to convey the sentiments of love.

BUT as the delicacy of her passion chose to reveal itself as little as possible before witnesses, she soon recovered the gaiety of her features, and addressing herself with a smile to her beloved peer, 'my lord,' said she, 'you are come in excellent time—the *Count* is entertaining us here with a very ingenious lecture on what it is we are to call the *world*.'

COUNT *Tag* was no stranger to his lordship, who perfectly knew, and heartily despised him for his foppery and affectation. Yet he was obliged now and then to submit to a visit from him; for being in possession of a title, the *Count*, who *haunted* all people of quality, would obtrude himself on his acquaintance contrary to his inclination; and good manners, as well as the natural candour of his temper, restrained him from expressing his detestation in too explicit terms. He had however no great desire at present to hear him upon a topic, where his impertinence would have so great a scope, and therefore endeavoured to turn the conversation to some other subject: but the *Count*, whose eyes sparkled (as they always did) on the appearance of a man of quality, no sooner saw him seated in his chair, than he fastened immediately upon him, and began to appeal to his lordship for a confirmation of his sentiments. 'My lord,' said he, 'I was endeavouring to convince the ladies, that if there is *no-body one knows*, *none of us*, in a public place, all the rest are to be considered in the light of porters and oyster-women. I dare say your lordship is of the same opinion.'

'INDEED sir, but I am not,' replied his lordship, 'and therefore I must desire you would not draw me into a participation of any such sentiments. The language of *people one knows*, and people *one does not know*, is what I very often hear in the world; but it seems to me the most contemptible jargon that ever was invented. Indeed for my own part, I don't understand it, and therefore I confess I am not qualified to talk about it. Whom pray are we to call the *people one knows?*'

'*O mon dieu!*' cries the *Count*, 'your lordship surely can't ask such a question. The people one knows, my lord, are the people who are in the round of assemblies and public diversions, people who have the *scavoir vivre*, the *ton de bonne compaigne*, as the *French* call it—in short, people who frize their hair in the newest fashion, and have their cloaths made at *Paris*.'

'AND are these the only people worth one's regard in life?' said his lordship.

'ABSOLUTELY, my lord!' cries the *Count*, 'I have no manner of idea or conception of any body else.'

'THEN I am most heartily sorry for you,' cries his lordship. 'I can readily allow that people of quality must in general live with one another; the customs of the world in good measure require it; but surely our station gives us no right to behave with insolence to people below us, because they have not their cloaths from *Paris*, or do not *frize* their hair in the newest fashion. And I am sure if people of quality have no such right, it much less becomes the fops and coxcombs in fashion, who are but the retainers on people of quality, who are themselves only in public by permission, and can pretend to no merit, but what they derive from an acquaintance with their betters. This surely is the most contemptible of all modern follies. For instance, because a man is permitted to whisper nonsense in a lady *Betty*'s or lady *Mary*'s ear, in the side-box at a play-house, shall he therefore fancy himself privileged to behave with impertinence to people infinitely his superiors in merit, who perhaps have not thought it worth their while to *riggle* themselves into a great acquaintance?—What say you, madam?' added he, addressing himself to *Theodosia*.

'YOUR observation,' she replied, 'is exceedingly just, my lord! but why do you confine it to your own sex? pray let ours come in for a share of the satire——For my part, I could name a great many trumpery insignificant girls about town, who having *riggled* themselves, as you say, into a polite acquaintance, give themselves ten times more airs, and are fifty thousand times more conceited, than the people to whose company they owe their pride. I have one now in my thoughts, who is throughout a composition of vanity and folly, and has been for several years the public jest and ridicule of the town for her behaviour.'

ALL this while the *Count* sat in some confusion. For tho' he had a wonderful talent, as indeed most people have, at warding off scandal from himself, and applying the satire he met with to his neighbours, he was here so plainly described, that it was hardly possible for him to be mistaken. *Aurora* saw this, and resolving to compleat his confusion, '*Count*,' said she, 'I have had it in my head this many a day to ask you a question—will you be so obliging as to tell me how you came by your title?' 'O pardon me, I have no title, madam,' cries the *Count*— 'mere *badinage* and ridicule, a nick-name given me by some of my friends, that's all—but another time for that. At present I am obliged to call upon lord *Monkeyman*, who desires my opinion of some pictures he is going to buy; after which I shall look in upon lady *Betty Vincent*, whom I positively have not seen for these three days.' Here he rose up, and made all the haste he could away, being exceedingly glad to escape the persecution, which he saw was preparing for him.

LITTLE *Pompey* was witness of many of these interviews, and began to think himself happily situated for life. He was a great favourite with *Aurora*, who caressed him with the fondest tenderness, and permitted him to sleep every night in a chair by her bed-side. When she awoke in a morning, she would embrace him with an ardour, which the happiest lover might have envied. Our hero's vanity perhaps made him fancy himself the genuine object of these caresses, whereas in reality he was only the representative of a much nobler creature. In this manner he lived with his new mistresses the greatest part of a winter, and might still have continued in the same happy situation, had he not ruined himself by his own imprudence.

AURORA had been dancing one night at a ridotta with her beloved peer, and retired late to her lodgings, with that vivacity in her looks, and transport in her thoughts, which love and pleasure always inspire. Animated with delightful presages of future happiness, she sat herself down in a chair, to recollect the conversation that had passed between them. After this, she went to bed, and resigned herself to the purest slumbers. She slept longer than usual the next morning, and it seemed as if some golden dream was pictured in her fancy; for her cheek glowed with unusual beauty, and her voice spontaneously pronounced, *my lord, I am wholly yours*.——— While her imagination was presenting her with these delicious ideas, little *Pompey*, who heard the sound, and thought she over-slept herself, leaped upon the bed, and waked her with his barking. To be interrupted in so critical a minute, while she was dreaming of her beloved peer, was an offence she knew not how to pardon. She darted a most enraged look at him, and resolved never to see him any more; but disposed of him that very morning to her milliner, who attended her with a new head-dress.

THUS was he again removed to new lodgings, and condemned to future adventures.

CHAPTER V

Relating the History of a Milliner.

THE fair Princess of Lace and Ribbands, who now took Possession of our Hero, had gone thro' a great Variety of Fortunes before she fell into her present Way of Life; some of which perhaps may be worth relating. She was originally Daughter of a Country Gentleman, who had lived, as it is called, *up to his Income*; by which Means he obtained the Character of a generous hospitable Man in his Neighbourhood, and died without making the least Provision for his Family. His Widow soon afterwards married a wealthy Lawyer in a large Market town, who like a great Vulture prey'd at large over the Country, and suffered no other Attorney to thrive within the Regions of his Plunder. The Gentlemen round-about made him Court-keeper-general of their Estates; and the poor People flocked to him with a kind of superstitious Opinion, that he could model the Laws according to his Pleasure. The Mayor and Aldermen too resorted to him for Advice in all dubious Cases, and he was a kind of petty Viceroy in the Town where he lived. Success had made him insolent and over-bearing, and when he flaunted thro' the Streets on a Market-day in his Night-gown,[1] he looked prouder than a Grandee of *Spain*.

THE young Lady, who was now to call him Father-in-Law,[2] was not at all pleased with her new Situation, thinking herself much degraded by her Mother's Marriage. When therefore the Wives and Daughters of the Town came to visit her in their best Gowns, she received them very coldly, disdained to be present at any of their public Tea-drinkings, and always affected to confound their Names. She was as little pleased with the Company of her new Father, and excepting the small Time spent at Meals, used to lock herself up all the rest of the Day in a little Closet, to read *Cowley*'s Poems, and the History of *Pamela Andrews*.[1] Gripe the Attorney soon observed and resented this Behaviour; and her Mother too, thinking it a Reflexion on the Choice she had made, began to take her roundly to Task about it. She told her, she wondered what she meant by giving herself such Airs, for she had no Fortune to support them: 'And pray, Madam, said she, what is your Birth, that you are so proud of, without Money?' To this the young Lady answer'd, 'that if some People could demean themselves, she saw no Reason why other People should be obliged to do the same; and for her Part, she found no Charms in the Company of Tradesmen and stinking Shop-keepers.' Many Altercations of this kind happened between them, till at length her Mother fairly told her, that if she disliked her present Condition, she might e'en seek for a better wherever she could. It was not long before she followed this Advice, and married a young Officer, who was quartered in the Town, without consulting any body's Inclinations but her own. This was a fair Pretence for her Parents to get rid of her; they complained loudly of her Disobedience in not asking their Advice, repre-sented her as a bold forward Hussy, and renounced all Correspondence with her for the future. The young Officer swaggered a little at first, talked much of his Honour, and threatened to cane her Father-in-law; but finding the Attorney despise his Menaces, he prudently suffered his Anger to cool, and proceded no farther than Words.

THE Regiment, to which this Gentleman belonged, was soon afterwards ordered into *Flanders*; and as the young Couple were then in the Honey-moon of their Love, the Bride prevailed to make a Campaign with her Husband. He consented, and fixed her in Lodgings at *Brussels*; near to which City the Army was at that Time quartered. There she had Leisure to observe the Lace Manufacture, and learnt the first Rudiments of Millinery, which afterwards became her Profession. In a little Time the News of a Battle arrived, and with it a Piece of News more terrible to the Ears of a young Bride, that her Husband was among the Number of the slain. This broke all her Measures and Hopes of Life, and she was obliged to return into *England*, with scarce Money enough to pay for her Voyage, or maintain her on the Road. On her Arrival she began to consider, whether she should not proceed to her Mother, and endeavour to obtain a Reconciliation; but Pride soon banished that Thought; her high Spirit would not suffer her to sue for Pardon, and she resolved, as a better Expedient, to go to Service. Accordingly, she procured herself the Office of a Waiting-Gentlewoman, in an agreeable Family, but unluckily there was no Table for upper Servants, and her Pride could not endure to sit down to Dinner with Menials. Preferably to this she would dine upon a Plate of cold Victuals in her Bed-chamber; thus gratifying her Vanity at the Expence of her Appetite.

FROM this Place she removed to another more agreeable to her Wishes, where there was a separate Apartment for the higher Servants, and her own Dominion was pretty considerable. In this Family all was Pleasure. The Lady of it having a Husband she despised, filled his House with eternal Parties of Company, studied to be expensive, and seemed resolved to see the End of his Estate before she died, without regarding what became of her Children after her Death. The Husband himself was almost an Idiot, and could hardly be said to live, for he spent his Days chiefly in dozing, and constantly fell asleep in his Chair after Dinner. His Wife treated him always with the highest Superiority, would sometimes spit in his Face, sometimes fling his Wig into the Fire, and never scrupled calling him Fool and Block-head before all Companies. This would now and then provoke him to mutter a surly Oath or two, but he had not Spirit or Courage to resent it in a proper manner. For her Part, she gave herself up to all the Luxuries of Life, and her House was a general Rendezvous of Pleasure, while her slumbring Spouse was considered both by herself and Servants as nothing better than a Cypher.

OUR Milliner having lived a few Years in this Family, in which Time she saved some Money, resolved now to execute a Project she had long been forming. She had always been a great Reader of Plays, Novels, Romances, and the like; and when she saw Tragedy-Queens sweeping the Stage with their Trains at the Play-house, her Imagination would be fired with Envy at the Sight: She longed to sit in a flowered Elbow-chair, surrounded with Guards and Attendants; and was quite wild to give herself Airs of High-life in the superior Parts of a Comedy. With these Hopes she offered herself to the Stage, and was received by the Managers of *Drury-Lane*: But her Genius did not make so quick a Progress as she imagined; her Ambition every Day was mortified with Refusals; and tho' she desired only to play the Part of Lady *Townly*,[1] as a Specimen at first, the ignorant Managers could not be brought to comply with her Sollicitations. In short, she trod the Stage near two Years without once wearing a Crown, or wielding a Scepter: The Parts alloted her, were always of the most trifling kind, and she had little else to do, than to appear on the Stage as a Mute, to make up the Retinue of a Princess, or sympathize in Silence with the Sorrows of a dying

Heroine, by applying a white Handkerchief to her Eyes.

BUT tho' she could not make a Fortune by her Genius, her Beauty was more successful, and she had the Luck to make a Conquest of one of those pretty Gentlemen, who appear in laced Frocks behind the Scenes, or more properly on the middle of the Stage. He attended her in the Green-Room every Evening, and at last made her the Offer of a Settlement, if she could be contented to sacrifice her Ambition to Love. She was at first a little unwilling to leave the Theatre, where she foresaw such Advantages from her Genius; but thinking her Merit not enough regarded, and despairing of better Treatment (for she had not yet been permitted to play Lady *Townly*) she resigned herself to the Proposals of her Gallant, and set out with him immediately for the Country. There they lived in Solitude and Retirement for a Year, and probably might have done longer, had not Death spitefully inter-rupted their Amour, and snatched away the fond Keeper from the Arms of his theatrical Mistress. In his Will she found herself rewarded for her Constancy with a Legacy of seventy Pounds *per Annum*; with which she returned to *London*, and set up a Milliner's Shop. She had a good Fancy at new Fashions, and soon recom-mended herself to the Notice of People of Quality; by which means in time she became a Milliner of Vogue, and had the Art to raise a considerable Fortune from Lace and Ribbands. The best Part of her House she let out for Lodgings, reserving to herself only a Shop, a Kitchen, and a little Parlour, which at Night served for a Bed-chamber.

SUCH was *Pompey*'s present Mistress, who now lived in great Ease and Comfort, after a Life of much Vexation and Disappointment.

CHAPTER VI

[Another long chapter of characters.]

THREE or four days after *Pompey* was settled in these
apartments, as he was frisking and sporting one
morning about the shop, a young lady, who lodged in
the house, came down stairs. and accosted his mistress in
the following terms: 'I want to see some ribbands if you
please, madam, to match my blue gown; for lady *Bab
Frightful* is to call upon mamma this evening, to carry
us to the play, to see *Othellor whore of Venus*, which they
say is one of the finest plays that ever was acted.' 'Yes
really, mem, 'tis a very engaging play to be sure,' replied
the milliner; 'indeed I think it one of the master-pieces
of the *English* stage—but you mistake a little, I fancy
miss, in the naming of it, for *Shakespear* I believe wrote
it *Othello* moor of *Venice*. *Venice*, mem, is a famous town
or city somewhere or other, where *Othello* runs away with
a rich heiress in the night-time, and marries her privately
at the fleet.[1] By very odd luck he was created lord high-
admiral that very night, and goes out to fight the *Turks*,
and takes his wife along with him to the wars; and there,
mem, he grows jealous of her, only because she happens
to have lost a handkerchief, which he gave her when he
came a courting to her. It was a muslin handkerchief,
mem, spotted with strawberries; and because she can't
find it, he beats her in the most unmerciful manner, and
at last smothers her between two feather-beds.' 'Does he
indeed?' cries the young lady; 'well, I hate a jealous
man of all things in nature; a jealous man is my particular
aversion—but however, no matter what the play is,
you know, ma'am, so we do but see it; for the pleasure
of a play is to shew one's self in the boxes, and see the
company, and all that——Yes, ma'am, this here is the
sort of ribbands I want, only if you please let me see
some of a paler blue.'

WHILE the milliner was taking down some fresh ban-boxes, the young lady turning round, happened to spy *Pompey* in a corner of the shop. 'O heavens!' cries she, as soon as she cast her eyes upon him, 'what a delightful little dog is there! Pray, dear Mrs. *Pincushion*, do tell me how long you have been in possession of that charming little beauty?' Mrs. *Pincushion* replied that he had been in her possession about a week, and was given her by a lady of celebrated beauty, whom she had the honour of serving. 'Well, if I am not amazed to think how she could part with him!' cries the young lady——'Sure, ma'am, she must be a woman of no manner of taste in the world, for I never saw any thing so charmingly handsome since the hour I was born. Pray, dear Mrs. *Pincushion*, what is his name?'

BEING informed that he was called *Pompey*, she snatched him up in her arms, kissed him with great transport, and poured forth the following torrent of nonsense upon him: 'O you sweet little *Pompey!* you most delightful little *Pompey!* you dear heavenly jewel! you most charming little perroquet! I will kiss you, you little beauty! I will—I will—I'll kiss you, and hug you, and kiss you to death.' Then turning again to the milliner, 'dear Mrs. *Pincushion*,' added she, 'you must give me leave to carry him up stairs, to shew him to papa and mamma, for in all my days I never beheld so divine a creature.' Being now served with her blue ribbands, and having received the milliner's consent to her request, she flew up stairs in all imaginable haste, with the dog in her arms: but before we relate the reception she met with, let us prepare the reader with a short description of her parents.

SIR *Thomas Frippery*, the father of this young lady, had formerly enjoyed a little post in queen *Anne*'s court, which entitled him to a knighthood in consequence of his office, tho' the salary of it was very inconsiderable, and by no means equal to the grandeur he affected. On the death of the queen he lost this employment, and was obliged to retire into the country; where he gave himself the airs of a minister of state, set up for an oracle of politics, and endeavoured to persuade his country-neighbours that he had been very intimate with lord *Oxford*,[1] and very deep in the transactions of those times.

THE same ridiculous vanity pursued him thro' every article of his life, and tho' his estate was known hardly to amount to three hundred pounds a year, he laboured to make people believe that it exceeded as many thousands. For this purpose, whatever he was obliged to do out of frugality, he was sure to put off with a pretence of *taste*, and always disguised his œconomy under the masque of fashion and the mode. For instance, when he laid down his coach, he boasted every where, how much better it was to hire job-horses as occasion required, than to run the hazard of accidents by keeping them—that coachmen were such villainous rascals, it was impossible to put any confidence in them—that going into dirty stables to overlook their management, and treading up to one's knees in horse-dung, was extremely disagreeable to people of fashion—and therefore for his part, he had laid down his coach to avoid the trouble and anxiety of keeping horses.

WHEN his country-neighbours dined with him, whose ignorance he thought he could impose on, he would give them alder-wine and swear it was hermitage,[2] call a gammon of bacon a *Bayonne* ham, and put off the commonest home-made cheese for the best *Parmasan* that ever came into *England*; which he said had been sent him as a present by a young nobleman of his acquaintance then on his travels.

ABOUT once in three years he brought his wife and family to town, which served for matter of conversation to them during the two intermediate years, that were spent in the country; and they looked forward to the winter of pleasure with as much rapture and expectation, as the Rev^d. Mr. *Wh*——*n*, and some other christians do to their *millennium*.[1]

DURING the time of his residence in *London*, Sir *Thomas* every morning attended the levees of ministers, to beg the restitution of his old place, or an appointment to a new one; which he said he would receive with the most grateful acknowledgments, and discharge in any manner they should please to prescribe. Yet whether it was that his majesty's ministers were insensible of his merits, or could find no place suited to his abilities, the unhappy knight profited little by his court-attendance, and might as well have saved himself the expence of a triennial journey to *London*.

BUT tho' these expeditions did not encrease his fortune, they added much to his vanity, and he returned into the country new-laden with stories to amuse his ignorant neighbours. He talked of *his old friend my* good lord——with the greatest familiarity, and related conversations that had passed at the duke of ——'s table, with as much circumstance and particularity as if he had been present at them.

THE last article of vanity we shall mention, were his cloaths; which gives the finishing stroke to his character: for he chose rather to wear the rags of old finery, which had been made up in the reign of queen *Anne*, than to submit to plain cloaths of a modern make and fashion. He fancied the poor people in his neighbourhood were to be awed with the sight of tarnished lace, and wherever he went, the gold-fringe fell from his person so plentifully, that you might at any time trace his footsteps by the relicks of finery, which he left behind him.

LADY *Frippery* his accomplish'd spouse, did not fall short of her husband in any of these perfections, but rather improved them with new graces of her own. For having been something of a beauty in her youth, she still retained all the scornful airs and languishing disdain, which she had formerly practised to her dying lovers.

THEY had one only daughter, who having been educated all her life at home under her parents, was now become a master-piece of folly, vanity and impertinence. She had not one gesture or motion that was natural; her mouth never opened without some ridiculous grimace; her voice had learnt a tone and accent foreign to itself; her eyes squinted with endeavouring to look alluring, and all her limbs were distorted with affectation. Yet she fancied herself so well-bred, genteel and engaging, that it was impossible for any man to look on her without admiration, and was always talking about *taste* and the *mode*.

IT happened now to be the *London* winter with this amiable family, and they were crowded into scanty lodgings on a milliner's first floor, consisting only of a dining-room, a bed-chamber and a closet. The dining-room was set apart for the reception of company, Sir *Thomas* and his lady took possession of the chamber, and miss slept in a little tent-bed occasionally[1] stuffed into the closet. Such was the family, to whom our hero was now to be introduced.

THERE is nothing more droll and diverting than the morning dresses of people, who being exceedingly poor, and yet exceedingly proud, affect to make a great figure with a very little fortune. The expence they are at abroad obliges them to double their frugality at home; and as their chief happiness consists in displaying themselves to the eye of the world, consequently when they are out of its eye, nothing is too dirty or too ragged for them to wear. Now as no-body ever had the vanity of appearance more than the family we have been describing, it will easily be believed, that in their own private apartments, behind the scenes of the world, they did not appear to the greatest advantage. And indeed there was something so singularly odd in their dress and employments, at the moment our hero was presented to them, that we cannot help endeavouring to set their image before the reader.

SIR *Thomas* was shaving himself before a looking-glass in his bed-chamber, habited in the rags of an old night-gown, which about thirty years before had been red damask. All his face, and more than half his head were covered with soap-suds; only on his crown hung a flimzy green silk night-cap, made in the shape of a sugar-loaf. He had on a very dirty night-shirt, richly tinctured with perspiration, for he had slept in it a fortnight; and over this, a much dirtier ribb'd dimitty wastecoat, which had not visited the wash-tub for a whole twelve-month past. To finish his picture, he wore on his feet a pair of darned blue satten slippers, made out of the remnants of one of his wife's old petticoats.

So much for Sir *Thomas*. Close by him sat his lady, combing her hoary locks before the same looking-glass, and drest in a short bed-gown, which hardly reached down to her middle. A night-shift, which likewise had almost forgot the washing-tub, shrouded the hidden beauties of her person. She was without stays, without a hoop, without ruffles, and without any linen about her neck, to hide those redundant charms, which age had a little embrowned.

THIS was their dress and attitude, when their daughter burst into the room, and earnestly called upon them to admire the beauties of a lap-dog. Her sudden entrance alarming them with the expectation of some mighty matter, Sir *Thomas* in turning hastily round, had the misfortune to cut himself with his razor: which put him in a passion, when he came to know the ridiculous occasion of all this hurry. 'Pox take the girl,' cries he, 'get away child, and don't interrupt me with your lap-dogs. I am in a hurry here to go to court this morning, and you take up my time with silly tittle-tattle about a lap-dog. Do you see here, foolish girl? you have made me cut myself with your ridiculous nonsense—Get away I tell you—what a figure do you think I shall make at the levees with such a scar upon my face?'

'BLESS me, papa!' cries the young lady, 'I protest I am vastly sorry for your misfortune, but I'm sure you'll forgive, if you will but look on this delightful heavenly little jewel of a dog.'

'D—MN your little jewel of a dog,' replies the knight; 'prithee stand out of my way——I tell you I am in a hurry to go to court, and therefore prythee don't trouble me with your whelps and your puppy-dogs.'

'O MONSTROUS! how can you call him such cruel names?' cries the daughter. 'I am amazed at you, papa, for your *want of taste*. How can any living creature be so utterly void of *taste*, as not to admire such a beautiful little monkey? do, dear mamma! look at him—I am sure you must admire him, tho' papa is so shamefully blind, and so utterly void of all manner of taste.'

'WHY sure, my dear, you are mad to-day,' replied the mother, 'one would think you was absolutely fuddled this morning. Taste, indeed! I declare you are void of all manner of understanding, whatever your taste may be, to interrupt us thus, when you see we are both in a hurry to be drest. Prythee girl! learn a little decency and good manners, before you pretend to talk of taste.'

THE young lady being reprimanded thus on both sides, began to look extremely foolish, when a servant entered to inform them that Mr. *Chace* was in the dining-room. 'Ay, ay, go,' cries Sir *Thomas*, 'go and entertain him with your taste, till I am able to wait on him; tell Mr. *Chace* I happen unfortunately to be dressing, but I'll be with him in a moment of time.'

MISS *Frippery* then, muttering some little scorn, hurried into the next room with the dog in her arms, to see if she could not persuade her lover, (for so he was) to discover more taste than her parents. And here indeed she had better success; for this gentleman, who was a great sportsman and fox-hunter, was consequently a great connoisseur in dogs; he was likewise what is called a *very pretty young fellow about town*, and had a taste so exactly correspondent with that of the lady, that it is no wonder they agreed in the same objects of admiration. Here follows his character.

MR. *Chace*, usually called *Jack Chace* among his intimates, possessed an estate of fifteen hundred pounds a year; which was just sufficient to furnish him with a variety of riding-frocks, jockey-boots, Khevenhullar hats,[1] and coach-whips. His great ambition was to be deemed a *jemmy fellow*,[2] for which purpose, he appeared always in the morning in a *New-Market* frock, decorated with a great number of green, red or blue capes; he wore a short bob wig, neat buck's-skin breeches, white-silk stockings, and carried a cane switch in his hand. He kept a phaeton-chaise, and four *bay cattle*; a stable of hunters, and a pack of hounds in the country. The reputation of being a coachman, and driving a set of horses with skill, or in his own phrase, *doing his business clean*, he esteemed the greatest character in human life, and thought himself seated on the very pinnacle of glory, when he was mounted up in a high-chaise at a horse-race. *New-Market* had not a more active spirit, where he was frequently his own jockey, and boasted always, as a singular accomplishment, *that he did not ride above eight stone and a half*. Tho' he was a little man, and not very healthy in his constitution, he desired to be thought capable of the greatest fatigue, and was always laying wagers of the vast journeys he could perform in a day. He had likewise an ambition to be esteemed a man of consummate debauch, and endeavoured to persuade you, that he never went to bed without first drinking three or four bottles of claret, lying with as

many wh—res, and knocking down as many watchmen.
In the mornings he attended Mr. *Broughton*'s amphitheatres,[1] and in the evenings, (if he was drunk in time,
which indeed he seldom failed to be) he came behind
the scenes of the play-house, in the middle of the third
act, and there heroically exposed himself to the hisses
of the galleries. Whenever he met you, he began constantly with describing his last night's debauch, or related
the arrival of a new wh—re upon the town, or entertained
you with the exploits of his bay cattle: and if you declined
conversing with him on these three illustrious subjects,
he swore you was a fellow of no soul or genius, and ever
afterwards shunned your company. Having a hunting
seat in the neighbourhood of Sir *Thomas Frippery*, he often
visited in the family of that worthy knight, and at last
made proposals of marriage to the young lady; which
were favourably enough received, as well by her, as her
parents, who, it must be confessed, had a very laudable
regard for Mr. *Chace*'s estate.

To this jemmy young gentleman, who was now seated
in Sir *Thomas*'s dining-room, Miss *Frippery* came running
with the dog in her arms, and much sparkling conversation passed between them, which perhaps might not be
unentertaining, if we were able to relate it; but as it
turned wholly upon *polite taste in dress*, and the *mode*, we
confess ourselves unequal to so difficult and delicate a
task.

CHAPTER VII

A sad Disaster befalls Sir Thomas Frippery *in the Night,*
and a worse in the Day.

AND now that we have drawn the Characters of so
many People, let us look a little into their Actions;
for Characters alone afford a very barren Entertainment
to the Reader.

OUR Hero was grown a great Favourite with the
Milliner, who presented him with a laced Ruff, made
in the newest Fashion, worn by Women of Quality, and
suffered him to play about the Shop, where he was taken
Notice of by all the Ladies, who came to traffic in Fans
and Lace, and was often stroked by the fairest Hands in
London. In Requital for these Favours, he one Night
preserved the Honour of his Mistress from the Attacks of
a desperate Ravisher, who came with a Design of invading
her Bed.

THE ancient Knight, described in the last Chapter,
had, in his Youth, been a Man of some Amour, and still
retained a certain liquorish Inclination, tho' he was
narrowly watched by the Jealousy of his Wife. From the
Time of his last Arrival in Town, he had cast the languishing Eyes of Affection on the fair Milliner with whom
he lodged, and had been projecting many Stratagems to
accomplish his Desires. He used frequently to call in at
the Shop, whenever he found the Coast clear, under
Pretence of buying little Presents for his Wife or Daughter,
and there indulged himself in certain amorous Freedoms,
such as Kisses, and the like, which would provoke her to
cry out, *Pray Sir—Don't, Sir* Thomas—*I vow I'll call out,*
if you offer to be rude. Inflamed with these little Preliminaries,
he once attempted a bolder Deed; and tho' she repulsed
him with great Disdain, still he nourished Hopes of
Success, and watched for a fair Opportunity of making
a second Attempt.

ONE Midnight, therefore, when his Wife was fast asleep, he stole gently out of her Bed, and with great Softness proceeded down Stairs, to find his Way to that of her Rival. But when he came to the Door, unfortunately it was locked, and the Noise he made against it awakened little *Pompey*, who lay watchful by his Mistress's Bed-side. Instantly the Dog took the Alarm, and fell to barking with so much Vehemence, that he roused his Mistress, who started, and cried out, *Who is there?* To this a gentle whispering Voice replied, *One—Pray let me in.* The Milliner, now no longer doubting but that her House was broke open by Thieves, rang her Bell with all her Might, to summon People to her Assistance, and *Pompey* seconded her with such outrageous Fits of Barking, that the amorous Knight thought it high Time to sheer off to his own Bed. As he was groping his Way up Stairs in the Dark, he ran against *Jack Chace*, who having heard the Noise, was descending intrepidly in his Shirt, to find out the Cause of it. They were both exceedingly alarm'd, and as Sir *Thomas* had some Reasons for not speaking, *Jack* was obliged to begin the Conference, which he did in the following Words, *What the Devil have we got here?* Sir *Thomas* now finding himself under a Necessity of replying, to prevent any farther Discoveries, answered with a gentle Voice, *Hush, hush Sir!—I have only been walking in my Sleep, that's all—You'll alarm the Family, Mr. Chace! Hush, for God's sake, and let me return to my Bed again.* This brought them to an Eclaircissement, and Sir *Thomas* repeating a Desire of returning to Bed with as little Noise as possible, *Jack Chace* lent him his Hand, and they were almost arrived at the Chamber-door, when the Maid, who had risen at the Sound of her Mistress's Bell, and with her Tinder-box struck a Light, met the noble Pair in their Shirts, on the Top of the Stair-case. She immediately screamed out, dropped her Candle, and ran back to her Garret with the utmost Precipitation.

Miss *Frippery*, who had long ago heard the Noise, and lay trembling in her little Bed, expecting every Moment some House-breaker to appear and cut her Throat, now began to be revived a little at the Sound of her Father's Voice, whom she heard talking with Mr. *Chace*, and took Courage to call out from her Cabin, *Heavens, Papa! What is the Matter, Papa?* By this Time, the worthy Knight was arrived at his Bed-side, and finding his Wife asleep, blessed his Stars for being so favourable to him; and then putting his Head into the Closet where his Daughter lay, desired her not to wake her Mother with any Noise, adding, *I have only been walking in my Sleep, my Dear! that's all; and Mr.* Chace *has been so kind to conduct me back again to my Bed.* So saying, he deposited himself once more by the Side of his sleeping Spouse, whose *gentle* Slumbers not all the Noise in the House had been able to disturb.

'Tis well observed, that Misfortunes never come single, and what happened to Sir *Thomas Frippery* will confirm this ancient Maxim; for the Disgrace he suffered in the Night, was followed by a more disastrous Accident the ensuing Day.

Out of Compliment to *Jack Chace*, who was then laying close Siege to his Daughter, our Knight had consented to make a Party to *Ruckolt-house*,[1] which was at that Time the fashionable Resort of all idle People, who thought it worth while to travel ten Miles for a Breakfast. Sir *Thomas*, and his Lady, went in a hired Chariot, and the Lovers shone forth in a most exalted *Phaeton*, which looked down with Scorn on all inferior Equipages, and seemed like the triumphal Carr of Folly. But alas! the Expedition set out under the Influence of some evil Star, and Fortune seemed to take a Pleasure in persecuting them with Mischances all the Day long. Sir *Thomas* had not long been landed at *Ruckolt*, before he found himself afflicted on a sudden with a most violent Fit of the Cholic; and the Agitation of his Bowels so distorted the Features of his Face, that his Companions began to think him angry with them, and begged Pardon if they had offended him. 'Zounds, cries he, I have got the Cholic to such a Degree, that I am ready to die; and 'tis so long since I have been at any of these youthful Places of Gaiety, that I know not where to go for Relief.' *Jack Chace* could not help laughing at the Distresses of his future Father-in-law, but conducted him, however, to one of the Temples of the Goddess *Cloacina*, whose Altars are more constantly and universally attended, than those of any other Deity. Here he was entering with great Rapidity, when, to his Surprize, he found two Female Votaries already in Possession of the Temple; and 'tis an inviolable Law in the Alcoran of this Goddess, as it was formerly in the Ceremonies of the *Bona Dea*,[1] that the two Sexes shall never communicate in Worship at the same Time. This put our Knight into the strangest Confusion, and he was obliged to retire, muttering to himself, *that Women were always in the Way*. The Consequences of this Disappointment I forbear to mention; only I cannot help lamenting, that Statesmen should be as subject to the Gripes as inferior Mortals; for I make no doubt, but the greatest Politicians have been sometimes invaded with this Disease in the most critical Junctures, and the Business of the Nation suspended, 'till a Minister could return from his Close-stool.

As the Party was returning home, *Jack Chace*, desirous of shewing his Coachmanship to the young Lady, whirled so rapidly round the Corner of a Street, that he overturned the Chaise, and it was next to a Miracle that they escaped with their Lives. But luckily the future Bride received no other Damage, than spoiling her best Silk Night gown (which I mention as a Warning to all young Ladies, how they trust themselves with Gentlemen in high Chaises) and little *Pompey*, who was in her Lap, came with great Dexterity upon his Feet. The Driver

himself indeed lost his Ear, which was torn off by the
Wheel in his Fall; but this he esteemed a Wound of
Honour, and boasted of it as much as disabled Soldiers
do of the Loss of their Legs and Arms. As for Sir *Thomas*,
he entirely disclaimed *Ruckolt* for the remaining Part of
his Life, which he swore abounded with Perils and
Dangers, and declared with much Importance, that
there was no such Place in being, when he and Lord
Oxford were at the Helm of Affairs.

CHAPTER VIII

A Description of a Drum.

BUT I hasten to describe an Event, which engrossed
the Attention of this accomplished Family for a
Fortnight, and was Matter of Conversation to them for
a Year afterwards. Lady *Frippery*, in Imitation of other
Ladies of her Rank and Quality, was ambitious of having
a Drum; tho' the Smallness of her Lodgings might well
have excused her from attempting that modish Piece of
Vanity.

A DRUM is at present the highest Object of Female
Vain-glory; the End whereof is to assemble as large a
Mob of Quality as can possibly be contained in one
House; and great are the Honours paid to that Lady,
who can boast of the largest Crowd. For this Purpose, a
Woman of superior Rank calculates how many People
all the Rooms in her House laid open can possibly hold,
and then sends about two Months beforehand *among the
People one knows*, to bespeak such a Number as she thinks
will fill them. Hence great Emulations arise among them,
and the Candidates for this Honour sue as eagerly for
Visiters, as Candidates for Parliament do for Votes at
an Election: For as it sometimes happens that two

Ladies pitch upon the same Evening for raising a Riot, 'tis necessary they should beat up in time for Voluntiers; otherwise they may chance to be defrauded of their Numbers, and one of them lie under the Ignominy of collecting a Mob of a hundred only, while the other has the Honour of assembling a well-drest Rabble of three or four hundred; which of course breaks the Heart of that unfortunate Lady, who comes off with this immortal Disgrace.

Now as the Actions of People of Quality are sure of being copied, hence it comes to pass that Ladies of inferior Rank, resolving to be in the Fashion, take upon them likewise to have Drums in Imitation of their Superiors: Only there is this Difference between the two Orders, that the Higher call nothing but a *Crowd* a *Drum*, whereas the Lower often give that Name to the commonest Parties, and for the sake of Honour call an ordinary Visit an Assembly.

THIS was the Case with Lady *Frippery*; her Acquaintance in Town was very small, and it seemed improbable that she could assemble above a dozen People at most, without making any Allowance for Colds, Head-achs, Vapors, hysteric Fits, Fevers upon the Spirits and other Female Indispositions; yet still she resolved to have a Drum, and the young Lady seconded her Mamma's Inclinations so vehemently, that Sir *Thomas* was obliged to comply.

FROM the Moment this great Event was resolved on, all their Conversations turned upon it, and it was pleasant to hear the Schemes and Contrivances they had about it. Their first and principal Care was to secure Lady *Bab Frightful*, the chief of Lady *Frippery*'s Acquaintance, and whose Name was to give a Lustre to the Assembly. Now Lady *Bab* being one of the Quality, it was possible she might have a previous Engagement, unless she was taken in time; and therefore a Card was dispatched to her in the first Place, to bespeak her for such an Evening; and it was resolved, that if any cross Accident prevented her coming, new Measures should be taken, and the Drum be deferred till another Night. Lady *Bab* returned for Answer, *that she would wait on Lady* Frippery, *if her Health permitted*. This dubious kind of Message puzzled them in the strangest manner, and was worse than a Denial; for without Lady *Bab* it was impossible to proceed, without Lady *Bab* the Assembly would make no Figure, and yet they were obliged to run the Hazard of her not coming in Consequence of her Answer. Every Day therefore, they sent to enquire after her Health, and their Hopes rose or fell according to the Word that was brought them; till on the Day before the Drum was to be held, a most calamitous Piece of News arrived, *that Lady* Bab *was disabled by her Surgeon*, who in cutting her Toe-nail had made an Incision in her Flesh; yet still she promised to be with them, *if it was possible for her to hobble Abroad*. 'Tis impossible to describe the Damp which this fatal Message struck into the whole Family; a general Consternation at once overspread their Faces, and they looked as if an Earthquake was going to swallow them up: But they were obliged to submit with Patience, and as a Glimpse of Hope still remained, they had nothing left but to put up their Prayers for Lady *Bab*'s Recovery.

At length the important Evening arrived, that was to decide all their Expectations and Fears. Many Consultations had been held every Day, and almost every Hour of the Day, that Things might be perfect and in Order, when the Time came: Yet notwithstanding all their Precautions, a Dispute arose almost at the last Moment, *whether Lady* Frippery *was to receive her Company at the Top or Bottom of the Stairs?* This momentous Question begat a warm Debate. Her Ladyship and Miss contended resolutely for the Top of the Stairs, Sir *Thomas* for the Bottom, and Mr. *Chace* observed a Neutrality; till at

length, after a long Altercation, the Knight was obliged
to submit to a Majority of Voices; tho' not without
condemning his Wife and Daughter for want of Politeness. 'My Dear,' said he, taking a Pinch of Snuff with
great Vehemence, I am amazed that you can be guilty
of such a Solecism in Breeding: It surprizes me, that you
are not sensible of the Impropriety of it—Will it not
shew much greater Respect and Complaisance to meet
your Company at the Bottom of the Stairs, than to stand
like an *Indian* Queen receiving Homage at the Top of
them?' 'Yes, my Dear! answered her Ladyship; but you
know my Territories do not commence till the Top of
the Stairs; our Territories do not begin below Stairs;
and it would be very improper for me to go out of my
own Dominions—Don't you see that, my Dear? I am
surprized at your want of Comprehension to-day, Sir
Thomas!' 'Well, well, I have given it up, answered he;
have your own Way, Child; have your own Way, my
Lady, and then you'll be pleased, I hope—but I am
sure, in my Days, People would have met their Company
at the Bottom of the Stairs. When I and Lord *Oxford*
were in the Ministry together, Affairs would have been
very different—but the Age has lost all its Civility, and
People are not half so well-bred as they were formerly.'

THIS Reflexion on modern Times piqued the Daughter's
Vanity, who now began to play her Part in the Debate.
'Yes, Papa, said she, but what signifies what People did
formerly? that is nothing at all to us at present, you
know; for to be sure all People were Fools formerly: I
always think People were Fools in former Days. They
never did any thing as we do now-a-days, and therefore
it stands to Reason they were all Fools and Idiots. 'Tis
very manifest they had no Breeding, and all the World
must allow, that the World never was so wise, and polite,
and sensible, and clever as it is at this Moment; and, for
my Part, I would not have lived in former Days for all

the World.' 'Pugh! said the Knight, interrupting her, you are a little illiterate Monkey; you talk without Book, Child! the World is nothing to what it was in my Days. Every thing is altered for the worse. The Women are not near so handsome. None of you are comparable to your Mothers.' 'Nay, there—said Lady *Frippery*, interposing, there, Sir *Thomas*, I entirely agree with you—there you have my Consent, with all my Heart. To be sure, all the celebrated Girls about Town are mere Dowdies, in Comparison of their Mothers; and if there could be a Resurrection of Beauties, they would shine only like *Bristol* Stones[1] in the Company of Diamonds.' 'Bless me, Mamma! cried the young Lady, with the Tears standing in her Eyes, how can you talk so? There never were so many fine Women in the whole World, as there are now in *London*; and 'tis enough to make one burst out a crying, to hear you talk—Come, Mr. *Chace*, why don't you stand up for us modern Beauties?'

IN the midst of this Conversation, there was a violent Rap at the Street-door; whereupon they all flew to the Window, crying out eagerly, *There——there is Lady* Bab— *I am sure 'tis Lady* Bab; *for I know her Footman's rap*. Yet, in spite of this Knowledge, Lady *Bab* did not arrive according to their Hopes; and it seemed as if her Lady-ship had laid a Scheme to keep them in Suspence; for of all the People, who composed this illustrious Assembly, Lady *Bab* came the last. They took care, however, to in-form the Company from time to time, that she was expected, by making the same Observation on the Arrival of every fresh Coach, and still persisting, that they knew her Footman's rap, tho' they had given so many Proofs to the contrary. At length, however, Lady *Bab Frightful* came; and it is impossible to express the Joy they felt on her Appearance; which revived them on a sudden from the Depth of Despair to the highest Exaltation of Happiness.

HER Ladyship's great Toe engrossed the Conversation for the first Hour, whose Misfortune was lamented in very pathetic Terms by all the Company, and many wise Reflexions were made upon the Accident which had happened; some condemning the Ignorance, and others the Carelessness of the Surgeon, who had been guilty of such a Trespass on her Ladyship's Flesh. Some advised her to be very careful how she walked upon it; others recommended a larger Shoe to her Ladyship, and Lady *Frippery*, in particular, continued the whole Evening to protest the vast Obligations she had to her, for favouring her with her Company under such an Affliction. But had I an hundred Hands, and as many Pens, it would be impossible to describe the Folly of that Night: Wherefore, begging the Reader to supply it by the Help of his own Imagination, I proceed to other Parts of this History.

CHAPTER IX

[In which several things are touched upon.]

WHEN this great affair was over, the marriage came next upon the carpet; the celebration of which was fixed for *Easter* week; but Mr. *Chace* recollecting in time that it would interfere with *Newmarket* races, procured a reprieve till the week following. At his return from those *Olympic* games, the nuptials were celebrated before a general assembly of their relations, and the happy couple were conducted to bed in publick with great demonstrations of joy. The bridegroom took possession of the bride, and Sir *Thomas* took possession of Mr. *Chace's* estate.

WHEN they had shewn their new cloaths a little in *London*, they set out in a body for the country; and in a few days afterwards, the lodgings on the first floor were taken by a lady, who passed under the fictitious name of Mrs. *Caryl*. The hasty manner, in which she made her agreement, infused a suspicion into our milliner from the very beginning; and many circumstances soon concurred to persuade her, that her new lodger was a wife eloped from her husband. For besides that she came into her lodgings late in the evening, she seemed to affect a privacy in all her actions, which plainly evidenced, that she was afraid of some discovery; and this increased our milliner's curiosity in proportion as the other seemed less inclined to gratify it. But an event soon happened to confirm her conjectures; for three days after the lady's arrival, a chair stopped at the door one evening near ten o'clock, from whence alighted a well-drest man about forty years old, who wrapping himself up in a red cloak, proceeded hastily up stairs, as if desirous to conceal himself from observation. This adventure savoured so strongly of intrigue, that it was no wonder our milliner contrived to meet him in the passage, to satisfy her curiosity with a survey of his features; for people, in whom that passion predominates, often find the greatest consolation from knowing the smallest trifles. *Pompey* was still more inquisitive than his mistress, and took courage to follow the gentleman into the dining-room, with a desire, I suppose, of hearing what passed in so fashionable an interview.

THE lady rose from her chair to receive this man of fashion, who saluted her with great complaisance, and hoped she was pleased with her new apartments. 'Yes, my lord,' answered she, 'the people are civilized people enough, and I believe have no suspicion about me—— but did they see your lordship come up stairs?' ''Pon my honour, madam,' said the peer, 'I can't tell; there was a female figure glided by me in the passage, but whether the creature made remarks[1] or not, I did not stay to observe——Well, madam, I hope now I may give you joy of your escape, and I dare say you will find yourself much happier than you was under the ill-usage of a tyrant you despised.' The lady then related, with great pleasantry, the manner of her escape, and the difficulties that attended the execution of it; after which she concluded with saying, 'I wonder, my lord, what my husband is now thinking on?' 'Thinking on!' answered the peer—that he's a fool and a blockhead, I hope, madam, and deserves to be hanged for abusing the charms of so divine a creature——Good God! was it possible for him to harbour an ill-natured thought, while he had the pleasure of looking in that angelic face?' 'My lord,' said the lady, 'I know I have taken a very ill step in the eye of the world; but I have too much spirit to bear ill-usage with patience, and let the consequences be what they will, I am determined to submit to them, rather than be a slave to the ill-humours of a man I despised, hated and detested.' 'Forbear madam,' said his lordship, 'to think of him; my fortune, my interest, my sword, are all devoted to your service, and I am ready to execute any command you please to impose upon me—but let us call a more agreeable topic of conversation.'

SOON after this a light, but elegant supper was placed upon the table, and the servants were ordered to retire; for there are certain seasons, when even the Great desire to banish ostentation. The absent husband furnished them with much raillery, and they pictured to themselves continually the surprize he would be in, when first he discovered his wife's elopement; nor did this man of gallantry and fashion finish his amorous visit till past two o'clock in the morning. As he was going down stairs, he found himself again encountered by the barking of little *Pompey*, whom he snatched up in his arms, and getting hastily into the chair, that waited for him at the door, carried him off with him to his own house.

THIS accomplished person was lord *Marmazet*,[1]

husband to that lady, who was so familiar and intimate with the sharper at *Bath*. He was a man of consummate intrigue, a most fortunate adventurer with the fair sex, and had the reputation of uncommon success in his amours. What made this success the more extraordinary was, that in personal charms he had nothing to boast of: nature had given him neither a face or figure to strike the eyes of women; but these deficiencies were abundantly recompensed by a most happy turn of wit, a very brilliant imagination, and extensive knowledge of the world. He had the most insinuating manner of address, the readiest flow of language, and a certain art of laughing women out of their virtue, which few could imitate. It was indeed scarce possible to withstand the allurements of his conversation; and what is odd enough, the number of affairs he had been concerned in, were so far from frightening ladies from his acquaintance, that on the contrary it was fashionable and modish to cultivate an intimacy with him. They knew the danger of putting themselves in his way, and yet were ambitious of giving him opportunities.

THE lady we have just now seen with him, had been his neighbour in the country, a very handsome woman under the tyranny of an ill-natured husband. This his lordship knew, and concluding that her aversion to her husband would make her an easy prey to a lover, watched every opportunity of being alone with her. In these stolen interviews he employed all his eloquence to seduce her, and won upon her so much by his flattering representation of things, that at length she courageously eloped from her tyrant, and put herself into private lodgings under the protection of his lordship. The reader need not be told that this ended in the utter ruin of the lady, who· finding her reputation lost, and her passionate lover soon growing indifferent, took refuge in citron waters, and by the help of those cordial lenitives of sorrow, soon bade adieu to the world and all its cares.

CHAPTER X

[*Matrimonial amusements.*]

WHEN our hero waked the next morning, and found himself in new apartments, the first thing he did was to piss on a pair of velvet breeches, which lay in a chair by his lordship's bedside; after which, the door being open, he travelled forth, and performed a much more disreputable action on a rich *Turkey* carpet in my lady's dining-room. Having thus taken possession of his new house by these two acts of *seisin*,[1] he returned to the bed-side, and reposed himself again to sleep till his lord should please to be stirring.

ABOUT ten o'clock lord *Marmazet* raised himself up in his bed, and rang his bell for servants to assist him in the fatigue of putting on his cloaths. The valet in chief immediately attended, undrew the curtains, and respectfully enquired his master's pleasure. In answer to which his lordship signifying that he would get up, *Guillaume* folded his stockings, placed his slippers by the bed-side, and was going to present him with his breeches —when lo! the crime our hero had been guilty of stared him full in the face, and gave such an air of surprize to his features, that his lordship could not help asking what was the matter. *Guillaume* then related the misdemeanor, at which his master was so far from being angry, that he only laughed at the astonishment of his valet, and calling the dog upon the bed, caressed him with as much tenderness, as if he had performed the most meritorious action in the world. Then turning again to his servant, 'what does the booby stare at, cries he, 'with such amazement? I wish to G—d the dog had pissed in thy mouth. Prythee get a fresh pair of breeches, and let me rise—or am I to lie a-bed till midnight?'

As soon as he was dressed in his morning dishabille,

he went down stairs to breakfast; in which our hero bore
him company, and had the honour of eating roll and
butter in great magnificence. When breakfast was over,
he recollected that it might now be time to send up
compliments to his lady, which he generally performed
every morning; and imagining that she would not be
displeased with the present of so pretty a dog, 'here,
Guillaume,' said he, 'take this little dog, and carry him
up stairs to your lady. My compliments, and desire to
know how her ladyship does this morning. Tell her I
found him—pox take him, I don't know where I found
him, but he's a pretty little fellow, and I am sure she
must be pleased with him.'

THO' the reader must from hence conclude that lord
and lady *Marmazet* reposed themselves in different beds
at night, he will not, I imagine, be surprised at such a
circumstance in this accomplished and fashionable age.
Her ladyship was a woman of great wit, pleasure and
amour, as well as her husband, only with a little more
reserve and caution, to save appearances with the world.
Her familiarity with a sharper at *Bath*, may have already
given the reader some little sketch of her character; and
for the rest it will be only necessary to inform him, that
she had spent the greatest part of her life in St. *James*'s
parish.[1] Her husband had married her without the
temptation of love, because she was a rich heiress of a
noble family; and she had consented to the match, with
an equal indifference, only because it preserved her rank
and station in the world. In consequence they soon grew
totally unconcerned about each other; but then, being
both of easy chearful tempers, their indifference did not
sour into hatred; on the contrary, they made it a topic
of wit, when they met, to railly one another on their
mutual amours. These meetings indeed were not very
frequent, once or twice a week perhaps at dinner, at
which times they behaved with the utmost politeness

and complaisance; or if they railed, it was done with so much gaiety and good-humour, that they only parted with the greater spirits to their evening amusements. In short, his lordship pursued his pleasures without any domestic expostulations, and her ladyship in return was permitted to live in all respects, as *Juvenal* expresses it,[1] *tanquam vicina mariti*, more like her husband's neighbour than his wife.

HER ladyship was now just awake, and taking her morning tea in bed, when *Guillaume* ascended the stairs, and knocked at her chamber-door. The waiting gentle-woman being ordered out to see who it was, returned immediately to the bed-side with a dog in her arms, and delivered the message that accompanied him. As her ladyship had never in her life discovered any fondness for these four-footed animals, she could not conceive the meaning of such a present, and with some disdain in her countenance ordered 'the fellow to carry back his puppies again to his master.' But when the servant was gone down stairs, bethinking herself that there might be some joke in it, which she did not perceive, and resolving not to be out-done by her husband in wit, she asked her maid eagerly, if there was any such thing as a cat in the house. 'A cat, my lady!' cries the waiting gentlewoman, 'yes, my lady, I believe there is such a thing to be found.' 'Well then,' said her ladyship, 'go and catch it directly, and carry it with my compliments to his lordship. Let him know I am infinitely obliged to him for his present, and have sent him a cat in return for his dog.'

THE maid simpered without offering to stir, as not indeed conceiving her mistress to be in earnest; but having the orders repeated to her, she set out immediately to fulfil them. After much laughter below stairs among the servants, a cat at length was catched, and the waiting-maid went with it in her arms to his lordship's dressing room. Having rapped at the door, and being ordered to enter, with a face half-blushing and half-smiling, she delivered her message in the following terms. 'My lady desires her compliments to your lordship, and begs the favour of you to accept of THIS, in return for your dog.' After which dropping the grave mouser on the floor, she was preparing to run away with all haste, being ready to burst with laughter. But his lordship, who was no less diverted, called her back, and having entertained himself with many jokes on the occasion, sent her up-stairs with a fresh message to her mistress. This was immediately returned on the part of her ladyship, and many little pieces of raillery were carried backwards and forwards, which perhaps might not be unentertaining: but as we are sensible with what contempt these little incidents will be received by the reader, if he happens to be a judge, a politician, or an alderman, we shall dwell no longer on them, and here put an end to the chapter.

CHAPTER XI

[Describing the miseries of a garretteer poet.]

Not long after this, as lord *Marmazet* was sitting in his study, reading some papers of state, with our hero under his chair; *Guillaume* entered the room, and informed him that Mr. *Rhymer* the poet was below. 'Curse Mr. *Rhymer* the poet, and you too for an egregious blockhead,' cries his lordship; 'why the devil did you let the fellow in? tell him, his last political pamphlet is execrable nonsense, and unintelligible jargon, and I am not at leisure to see him this morning.' 'My lord,' replied the valet, 'he begged me to present his humble duty to your lordship, and to inform you, that a small gratuity would be very acceptable at present, for it seems his wife is ready to lie-in, and he says, he has not six-pence

to defray the expences of her groaning.' 'How,' cries his
lordship, 'has that fellow the impudence to beget children?
the dog pretends here to be starving, and yet has the
assurance to deal in procreation——Prythee, *Guillaume*,
what sort of a woman is his wife? have you ever seen
her?' 'Yes, my lord,' answered the trusty valet; 'I have
had the honour of seeing the lady, but I am afraid she
would have no great temptations for your lordship; for
the poor gentlewoman has the misfortune to squint a
little, which does not give a very bewitching air to her
countenance, besides which, she has the accomplishment
of red hair into the bargain.' 'Well then,' cries the peer,
turn the hound out of doors, and bid him go to the devil.
Pox take him, if he had a handsome wife, I might be
tempted to encourage him a little; but how can he expect
my favour without doing any thing to deserve it?' 'Then
your lordship won't be pleased to send him a small
acknowledgment,' said the valet de chambre. 'No,'
replied the peer, 'I have no money to fling away on poets
and hackney-writers; let the fellow eat his own works,
if he is hungry.——Hold, stay, I have thought better of
it; here *Guillaume*, take this little dog, since my wife
won't have him, and carry him to the poet. My service
to the gentleman, and desire him to keep him for my
sake.'

GUILLAUME was a man of some little humour, which
had promoted him to the dignity of first pimp in ordinary
to his lordship, and perceiving that his master had a
mind to divert himself this morning with the miseries of
an unhappy poet, he resolved that the joke should not
be lost in passing through his hands. Taking the dog
therefore from his lordship, he made haste down stairs,
and accosted the expecting bard in the following manner:
'Sir! his lordship is very busy this morning, and not at
leisure to see you, but he speaks very kindly of you, and .
begs you would do him the favour to accept of this

beautiful little *Bologna* lap-dog.' 'Accept of a lap-dog,'
cried the poet with astonishment; 'bless me! what is the
matter? surely there must be some mistake, Mr. *Guillaume!*
for I cannot readily conceive of what use a *Bologna* lap-
dog can be to me.' 'Sir,' replied the valet-de-chambre,
'you may depend upon it, his lordship had some reason
for making you this present, which it does not become us
to guess at.' 'No,' said the bard, 'I would not presume
to dive into his lordship's councils; but really now, Mr.
Guillaume, a few guineas in present cash would be rather
more serviceable to me than a *Bologna* lap-dog, and more
comfortable to my poor wife and children.' 'Sir,' said the
valet, 'you must not distrust his lordship's generosity:
great statesmen, Mr. *Rhymer*, always do things in a
different manner from the rest of the world: there is
usually something a little mysterious in their conduct;
but assure yourself, sir, this dog will be the fore-runner
of a handsome annuity, and it would be the greatest
affront imaginable not to receive him.——You must
never refuse any thing, which the Great esteem a favour,
Mr. *Rhymer*, on any account; even tho' it should involve
you and your family in everlasting ruin. His lordship
desired that you would keep the dog for his sake, sir, and
therefore you may be sure he has a particular regard
for you, when he sends you such a memorial of his
affection.'

THE unhappy poet finding he could extort nothing
from the unfeeling hands of his patron, was obliged to
retire with the dog under his arm, and climbed up in a
disconsolate mood to his garret, where he found his wife
cooking the scrag end of a neck of mutton for dinner.
The mansions of this son of *Apollo* were very contracted,
and one would have thought it impossible for one single
room to have served so many domestic purposes; but
good housewifery finds no difficulties, and penury has a
thousand inventions, which are unknown to ease and

wealth. In one corner of these poetical apartments stood
a flock-bed, and underneath it, a green jordan[1] presented
itself to the eye, which had collected the nocturnal urine
of the whole family, consisting of Mr. *Rhymer*, his wife,
and two daughters. Three rotten chairs and a half
seemed to stand like traps in various parts of the room,
threatning downfals to unwary strangers; and one
solitary table in the middle of this aerial garret, served to
hold the different treasures of the whole family. There
were now lying upon it the first act of a comedy, a pair
of yellow stays, two political pamphlets, a plate of bread-
and-butter, three dirty night-caps, and a volume of
miscellany poems. The lady of the house was drowning a
neck of mutton, as we before observed, in meagre soup,
and the two daughters sat in the window, mending their
father's brown stockings with blue worsted. Such were
the mansions of Mr. *Rhymer*, the poet, which I heartily
recommend to the repeated perusal of those unhappy
gentlemen, who feel in themselves a growing inclination
to that mischievous, damnable, and destructive science.

As soon as Mr. *Rhymer* entered the chamber, his wife
deserted her cookery, to enquire the success of his visit,
on which the comforts of her lying-in so much depended;
and seeing a dog under her husband's arm, 'Bless me,
my dear!' said she, 'why do you bring home that filthy
creature, to eat up our victuals? Thank heaven, we have
got more mouths already, than we can satisfy, and I am
sure we want no addition to our family.' 'Why, my dear,'
answered the poet, 'his lordship did me the favour to
present me this morning with this beautiful little *Bologna*
lap-dog.' 'Present you with a lap-dog,' cried the wife
interrupting him, 'what is it you mean, Mr. *Rhymer*?
but, however, I am glad his lordship was in so bountiful
a humour, for I am sure then he has given you a purse
of guineas to maintain the dog.——Well, I vow it was
a very genteel way of making a present, and I shall love

the little fool for his master's sake.—Great men do things with so much address always, that one is transported as much with their politeness as their generosity.' Here the unhappy bard shook his head, and soon undeceived his wife, by informing her of all that had passed in his morning's visit. 'How,' said she, 'no money with the dog? Mr. *Rhymer*, I am amazed that you will submit to such usage. Don't you see that they make a fool, and an ass, and a laughing-stock of you? Why did you take their filthy dog? I'll have his brains dashed out this moment.— Mr. *Rhymer*, if you had kept on your tallow-chandler's shop, I and mine should have had wherewithal to live; but you must court the draggle-tail muses forsooth, and a fine provision they have made for you.—Here I expect to be brought to bed every day, and you have not money to buy pap and caudle.[1]—O curse your lords and your political pamphlets! I am sure I have reason to repent the day that ever I married a poet.' 'Madam,' said *Rhymer*, exasperated at his wife's conversation, 'you ought rather to bless the day, that married you to a gentleman, whose soul despises mechanical trades, and is devoted to the noblest science in the universe. Poetry, madam, like virtue, is its own reward; but you have a vulgar notion of things, you have an illiberal attachment to money, and had rather be frying grease in a tallow-chandler's shop, than listening to the divine rhapsodies of the *Heliconian* maids.[2] 'Tis true, madam, his lordship has not recompensed my labours according to expectation this morning, but what of that? he bid me proceed in the execution of my design, and undoubtedly means to reward me. Lords are often destitute of cash, as well as poets, and perhaps I came upon him a little unseasonably, when his coffers were empty; but I auspicate great things from his present of a dog.—A dog, madam, is the emblem of fidelity.' 'The emblem of a fiddle-stick!' cried the wife, interrupting him, 'I tell you, Mr. *Rhymer*, you are a fool, and have ruined your family by your senseless whims and projects.——A gentleman, quotha! Yes, forsooth, a very fine gentleman truly, that has hardly a shirt to his back, or a pair of shoes to his feet.—Look at your daughters there in the window, and see whether they appear like a gentleman's daughters; and for my part, I have not an under-petticoat that I can wear.— You have had three plays damned, Mr. *Rhymer*, and one would think that might have taught you a little prudence ; but, deuce fetch me, if you shall write any more, for I'll burn all this nonsense that lies upon the table.' So saying, she flew like a *Bacchanal* fury at his works, and with savage hands was going to commit them to the flames, had she not been interrupted by her husband's voice, crying out with impatience, 'see, see, see, my dear! the pot boils over, and the broth is all running away into the fire.' This luckily put an end to their altercation, and postponed the sacrifice that was going to be made; they then set down to dinner without a table-cloth, and made a wretched meal, envying one another every morsel that escaped their own mouths. And 'tis highly probable poor *Pompey* would soon have fallen a sacrifice to hunger, and been served up at Mr. *Rhymer*'s poetical table, had not an accident luckily happened, to relieve him from this scene of misery, squallidness, and poesy.

CHAPTER XII

[A poetical feast, and squabble of authors.]

AFTER dinner was over, Mr. *Rhymer* sat himself down to an epic poem, which was then on the anvil, and his head not being clouded with any fumes of indigestion, he worked at it very laboriously till eight or nine o'clock in the evening. Then he took his hat, and went out to meet a club of authors, who assembled every *Monday* night, at a little dirty dog-hole of a tavern in *Shire-lane*,[1] to eat tripe, drink porter, and pass their judgments on the books of the preceding week. *Pompey* waited on his master; for as Mrs. *Rhymer* had resolutely vowed his destruction, the good-natured bard did not chuse to leave him at her mercy.

ON their arrival in the club-room, they found there assembled a free-thinking writer of moral essays, a no-thinking scribler of magazines, a *Scotch* translator of *Greek* and *Latin* authors, a *Grub-street* bookseller, and a *Fleet* parson.[2] These worthy gentlemen immediately surrounded Mr. *Rhymer* with great vociferation, and began to curse him for staying so long, declaring it would be entirely his fault, if the tripe was spoilt, which they very much feared. To prevent which however, they now ordered it to be served up with all possible expedition, and on its appearance, fell to work with the quickest dispatch. The reader will believe that little or no conversation passed among them at table, their mouths being much too busily employed to have any leisure for discourse; but when the tripe was quite consumed, and innumerable slices of toasted cheese at the end of it, they then began to exercise their tongues as readily as they had before done their teeth.

BY odd luck, every one of these great advancers of modern literature, happened to have a dog attending him; and as the gentlemen drew round the fire after supper in a ring, the dogs likewise made an interior semi-circle, sitting between the legs of their respective masters. This could not escape the observation of the company, and many trite reflections began to be made on their fidelity, their attachment to man, and above all, on the felicity of their condition; for a dog sleeping before a fire, is by all people esteemed an emblem of complete happiness. At length, they struck into a higher conversation. 'Gentlemen!' says the free-thinker, 'I should be glad to hear your sentiments concerning reason and instinct. I have a curious treatise now by me, which I design very soon to astonish the world with. 'Tis upon a subject perfectly new, and those dogs there put me in the head of it. The clergy I know will be up in arms against me, but no matter; I'll publish my opinions in spite of all the priests in *Europe*.'

HERE the *Fleet* parson, thinking himself concerned, took his pipe from his mouth with great deliberation, and said, 'I don't know what your opinions may be, but I hope you don't design to publish any thing to the disadvantage of that sacred order to which I belong: if you do sir, I believe you'll find pens enow ready to answer you.'

'YES, sir, no doubt I shall,' replied the free-thinker, 'and who cares for that? perhaps you, sir, may do me the honour to be my antagonist, but I defy you all!—I defy the whole body of the priesthood. Sir, I love to advance a paradox; I love a paradox at my heart, sir! and I'll—I'll shew you some sport very shortly.'

'WHAT do you mean by sport, sir?' cries the doctor ——'If you write as you talk, I hope you'll be set in the pillory for your sport.'

'YOU are bloody complaisant, sir,' returned the free-thinker; 'but I'd have you to know we are not come to such a pass yet in this country, as to persecute people for searching after truth. You priests I know would be glad to keep us all in ignorance, but the age won't be priest-ridden any longer. There is a noble spirit and freedom of enquiry now subsisting in the nation: people are determined to canvass things freely, and go to the bottom of all subjects, without regarding base prejudices of education. The shops abound with a number of fine treatises written every day against religion, to the honour and glory of the nation.'

'TO its shame and damnation rather,' cries the *Fleet* parson; 'but what is your paradox, sir?'

'WHY this is my paradox, sir,' replied the free-thinker; 'I undertake to prove that brutes think and have intellectual faculties. That perhaps you'll say is no novelty, because many others have asserted the same thing before me; but I go farther sir, and maintain that they are reasonable creatures, and moral agents.'

'AND I will maintain that they are mere machines,' cries the parson, 'against you and all the atheists in the world.[1] Sir, you may be ashamed to prostitute the noble faculty of reason to the beasts of the field.'

'DON'T tell me of reason,' said the free-thinker; 'I don't care one half-penny for reason—what is reason, sir?'

'WHAT is reason, sir?' resumed the doctor; 'why reason sir, is a most noble faculty of the soul, the noblest of all the faculties. It discerns and abstracts, and compares and compounds, and all that.'—

'AND roasts eggs too, does it not? you forget one of its noble faculties,' cries the other: 'but I will maintain that brutes are capable of reason, and they have given manifest proofs of it. Did you never hear of Mr. *Locke*'s parrot, sir, that held a very rational conversation with prince *Maurice* for half an hour together?[2] what say you to that, sir?'

'BY my faith, gentlemen!' said the *Scotch* translator interrupting them, 'upon my word you are got here into a very deep mysterious question, which I do not very well understond what to make of; but by my faith I have always thought brutes to have something particular in the intellectual faculties of their souls, ever since I read what-d'ye-callum there——the *Roman* historian; for why? you know he tells us how the geese discovered to the *Romans* that the *Gauls* were coming to plunder the capitol.[3] Now by my soul, they must have been a d—mn'd sensible flock of geese, and very great lovers of their country too, which let me tell you, is the greatest virtue under heaven. Besides, doth not *Homer* teach us, that *Ulysses*'s dog *Argus* knew his old master at his return home, after he had been absent ten or twelve years at the siege of *Troy?*[1] now by *Jove* he was a plaguy cunning dog, and had a devilish good memory, otherwise he could not have remembered his old chrony so long.'

BEFORE the *Scotchman* had finished his speech, the two other disputants, whose spirits were kindled with controversy, resumed their argument, and fell upon one another again with so much impetuosity, that no voices could be heard but their own. The scene which now ensued, consisted chiefly of noise and scolding, equal to any thing that passes among the orators at *Robin-Hood*'s ale-house.[2] In short, there was not a scurrilous term in the *English* language, which was not vented on this occasion; till at length, the *Fleet* parson heated with rage and beer, flung his pipe at his antagonist, and was proceeding to blows, had he not been restrained by the rest of the company. The festivity of the evening being by this means destroyed, the club soon afterwards broke up, and the several members of it retired to their several garrets.

As Mr. *Rhymer* was walking home in a pensive solitary mood, wrapped up in contemplation on the stars of heaven, and perhaps forgetting for a few moments that he had but three-pence half-penny in his pocket, two young gentlemen of the town, who were upon the hunt after amorous game, followed close at his heels. They quickly smoked him for *a queer fish*,[3] as the phrase is, and began to hope for some diversion at his expence. The moon now shone very bright, and Mr. *Rhymer*, whose eyes were fixed with rapture on that glorious luminary, began to apostrophize her in some poetical strains from *Milton*,[4] which he repeated with great emphasis aloud. In the midst of this, the two gentlemen broke out in a profuse fit of laughter, at which the bard turned round in surprize, but soon recovering himself, he cast a most contemptuous look at them for their ignorance and want of taste. However, as the chain of ideas in his mind was by this means disturbed, he thought it most adviseable to make the best of his way home, and for that purpose called *Pompey* to follow him. *Pompey* indeed made many efforts, and seemed desirous to obey; but in vain the poet called, in vain the dog endeavoured to follow; and it was a long while before Mr. *Rhymer*, whose thoughts were a little muddled with contemplation and porter, found out that the two gentlemen had tied a handkerchief round his neck. He then stopt to demand his property, but finding himself pretty roughly handled, he began to think his own person in danger. Taking to his heels therefore, he ran away with the utmost precipitation, and left his dog behind him; who on his part was not at all sorry to be delivered from such a master.

CHAPTER XIII

Shewing the ill Effects of Ladies having the Vapours.

OUR Hero wandered about the Streets for two or three Hours, 'till being tired of his Peregrination, he took Shelter in a handsome House, where the Door stood hospitably open to receive him. Here he was soon found by the Servants, and the Waiting-gentlewoman carried him up Stairs, as a Beauty, to her Mistress, whom she found in a Fit, and consequently was obliged to defer the Introduction of *Pompey*, to assist her Lady with Hartshorn,[1] and other physical Restoratives, with which her Chamber was plentifully stored.

THIS Lady, by Name Mrs. *Qualmsick*, had the Misfortune to be afflicted with that most terrible Sickness, which arises only from the Imagination of the Patient, and which it is no Wonder Physicians find such a Difficulty to cure, as it has neither Name, Symptoms, or Existence. She was, in reality, eaten up with the Vapours; by which Means her whole Life became an uninterrupted Series of Miseries, which she had been ingenious enough to invent for herself, because neither Nature nor Fortune had bestowed any upon her. Her Constitution originally was very good and healthy, but she had so many Years been endeavouring to destroy it, by the Advice and Assistance of Physicians, that she had now physicked herself into all kinds of imaginary Disorders, and was unhealthy from the very Pains she took to preserve her Health. Her meek-spirited Husband possessed an Estate of Two Thousand Pounds a Year, the far greatest Part whereof his indulgent Wife lavished away on Physicians and Apothecaries Bills; and tho' she took all Pains to render herself unlovely in the Eyes of a Husband, the good-natured simple Man was so enamoured of her sickly Charms, that he still adored her as a Goddess, and paid a blind Obedience to her Will in every Thing. As her *weak Nerves* seldom permitted her to go abroad herself, she kept her obsequious Spouse almost constantly confined in her Bed-chamber, as a Companion to her in her Afflictions: and besides the Confinement he underwent, he was obliged likewise, at all Seasons, to conform himself to the present State of her Nerves. For, sometimes, the Sound of a Voice was Death to her, and then he was enjoined inviolable Silence: At other Times, she chose to be diverted with a Book, and then he was to read *Hervey*'s Meditations among the Tombs:[1] Again, at other Times, when her Imagination was a little more chearful than usual, she would amuse herself with conjugal Dalliances, toy with her Husband, stroke his Face, and provoke him to treat her with little amorous Endearments.

As a Reward for this Humility, and Readiness to

comply with her Humours, she would do him the Favour, every now and then, to take him abroad in her Coach, when her Physicians prescribed her an Airing: Tho' it may be doubted whether he received any great Enjoyment of this uncommon Favour, as the Glasses and Canvasses were constantly drawn up, while the sick Lady lay along like a fat Corpse, on one whole Seat of the Coach, gasping for Air, and complaining of the uneasy Motion.

As these kinds of Distempers are very fantastical, she was often seized with the strangest Whims, and would imagine herself converted into all kinds of living Creatures; nay, when her Phrenzy was at the highest, it was not unusual for her to fancy herself a Glass-bottle, a Tea-pot, a Hay-rick, or a Field of Turnips.[1] The Furniture of her Rooms was likewise altered once a Month, to comply with the present Fit of Vapours: For, sometimes, Red was too glaring for her Eyes; Green put her in Mind of Willows, and made her melancholic; Blue remembered her of her dear Sister, who had unfortunately died ten Years before in a blue Bed; and some such Reason was constantly found for banishing every Colour in its Turn. But a little Specimen of her Conversation one Day with her Doctor, and the Consequences of it afterwards on her Husband, will give the best Description of her Character.

THE Gentleman of the *Esculapian* Art came to attend her one Morning, and she began as usual, with informing him of the deplorable State in which he found her. 'O, Doctor, said she, my Nerves are so low to-day, that I can hardly fetch my Breath. There is such a Damp and Oppression upon my Spirits, that 'tis impossible for me to live a Week longer. Do you think, Sir, I can possibly live a Week longer?' 'A Week longer, Madam! answered the Physician, Oh, bless me! yes, yes, many Years, I hope——Come, come, Madam, you must not give way to such Imaginations. 'Tis the Nature of your Disorder to be attended with a Dejection of Spirits——Perhaps some external Object may have presented itself, that has excited a little Fume of Melancholy; or perhaps your Ladyship may have heard a disagreeable Piece of News; or perhaps the Haziness of the Weather may have cast a kind of a—a kind of a Lethargy over the animal Spirits, or perhaps mere want of Sleep may have left a *Tedium* on the Brain; or a thousand Things may have contributed —but you must not be alarmed, you must not be alarmed, Madam! we shall remedy all that; we shall brace up your Nerves, and give a new Flow to the Blood.' 'O Doctor, said she, interrupting him, I am afraid you comfort with vain Hopes. My Blood is quite in a State of Stagnation, Doctor; and I believe it will never flow any more——Do, feel my Pulse, Doctor!' 'Let us see, let us see, answered the Physician, taking hold of her Hand, 'Stagnation! bless us, Madam! No, no, your Pulse beats very regularly and floridly, I protest, and your Ladyship will do very well again in time—but you must take time, Madam! That Plexus of Nerves upon the Stomach, which I have often described to you as the Seat of your Disorder, wants some corroborating Help to give them a new Springiness and Elasticity; and when Things are relaxed, you know, Madam, they will be out of Order. You see it is the Case in all mechanical Machines, and of course it must be the same in the human Œconomy; for we are but Machines, we are nothing but Machines, Madam!' 'O Sir, replied the Lady, I care not what we are; but do, for Heaven's sake, redeem me from the Miseries I suffer.' 'I will, Madam, returned the Doctor; I'll pawn my Honour on your Recovery; but you must take time, Madam, your Ladyship must have Patience, and not expect Miracles to be wrought in a Day. Time, Madam, conquers every thing, and you need not doubt but we shall set you up again—in time. How do you find your Appetite? Do you eat, Madam?' 'Not at all, Sir, answered the Lady, not at all; I have neither Stomach, nor Appetite, nor Strength, nor any thing in the World; and I believe verily, I can't live a Week longer—I drank a little Chocolate yesterday Morning, Sir, and got down a little Bason of Broth at Noon, and eat a Pigeon for my Dinner, and made a shift to get down another little Bason of Broth at Night—but I can't eat at all, Sir; my Appetite fails me more and more every Day, and I live upon mere nothing.'

MUCH more of this kind of Conversation passed between them, which we will not now stay to relate. When the Doctor had taken his Leave, the good-natured Husband met him at the Bottom of the Stairs, and very tenderly enquired how he had left his Spouse? To this, the Son of *Esculapius* answered, *Quite brave, Sir*; and assured him there was no doubt to be made of her Recovery; adding at the same time, 'If you can persuade her to believe herself well, Sir, you will be her best Physician. 'Do you think so, Doctor?' said *Qualmsick*, with a silly Smile. 'Sir, I am sure of it,' answered the Physician: After which Words he flew to his Coach, and drove away to the Destruction of other Patients.

QUALMSICK immediately posted up Stairs to his Wife's Apartment to try the Effect of his Persuasions upon her, little thinking what a dangerous Office he was about to undertake. He began with congratulating her on the Amendment of her Health, and said he was very glad to find from the Account her Physician had been giving, that she was in a very fair way of Recovery. This extremely surprized her, and weak as she was, she began to put much Resentment into her Countenance; which *Qualmsick* observing, proceeded in the following manner. 'Come, come, my Dear, you must not deceive us any longer—we know how it is; we know you are well enough, my Dear, if you would but fancy yourself so—Do but lay aside your Vapours and Imaginations, and I warrant you will have your Health for the future.'

THIS was the first time that *Qualmsick* ever presumed to talk in this audacious Strain to his Wife; which incensed her so much, that she immediately burst out in Tears, and fell upon him with all the Bitterness of Passion. 'Barbarous Monster, cried she, how dare you insult over my Miseries, when I am just at the Point of Death? You might as well take a Knife and stab me to the Heart, you might—brutal, inhuman Wretch, thus to ridicule my Afflictions!—Get out of the Room, go, and let me never see your Face any more.'

QUALMSICK was so astounded at the *Premunire*[1] he had drawn himself into, that he knew not at first what to think or answer; but when he had a little recovered his Wits, which were none of the best, he endeavoured to lay the Blame on the Physician, and assured his Wife, that whatever he had uttered, was by the Advice and Instigation of her Doctor. ''Tis a Lie, cried she blubbering, 'tis a horrid Lie; the Doctor has too much Humanity to contradict me, when I tell him I am at the Point of Death—No; 'tis your own Artifice, inhuman Monster! you want to get rid of me, Barbarian! and this is the Method you have taken to murder me. I am going fast enough already, but thou wilt not suffer me to die in Peace—— Get out of the Room, Cannibal, and never presume to come into my Presence any more.'

WITH this terrible Injunction he was obliged to comply, and it was near a Fortnight before she admitted him to make his Peace; which, however, he did at length, with many Protestations of Sorrow for his past Offence, and repeated Assurances of behaving with more Humility for the future. The Physician, who gave Occasion to this Dispute, now fell a Sacrifice to it, and was immediately discarded for daring to suppose that a Lady was well, when she had made such a vehement Resolution to be ill.

CHAPTER XIV

Our Hero goes to the University of Cambridge.

Pompey had the good Fortune to bark one Day,
when his Lady's Head was at the worst; whether
designedly, or not, is difficult to determine; but the
Sound so *pierced her Brain*, and *affected her Nerves*, that she
resolved no longer to keep him in her own Apartments.
And thus the same Action, which had unfortunately
banished him from the Presence of *Aurora*, was now
altogether as favourable in redeeming him from the sick
Chamber, or rather Hospital of Mrs. *Qualmsick*.

Mrs. *Qualmsick* had a Son, who was about this Time
going to the University of *Cambridge*, and as the young
Gentleman had taken a Fancy to *Pompey*, he easily prevailed to carry him along with him, as a Companion
to that great Seat of Learning.

Young *Qualmsick* inherited neither the hypochon-
driacal Disposition of his Mother, nor the insipid Meek-
ness of his Father; but, on the contrary, was blessed with
a good Share of Health, had a great Flow of Animal
Spirits, and a most violent Appetite for Pleasure. He
received the first Part of his Education at *Westminster*
School, where he had acquired what is usually called,
a very pretty Knowledge of the Town; that is to say, he had
been introduced, at the Age of Thirteen, into the most
noted Bagnios,[1] knew the Names of the most celebrated
Women of Pleasure, and could drink his two Bottles of
Claret in an Evening, without being greatly disordered
in his Understanding. At the Age of Seventeen, it was
judged proper for him, merely out of Fashion, and to be
like other young Gentlemen of his Acquaintance, to take
Lodgings at a University; whither he went with a hearty
Contempt of the Place, and a determined Resolution
never to receive any Profit from it.

HE was admitted under a Tutor, who knew no more of the World than if he had been bred up in a Forest, and whose sour pedantic Genius was ill-qualified to cope with the Vivacity and Spirit of a young Gentleman, warm in the Pursuit of Pleasure, and one who required much Address, and very artful Management, to make any kind of Restraint palatable and easy to him.

HE was admitted in the Rank of a Fellow-commoner, which, according to the Definition given by a Member of the University in a Court of Justice, is one who sits at the same Table, and *enjoys the Conversation* of the Fellows. It differs from what is called a Gentleman-commoner at *Oxford*, not only in the Name, but also in the greater Privileges and Licenses indulged to the Members of this Order; who do not only *enjoy the Conversation of the Fellows*, but likewise a full Liberty of following their own Imaginations in every Thing. For as Tutors and Governors of Colleges have usually pretty sagacious Noses after Preferment, they think it impolitic to cross the Inclinations of young Gentlemen, who are Heirs to great Estates, and from whom they expect Benefices and Dignities hereafter, as Rewards for *their Want of Care of them*, while they were under their Protection. From hence it comes to pass, that Pupils of this Rank are excused from all public Exercises, and allowed to absent themselves at Pleasure from the private Lectures in their Tutor's Rooms, as often as they have made a Party for Hunting, or an Engagement at the Tennis-court, or are not well recovered from their Evening's Debauch. And whilst a poor unhappy Soph, of no Fortune, is often expelled for the most trivial Offences, or merely to humour the capricious Resentment of his Tutor, who happens to dislike his Face; young Noblemen, and Heirs of great Estates, may commit any Illegalities, and, if they please, overturn a College with Impunity.

YOUNG *Qualmsick* very early began to display his

Genius, and was soon distinguished for one of the most enterprizing Spirits in the University. No-body set Order and Regularity at greater Defiance, or with more heroic Bravery than he did; which made him quickly be chosen Captain-general by his Comrades, in all their Parties of Pleasure, and Expeditions of Jollity. Many Pranks are recorded of his performing, which made the Place resound with his Name; but one of his Exploits being attended with Circumstances of a very droll Nature, we cannot forbear relating it.

THERE was in the same College, a young Master of Arts, *Williams* by Name, who had been elected into the Society, in Preference to one of greater Genius and Learning, because he used to make a lower Bow to the Fellows, whenever he passed by them, and was not likely to disgrace any of his Seniors by the Superiority of his Parts. This Gentleman concluding now there was no farther Occasion of Study, after he had obtained a Fellowship, which had long been the Object of his Ambition, gave himself over to Pursuits more agreeable to his Temper, and spent the chief of his Time in drinking Tea with Barber's Daughters, and other young Ladies of Fashion in the University, who there take to themselves the Name of *Misses*, and receive amorous Gownsmen at their Ruelles. For nothing more is necessary to accomplish a young Lady at *Cambridge*, than a second-hand Capuchin, a white washing Gown,[1] a Pair of dirty Silk Shoes, and long Muslin Ruffles; in which Dress they take the Air in the public Walks every *Sunday*, to make Conquests, and receive their Admirers all the rest of the Week at their Tea-tables. Now *Williams*, having a great deal of dangling Good-nature about him, was very successful in winning the Affections of these Academical Misses, and had a large Acquaintance among them. The three Miss *Higginses*, whose Mother kept the Sun Tavern; Miss *Polly Jackson*, a Baker's Daughter; the celebrated *Fanny*

Hill,[1] sole Heiress of a Taylor, and Miss *Jenny* of the Coffee-house, were all great Admirers of our College-gallant; and Fame reported, that he had Admission to some of their Bed-chambers, as well as to their Tea-tables. Upon this Presumption, young *Qualmsick* laid his Head together with other young Gentlemen, his Comrades, to play him a Trick, which we now proceed to disclose.

ABOUT This Time, a Bed-maker of the College was unfortunately brought to Bed, without having any Husband to father the Child; and as our Master of Arts was suspected, among others, to have had a Share in the Generation of the new-born Infant, being a Gentleman of an amorous Nature, it occurred to young *Qualmsick* to make the following Experiment upon him.

As Mr. *Williams* was coming out of his Chamber one Morning early to go to Chapel, he found a Basket standing at his Door on the top of his Stair-case, with a Direction to himself, and a Letter tied to the Handle of the Basket. He stood some little time guessing from whom such a Present could come, but as he had expected a Parcel from *London* by the Coach for a Week before, he naturally concluded this to be the same, and that it had been brought by a Porter from the Inn, and left at his Door before he was awake in the Morning. With this Thought he opened the Letter, and read to the following Effect.

> *Honorable Sir,*
>
> AM surprized should use me in such a manner; have never seen one Farthing of your Money, since was brought To-bed, which is a Shame and a wicked Sin. Wherefore have sent you your own Bastard to provide for, and am your dutiful Sarvant to command tell Death——
>
> *Betty Trollop.*

THE Astonishment, which seized our Master of Arts at the perusal of this Letter, may easily be imagined, but not so easily described: He turned pale, staggered,

and looked like *Banquo*'s Ghost in the Play; but as his
Conscience excused him from the Crime laid to his
Charge, he resolved (as soon as his Confusion would
suffer him to resolve) to make a public Example of the
Wretch, that had dared to lay her Iniquities at his Door.
To this end, as soon as Chapel was over, he desired the
Master of the College to convene all the Fellows in the
Common-room, for he had an Affair of great Consequence
to lay before them. When the Reverend Divan[1] was met
according to his Desire, he produced the Basket, and with
an audible Voice read the Letter, which had been annexed
to it: After which he made a long Oration on the un-
parallelled Impudence of the Harlot, who had attempted
to scandalize him in this audacious Manner, and concluded with desiring the most exemplary Punishment
might be inflicted on her; for he said, unless they dis-
couraged such a Piece of Villainy with proper Severity,
it might hereafter be their own Lots, if they were remiss
in punishing the present Offender. They all heard him
with great Astonishment, and many of them seemed to
rejoice inwardly, that the Basket had not travelled to
their Doors; as thinking, perhaps it would have been
unfatherly and unnatural to have refused it Admittance.
But the Master of the College taking the thing a little
more seriously, declared that if Mr. *Williams* had not
been known to trespass in that Way, the Girl would
never have singled him out to father her Iniquities upon
him; however as the thing had happened, and he had
protested himself innocent, he said he would take care
the Strumpet should be punished for her Impudence.
He then ordered the Basket to be unpacked; which was
performed by the Butler of the College, in Presence of
the whole Fraternity; when lo!——instead of a Child,
puling and crying for its Father, out leaped *Pompey*, the
little Hero of this little History; who had been enclosed
in that Osier Confinement by young *Qualmsick*, and

convey'd very early in the Morning to Mr. *Williams*'s Chamber-door. The grave Assembly was astonished and enraged at the Discovery, finding themselves convened only to be ridiculed; and all of them gazed on our Hero with the same kind of Aspect, as did the Daughters of *Cecrops* on the deformed *Erichthonius*, when their Curiosity tempted them to peep into the Basket, which *Minerva* had put into their Hands, with positive Commands to the contrary.[1]

CHAPTER XV

[*Adventures at* Cambridge.]

WILLIAMS, tho' much ashamed and out of countenance, was yet in his heart very glad to be relieved from the apprehensions of maintaining a bastard, which he imagined would add no great lustre to his reputation as fellow of a college. When therefore *Pompey* escaped out of his wicker prison, he was in reality pleased with the discovery, which put an end to his fears, and feigning himself diverted with the thing, took the little dog home to his own chambers.

THIS was an adventure of the comic kind, attended with no ill consequences to our hero; but we now proceed to relate one of a very tragic nature indeed, which fortune seems to have reserved in store, as the utmost stretch of her malice, to compleat the miseries of his unhappy life.

THERE flourished in this college, or rather was beginning to flourish, a young physician, who now stood candidate for fame and practice. He had equipped himself with a gilt-headed cane, a black suit of cloaths, a wise mysterious face, a full-bottomed flowing peruke, and all other externals of his profession: so that, if according to the inimitable *Swift*, the various members of a commonwealth are only so many different suits of cloaths,[1] this gentleman was amply qualified for the discharge of his office. But not chusing to rely totally on his dress to introduce him into business, he was willing to add to it a supplemental, and as many think, superfluous knowledge of his art.

ABOUT this time, a member of the university died in great torments of the iliac passion,[2] and some peculiarities in his case made a noise among the faculty of *Cambridge*. The theory of this terrible disorder, caused by the cessation of the peristaltic motion of the guts, our young doctor very well understood; but not contenting himself with theory only, he resolved to go a step farther, and for this purpose, cast his eyes about after some dog, intending to dissect him alive for the satisfaction of his curiosity.

A DOG might have been the emblematic animal of *Esculapius* or *Apollo*, with as much propriety as he was of *Mercury*; for no creatures I believe have been of more eminent service to the healing tribe than dogs. Incredible is the number of these animals, who have been sacrificed from time to time at the shrines of physic and surgery. Lectures of anatomy subsist by their destruction; *Ward* (says Mr. *Pope*) tried his drop on puppies and the poor;[3] and in general all new medicines and experiments of a doubtful nature are sure to be made in the first place on the bodies of these unfortunate animals. Their very ordure is one of the chief articles of the *Materia Medica*; and I am persuaded, if the old *Egyptians* had any physician among them, they certainly described him by the hieroglyphic of a dog.

BUT not to spend too much time in these conjectures, our young doctor had no sooner resolved to satisfy himself concerning the peristaltic motion of the guts, than unluckily, in an evil hour, *Pompey* presented himself to his eye. More unluckily for him still, neither his master Mr. *Williams*, nor any other of his college-friends happened to be present, or within view at this moment. *Machaon*[1] therefore very boldly seized him as a victim, and conveyed him into a little dark place near his room, which he called his cellar, and in which he kept his wine. There he shut him up three or four days in the condemned hole, while he prepared his chirurgical instruments, and invited some other young practitioners in physic of his acquaintance to be present at our hero's dissection.

THE day being soon appointed for his death, the company assembled at their friend's room in the morning at breakfast, where much sapient discourse passed among them concerning the operation in hand, not material to be now related. At length cries the hero of the party, 'Come gentlemen! we seem I think to have finished our breakfasts, let us now proceed to business:' after which, the tea-things were removed, the instruments of dissection placed on the table, and the doctor went to his cellar to bring forth the unhappy victim.

AND here, good-natured reader, I am sure it moves thy compassion to think that poor *Pompey*, after suffering already so many misfortunes, must at last be dissected alive to satisfy a physician concerning the peristaltic motion of the guts. The case would indeed be lamentable, if it had happened: but when the doctor came to call him forth to execution, to his great surprize no dog was there to be found. He found however something else not entirely to his satisfaction, and that was his wine streaming in great profusion about his cellar. The truth is, our hero, being grown desperate with hunger, had in his struggles for liberty broke all the bottles, and at last forcibly gnawed his way thro' a deal board, that composed one side of the cellar. The danger however which he had been in, made him sick of universities, and he wished earnestly for an accident, which soon happened, to relieve him from an academic life.

CHAPTER XVI

Another College-Character.[1]

ABOUT this Time three Ladies happened to be returning out of the *North*, whither they had been to make a Summer-Visit, and were inclined to take *Cambridge* in their way Home; which Place they believed to be worthy of their Curiosity, having never seen it. For this Purpose they procured a double Recommendation to two Gentlemen of different Colleges, lest one of them should happen to be absent at the Time of their Arrival. One of these Gentlemen was the Reverend Mr. *Williams*, who received a Letter from a Friend of his, advertising him of the Arrival of three Ladies, and desiring he would assist their Curiosity in shewing them the University. At the same time came another Letter from another Gentleman to an ancient Doctor of Divinity, whose Character we shall here disclose.

THIS Gentleman in his Youth, when his Friend was at College, had been a Man of great Gaiety, and stands upon Record for the first Person who introduced Tea-drinking into the University of *Cambridge*. He had good Parts, improved by much classical Reading; but it was his Misfortune very early in Life to fall in Love with an Apothecary's Daughter, with whom he maintained a Courtship near Twenty Years; in which Time he laboured by all means in his Power, but without Success, to obtain a Living, as the Foundation of Matrimony. For tho' his Vivacity had rendered him agreeable to many young Gentlemen of Fortune, who were his Cotemporaries at College, he found himself forgotten by them, when they came into the World, and too late experienced the Difference between a Companion and a Friend. Disappointed in all his Hopes, and growing sick of a tedious Courtship, he shut himself up in his Chamber, and there abandoned himself to Melancholy: He shunned all his Friends, and became a perfect Recluse; appeared but seldom at Meals in the College-hall, and then with so wild a Face and unfashionable a Dress, that all the younger Part of the College, who knew nothing of his History, esteemed him a Madman. This was the Person recommended to conduct Ladies about the University; for his Friend unluckily made no Allowance for the Fifty Years that had elapsed since his own leaving the College, but concluded his old Acquaintance to be the same Man of Gallantry in his Age, which he had formerly remembered him in his Youth.

WHEN the Ladies arrived at *Cambridge*, accompanied by a Gentleman, who was their Relation, they laid their Heads together to consider what Measures they should pursue; and all agreeing that it would be proper to pay the Doctor a Visit at his Chamber, they set out in a Body for that Purpose. Being directed to his College, and having with Difficulty found out his Stair-Case, they mounted it with many wearisome Steps, and knocked at the Door for Admittance. It was a long while before the Sound pierced thro' the sevenfold Night-caps of the old Doctor, who sat dozing half-asleep in an Elbow-chair by a Fire almost extinguished. When he had opened the Door, he started back at the Sight of Ladies with as much Amazement as if he had seen a Ghost, and kept the Door half-shut in his Hand, to prevent their Entrance into his Room. Indeed his Apartment was not a Spectacle that deserved Exhibition, for it seemed not to have been swept for Twenty Years past, and lay in great Disorder, scattered over with mouldy Books and yellow Manuscripts. The Cobwebs extended themselves from one Corner of the Room to the other, and the Mice and Rats took their Pastime about the Floor with as much Security as if it had been uninhabited. On a Table stood a Can of stale Small Beer, and a Plate of Cheese-parings, the Relicks of his last Night's Supper: All which Appearances created such Astonishment in his Visiters, that they began to believe themselves directed to a wrong Person, and thought it impossible for this to be the gay Gentleman, who had been recommended to them as the Perfection of Courtesy and Good-breeding.

WHEN therefore they had suppressed their Inclination to laugh as well as they could, the Gentleman who was Spokesman of the Party, began to beg Pardon for the Disturbance they had given in consequence of a wrong Information, and desired to be directed to the Chambers of Doctor *Clouse*. 'Oho, said the Doctor, What—I warrant you are the *Folks* that I received a Letter about last Week!' The Gentleman then assured him they were the same, and begged the favour of his Assistance, if it was not too much Trouble, to shew the Ladies the University, which they would acknowledge as a very particular Favour. 'A-lack-a-day! answered he with a stammering Voice, I should be very glad, Sir, to do the Ladies any Service in my Power; but really I protest, Sir, I have almost forgot the University. 'Tis many Years since I have ventured out of my own College, and indeed it is not often that I go out of my Room——You'll find some younger Man, Ladies, that knows more of the Matter than I do; for I suppose every Thing is altered since my Time, and I question whether I should know my Way about the Streets.' After which Words he made a Motion to retire into his Chamber, which the Company observing, asked Pardon once more for the Disturbance they had given, and made haste away to laugh at this uncommon Adventure.

CHAPTER XVII

A prodigious short Chapter.

WHEN the Gentleman and Ladies were got back to their Inn, they diverted themselves with much Raillery at the old Doctor's Expence, and began to despair of any better Success from their second Recommendation, charitably concluding that all the Members of the University were like the Gentleman they had seen. They resolved therefore not to be at the Trouble of visiting Mr. *Williams*, but sent a Messenger from the Inn to inform him of their Arrival, and beg the Favour of his Company at Supper; which Invitation, however, they would gladly have excused him from accepting, for they were grown sick of the Place, and determined to leave it early the next Morning.

WILLIAMS, who had lived in Expectation of their coming several Days, posted away to the Inn with all imaginable Dispatch, and with many academical Compliments, welcomed them to *Cambridge*. He staid Supper, and the Evening was spent with a good deal of Mirth; for when the Ladies found they had to do with a human Being, they recounted the Adventure of the old Doctor, and *Williams*, in return, entertained them with several others of a similar Nature. Nor did he depart to his College, till he had made them promise to dine with him at his Chambers the next Day. [And this gives us an opportunity of explaining some farther particulars in that gentleman's character, being not an uncommon one, I believe, in either of our universities.

IF we were in a hurry to describe him, it might be done effectually in two or three words, by calling him *a most egregious trifler*; but as we have leisure to be a little more circumstantial, the reader shall be troubled with a day's journal of his actions.

MR. *Williams* was, in the first place, a man of the most punctilious neatness; his shoes were always blacked in the nicest manner, his wigs were powdered with the exactest delicacy, and he would scold his laundress for a whole morning together, if he discovered a wry plait in the sleeve of his shirt, or the least speck of dirt on any part of his linen. He rose constantly to chapel, and proceeded afterwards with great importance to breakfast, which, moderately speaking, took up two hours of his morning. When this was over, he amused himself either in paring his nails, or watering two or three orange-trees, which he kept in his chamber, or in tilling a little spot of ground, about six feet square, which he called his garden, or in changing the situation of the few books in his study. The *Spectators* were removed into the place of the *Tatlers*, and the *Tatlers* into the place of the *Spectators*. But generally speaking, he drew on his boots immediately after breakfast, and rode out for the air, having been told that a sedentary life is destructive of the constitution, and that too much study impairs the health. At his return home, he had barely time to wash his hands, clean his teeth, and put on a fresh-powdered wig, before the college-bell summoned him to dinner in the public hall. His afternoons were spent in drinking tea with the young ladies above-mentioned, who all esteemed him a prodigious genius, and were ready to laugh at his wit, before he opened his mouth. In these agreeable visits he remained till the time of evening chapel; after which, supper succeeded to find him fresh employment; from whence he repaired to the coffee-house, and then to some engagement at a friend's room, for the remaining part of the evening. By this account of his day's transactions, the reader will see how very impossible it was for him to find leisure for study, in the midst of so many important avocations; yet notwithstanding this great variety of business, he made a shift sometimes to play half a tune on the *German* flute in a morning, and once in a quarter of a year, took the pains to transcribble a sermon out of various authors.

ANOTHER part of his character was a great affectation of politeness, which is more pretended to in universities, where less of it is practised, than in any other part of the kingdom. Thus Mr. *Williams* was always talking of *genteel life*, to which end he was plentifully provided with stories by a female cousin, who kept a milliner's shop in *London*, and never failed to let him know by letters what passed among *the Great*; tho' she frequently mistook the names of people, and attributed scandal to one lord, which was the property of another. Her cousin however did not find out the mistakes, but retailed her blunders about the colleges with great confidence and security.

BUT nothing pleased him more than shewing the university to strangers, and especially to ladies, which he thought gave him an air of acquaintance with the genteel world; and on such occasions he would affect to make expensive entertainments, which neither his private fortune, or the income of his fellowship could afford.

EARLY in the Morning then he rose with the Lark, and held a Consultation with the College Cook concerning the Dinner, and other Particulars of the Entertainment: For as he had never yet been honoured with Company of so high a Rank, he resolved to do what was handsome, and send them away with an Opinion of his Politeness. Among many other Devices he had *to be genteel*, one very well deserves mentioning, being of a very academical Nature indeed; for he was at the Expence of purchasing a *China Vase* of a certain Shape, which sometimes passes under a more vulgar Name, to set in his Bed-chamber; that if the Ladies should chuse to retire after Dinner, for the sake of *looking at the Pattern of his Bed*, or to *see the Prospect out of his Window*, or from any other Motive of

Curiosity, they might have the Pleasure of *being served in China*.

WHEN these Affairs were settled, he dressed himself in his best Array, and went to bid the Ladies good-morrow. As soon as they had breakfasted, he conducted them about the University, and shewed them all the Rarities of *Cambridge*. They observed, *that such a thing was very grand, another thing was very neat, and that there were a great many Books in the Libraries, which they thought it impossible for any Man to read through, tho' he was to live as long as* Methuselah.

WHEN their Curiosity was satisfied, and *Williams* had indulged every Wish of Vanity, in being seen to escort Ladies about the University, and to hand them out of their Coach, they all retired to his Chambers to Dinner. Much Conversation passed, not worth recording, and when the Cloth was taken away, little *Pompey* was produced on the Table for the Ladies to admire him. They were greatly struck with his Beauty; and one of them took Courage to ask him as a Present, which the complaisant Master of Arts, in his great Civility, complied with, and immediately delivered him into the Lady's Hands. He likewise related the Story, how he came into his Possession, which another Person perhaps would have suppressed; but *Williams* was so transported with his Company, that he was half out of his Wits with Joy, and his Conversation was as ridiculous as his Behaviour.

CHAPTER XVIII

Pompey *returns to* London, *and occasions a remarkable Dispute in the* Mall.

ONCE more then our Hero set out for the Metropolis of *Great-Britain*, and after an easy Journey of two Days arrived at a certain Square, where his Mistresses

kept their Court. To these Ladies, not improperly might
be applied the Question which *Archer* asks in the Play,
Pray which of you three is the old Lady?[1] the Mother being
full as youthful and airy as the Daughters, and the
Daughters almost as ancient as the Mother.

Now as Fortune often disposes Things in the most
whimsical and surprizing Manner, it so happened, that
one of his Mistresses took him with her one Morning
into St. *James*'s *Park*, and set him down on his Legs
almost in the very same Part of the *Mall*, from whence
he had formerly made his Escape from Lady *Tempest*
near eight Years before, as is recorded in the first Part
of his History. Her Ladyship was walking this Morning
for the Air, and happened to pass by almost at the very
Instant that the little Adventurer was set on his Legs to
take his Diversion. She spied him in a Moment, with
great Quickness of Discernment, and immediately recollecting her old Acquaintance, caught him up in her
Arms, and fell to kissing him with the highest Extravagance
of Joy. His present Owner perceiving this, and thinking
only that the Lady was pleased with the Beauty of her
Dog, and had a mind to compliment him with a few
Kisses, passed on without interrupting her: But when
she saw her Ladyship preparing to carry him out of the
Mall in her Arms, she advanced hastily towards her, and
redemanded her Favourite in the following Terms:
'Pray, Madam, what is your Ladyship going to do with
that Dog?' Lady *Tempest* replied, 'Nothing in the World,
Madam, but take him home with me.' 'And pray, Madam,
what Right has your Ladyship to take a Dog that belongs
to me?' 'None, my dear! answered Lady *Tempest*; but I
take him, Child, because he belongs to me.' ''Tis false,
said the other Lady, I aver it to be false; he was given
me by a Gentleman of *Cambridge*, and I insist upon your
Ladyship's replacing him upon his Legs, this individual
Moment.' To this, Lady *Tempest* replied only with a

Sneer, and was walking off with our Hero; which so greatly aggravated the Rage of her Antagonist, that she now lost all Patience, and began to exert herself in a much higher Key. 'Madam, said she, I would have you to know, Madam, that I am not to be treated in this *superlative Manner*. Your Ladyship may affect to sneer, if you please, Madam, and shew a Contempt, Madam, which is more due to your own Actions than to me, Madam; for thank Heaven, I have some Regard to Decency in my Actions.' 'Dear, Miss! don't be in a Passion, replied Lady *Tempest*; it will spoil your Complexion Child, and perhaps ruin your Fortune——but will you be pleased to know, my Dear, that I lost this Dog eight Years ago in the *Mall*, and advertized him in all the News-papers, tho' you or your Friend at *Cambridge*, who did me the Favour to steal him, were not so obliging as to restore him?—And will you be pleased to know likewise, young Lady, that I have a Right to take my Property wherever I find it.' ''Tis impossible, cried the other Lady, tossing back her Head, 'tis impossible to remember a Dog after eight Years absence; I aver it to be impossible, and nothing shall persuade me to believe it.' 'I protest, my Dear, answered Lady *Tempest*, I know not what Sort of a Memory you may be blest with, but really, I can remember Things of a much longer Date; and as a fresh Instance of my Memory, I think, my Dear, I remember you representing the Character of a young Lady for near these twenty Years about Town.' 'Madam, returned the Lady of inferior Rank, now inflamed with the highest Indignation; you may remember yourself, Madam, representing a much worse Character, Madam, for a greater Number of Years. It would be well, Madam, if your Memory was not altogether so good, Madam, unless your Actions were better.'

THE War of Tongues now began to rage with the greatest Violence, and nothing was spared that Wit could suggest on the one side, or Malice on the other. The Beaux, and Belles, and Witlings,[1] who were walking that Morning in the *Mall*, assembled round the Combatants at first, out of Curiosity, and for the sake of Entertainment; but they soon began to take Sides in the Dispute, 'till at length it became one universal Scene of Wrangle; and no Cause in *Westminster-Hall*[2] was ever more puzzled by the Multitude of Voices all contending at once for the Victory. At last, Lady *Tempest* scorning this ungenerous Altercation, told her Adversary, 'Well, Madam, if you please to scold for the publick Diversion, pray continue; but for my Part, I shall no longer make myself the *Spectacle* of a Mob.' And so saying, she walked courageously off with little *Pompey* under her Arm. It was impossible for her Rival to prevent her; who likewise immediately after quitted the *Mall*, and flew home, ready to burst with Shame, Spite, and Indignation.

LADY *Tempest* had not been long at her Toilette, before the following little Scroll was brought to her; and she was informed, that a Footman waited below in great Hurry for an Answer. The Note was to this Effect.

Madam,

IF it was possible for me to wonder at any of your Actions, I should be astonished at your Behaviour of this Morning. Restore my Dog by the Bearer of this Letter, or by the living G—d, I will immediately commence a Prosecution against you in Chancery, and recover him by Force of Law.

Yours——

LADY *Tempest*, without any Hesitation, returned the following Answer.

Madam,

I HAVE laughed most heartily at your ingenious

Epistle; and am prodigiously diverted with your
Menaces of a Law-Suit. *Pompey* shall be ready to put in
his Answer, as soon as he hears your Bill is filed against
him in Chancery.

I am, dear Miss, yours,
TEMPEST.

CHAPTER XIX

*A terrible Misfortune happens to our Hero, which brings his
History to a Conclusion.*

THIS Letter inflamed the Lady so much, that she
immediately ordered her Coach, and drove away to
Lincoln's-Inn, to consult her Sollicitor. She found him in
his Chambers, surrounded with Briefs, and haranguing
to two Gentlemen, who had made him Arbitrator in a
very important Controversy, concerning the Dilapidations
of a Pig-stye. On the Arrival of our Lady, the Man of
Law started from his Chair, and conducted her with
much Civility to a Settee which stood by his Fire-side;
then turning to his two Clients, whom he thought he had
already treated with a proper Quantity of Eloquence,
'Well, Gentlemen, said he, when your respective Attornies
have drawn up your several Cases, let them be sent to
me, and I'll give Determination upon them with all
possible Dispatch.' This Speech had the desired Effect
in driving them away, and as soon as they were gone,
addressing himself with an Affectation of much Politeness
to the Mistress of little *Pompey*, he began to enquire after
the *good Lady her Mother*, and *the good Lady her Sister*—
but our Heroine was so impatient to open her Cause,
that she hardly allowed herself Time to answer his
Questions, before she began in the following Manner.
'Sir, I was walking this Morning in the *Mall*, when a

certain extraordinary Lady, whose Actions are always of
a very extraordinary Nature, was pleased, in a most
peculiar Manner, to steal my Lap-dog from me.' 'Steal
your Lap-dog from you, Madam! said the Man of Law;
I protest, a very extraordinary Transaction indeed!
And pray, Madam, what could induce her to be guilty
of such a Misbehaviour?' 'Induce her! cried the Lady
eagerly; Sir, she wants no Inducement to be guilty of
any thing that is audacious and impudent.—But, Sir, I
desire you would immediately commence a Suit against
her in Chancery, and push the Affair on with all possible
Rapidity, for I am resolved to recover the Dog, if it costs
me Ten Thousand Pounds.' The Counsellor smiled, and
commended her Resolutions; but paused a little, and
seemed puzzled at the Novelty of the Case. 'Madam,
said he, undoubtedly your Ladyship does right to assert
your Property, for we should all soon be reduced to a
State of Nature, if there were no Courts of Law; and
therefore your Ladyship is highly to be applauded—but
there is something very peculiar in the Nature of Dogs—
There is no Question, Madam, but they are to be considered under the Denomination of Property, and not
to be deemed *feræ Naturæ*, Things of no Value,[1] as ignorant
People foolishly imagine; but I say, Madam, there is
something very peculiar in their Nature, Madam.—
Their prodigious Attachment to Man inclines them to
follow any body that calls them, and that makes it so
difficult to fix a Theft.—Now, if a Man calls a Sheep, or
calls a Cow, or calls a Horse, why he might call long
enough before they would come, because they are not
Creatures of a *following Nature*, and therefore our penal
Laws have made it Felony with respect to those Animals;
but Dogs, Madam, have a strange undistinguishing
Proneness to run after People's Heels.' 'Lord bless me,
Sir! said the Lady, somewhat angry at the Orator's
Declamation; What do you mean, Sir, by following

People's Heels? I do protest and asseverate, that she took him up in her Arms, and carried him away in Defiance of me, and the whole *Mall* was Witness of the Theft.' 'Very well, Madam, very well, replied the Counsellor, I was only stating the Case fully on Defendant's side, that you might have a comprehensive View of the whole Affair, before we come to unravel it all again, and shew the Advantages on the side of Plaintiff.—Now tho' a Dog be of *a following Nature*, as I observed, and may be sometimes tempted, and seduced, and inveigled away in such a Manner, as makes it difficult—do you observe me—makes it difficult, I say, Madam, to fix a Theft on the Person seducing; yet, wherever Property is discovered and claimed, if the Possessor refuses to restore it on Demand,—on Demand, I say, because Demand must be made—refuses to restore it, on Demand, to the proper, lawful Owner, there an Action lies, and, under this Predicament, we shall recover our Lap-dog.' The Lady seeming pleased with this Harangue, the Orator continued in the following Manner; 'If therefore, Madam, this Lady—whosoever she is, *A.* or *B.* or any Name serves our Purpose—if, I say, this extraordinary Lady, as your Ladyship just now described her, took your Dog before Witnesses, and refused to restore it on Demand, why then we have a lawful Action, and shall recover Damages.——Pray, Madam, do you think you can swear to the Identity of the Dog, if he should be produced in a Court of Justice?' The Lady answered, 'Yes, she could swear to him amongst a Million, for there never was so remarkable a Creature.' 'And you first became possessed of him, you say, Madam, at the University of *Cambridge*.— Pray, Madam, will the Gentleman, who invested you with him, be ready to testify the Donation?' She answered affirmatively. 'And pray, Madam, what is the Colour of your Dog?' 'Black and White, Sir!' 'A Male, or Female, Madam?' To this the Lady replied; *She positively could not tell*; whereupon, the Counsellor, with a most sapient Aspect, declared he would search his Books for a Precedent, and wait on her, in a few Days, to receive her final Determinations; but advised her, in the mean while, to try the Effect of another Letter upon her Ladyship, and once more threaten her with a Prosecution. He then waited upon her to her Chariot, observed that *it was a very fine Day*, and promised to use his utmost Endeavours to reinstate her in the Possession of her Lap-dog.

THIS was the State of a Quarrel between two Ladies for a Dog, and it seemed as if all the Mouths of the Law would have opened on this important Affair (for Lady *Tempest* continued obstinate in keeping him) had not a most unlucky Accident happened to balk those honourable Gentlemen of their Fees, and disappoint them of so hopeful a Topic for shewing their Abilities. This unfortunate Stroke was nothing less than the Death of our Hero, who was seized with a violent Pthisic, and after a Week's Illness, departed this Life on the Second of *June*, 1749, and was gathered to the Lap-dogs of Antiquity.

FROM the Moment that he fell sick, his Mistress spared no Expence for his Recovery, and had him attended by the most eminent Physicians of *London*; who, I am afraid, rather hastened than delayed his Exit, according to the immemorial Custom of that right venerable Fraternity. The Chamber-maids took it by Turns to sit up with him every Night during his Illness, and her Ladyship was scarce ever away from him in the Day-time; but, alas! his Time was come, his Hour-glass was run out, and nothing could save him from paying a Visit to the *Plutonian* Regions.

IT is difficult to say, whether her Ladyship's Sorrow now, or when she formerly lost him in the *Mall*, most exceeded the Bounds of Reason. He lay in State three Days after his Death, and her Ladyship, at first, took a Resolution of having him embalmed, but as her Physicians informed her the Art was lost, she was obliged to give over that chimerical Project; otherwise, our Posterity might have seen him, some Centuries hence, erected in a public Library at a University; and, perhaps, some Doctor, of great Erudition, might have undertaken to prove, with Quotations from a Thousand Authors, that he was formerly the *Egyptian Anubis.*

HOWEVER, tho' her Ladyship could not be gratified in her Desires of embalming him, she had him buried, with great Funeral Solemnity, in her Garden, and erected over him an elegant Marble Monument, which was inscribed with the following Epitaph, by one of the greatest Elegiac Poets of the present Age.

King of the Garden, blooming Rose!
Which sprang'st from Venus' *heavenly Woes,*
When weeping for Adonis *slain,*
Her pearly Tears bedew'd the Plain,
Now let thy dewy Leaves bewail
A greater Beauty's greater Ill;
Ye Lillies! hang your drooping Head,
Ye Myrtles! weep for Pompey *dead;*
Light lie the Turf upon his Breast,
Peace to his Shade, and gentle Rest.

CHAPTER XX

The CONCLUSION.

HAVING thus traced our Hero to the Fourteenth Year of his Age, which may be reckoned the Three-score and Ten of a Lap-dog, nothing now remains, but to draw his Character, for the Benefit and Information of Posterity. In so doing we imitate the greatest, and most

celebrated Historians, Lord *Clarendon*, Dr. *Middleton*,[1]
and others, who, when they have put a Period to the
Life of an eminent Person (and such undoubtedly was
our Hero) finish all with a Description of his Morals, his
Religion, and private Character: Nay, many Biographers
go so far, as to record the Colour of their Hero's Complexion, the Shade of his Hair, the Height of his Stature,
the Manner of his Diet, when he went to Bed at Night,
at what Hour he rose in the Morning, and other equally
important Particulars; which cannot fail to convey the
greatest Satisfaction and Improvement to their Readers.
Thus a certain Painter,[2] who obliged the World with a
Life of *Milton*, informs us, with an Air of great Importance,
that he was a short thick Man, and then recollecting himself,
informs us a second Time, upon maturer Deliberation,
*that he was not a short thick Man, but if he had been a little
shorter, and a little thicker, he would have been a short thick
Man*; which prodigious Exactness, in an Affair of such
Consequence, can never be sufficiently applauded.

Now as to the Description of our Hero's Person, that
has already been given in an Advertisement, penned by
one of his Mistresses, when he had the Misfortune to be
lost in *St. James's Park*, and therefore we will not trouble
our Reader with a needless Repetition of it, but proceed
to his Religion, his Morals, his Amours, &c. in Conformity
to the Practice of other Historians.

It is to be remembered, in the first Place, to his Credit,
that he was a Dog of the *most courtly Manners*, ready to
fetch and carry, at the Command of all his Masters,
without ever considering the Service he was employed
in, or the Person from whom he received his Directions:
He would fawn likewise with the greatest Humility, on
People who treated him with Contempt, and was always
particularly officious in his Zeal, whenever he expected
a new Collar, or stood Candidate for a Ribbon[3] with
other Dogs, who made up the Retinue of the Family.

FAR be it from us to deny, that in the first Part of his Life he gave himself an unlimited Freedom in his Amours, and was extravagantly licentious, not to say debauched, in his Morals; but whoever considers that he was born in the House of an *Italian* Courtesan, that he made the grand Tour with a young Gentleman of Fortune, and afterwards lived near two Years with a Lady of Quality, will have more Reason to wonder that his Morals were not entirely corrupted, than that they were a little tainted by the ill Effect of such dangerous Examples: Whereas, when he became acquainted with a Philosophic Cat, who set him right in his mistaken Apprehensions of Things, he lived, afterwards, a Life of tolerable Regularity, and behaved with much Constancy to the Ladies, who were so happy as to engage his Affections.

As to Religion, we must ingenuously confess that he had none; in which Respect he had the Honour to bear an exact Resemblance to all the well-bred People of the present Age, who have long since discarded Religion, as a needless and troublesome Invention, calculated only to make People wise, virtuous, and unfashionable; and whoever will be at the Pains of perusing the Lives and Actions of the Great World, will find them, in all Points, conformable to such prodigious Principles.

IN Politics, it is difficult to say whether he was Whig or Tory, for he never was heard, on any Occasion, to open his Mouth on that Subject, tho' he once served a Lady, whom Love engaged very deeply in Party, and perhaps might have been admitted to vote at a certain Election, among the Numbers that composed that stupendous Poll.[1]

FOR the latter Part of his Life, his chief Amusement was to sleep before the Fire, and Indolence grew upon him so much, as he advanced in Age, that he seldom cared to be disturbed in his Slumbers, even to eat his Meals: His Eyes grew dim, his Limbs failed him, his Teeth dropped out of his Head, and, at length, a Pthisic came very seasonably to relieve him from the Pains and Calamities of long Life.

THUS perished little *Pompey*, or *Pompey the Little*, leaving his disconsolate Mistress to bemoan his Fate, and me to write his eventful History.

FINIS.

APPENDIX

[*From Book II ch. ix of the first edition.*]

THE next Morning, when our Hero waked, and took a Survey of his new Apartments, he had great Reason to rejoice in the Change he had made: The Magnificence of the Furniture evidently shewed that he was in the House of a Man of Quality; and the Importance which discovered itself in the Faces of all the Domestics, seemed likewise to prove that their Master belonged to the Court. The Porter in particular appeared to be a Politician of many Years standing, for he never deliver'd the most ordinary Message but in the Voice of a Whisper, accompanied with so many Nods, Winks, and other mysterious Grimaces, that he passed among his Acquaintance for a Statesman of no common Capacity.

ABOUT Nine o'Clock in the Morning Lord *Danglecourt* was pleased to raise himself up in his Bed, and summoned his Valets to assist him in putting on his Cloaths. As soon as it was reported through the House that his Lordship was stirring, the Multitudes who were waiting to attend his Levee, put themselves in Order in his Antichamber to pay their Morning Homage, as soon as he pleased to appear. Several of them, however, who came on particular Business, or were necessary Agents under his Lordship, were selected from the common Groupe, and introduced into the Bed-chamber; where they had the inexpressible Honour and Pleasure to see his Lordship wash his Hands and buckle on his Shoes in private.

BUT his Lordship was condemned this Morning to give private Audience to the chief Inhabitants of a Borough-Town, of which (to use the common Phrase) he *made the Members*,[1] and consequently was obliged to treat them with that ceremonious Respect, which *Free-Britons* always demand in exchange for their Liberty.

These Gentlemen were ambitious of having their Town erected into a Corporation, and now waited on Lord *Danglecourt* with a Petition, setting forth the Nature of their Request, and begging his Lordship's Interest to obtain a Charter for them. They were conducted into a private Room, where his Lordship soon presented himself to them, and after saluting them all round, begged to know if he could have the Honour of serving them in any thing, making many Protestations of his particular Regard for them and eternal Devotion to their Interest. This seemed to answer their Wishes; whereupon one of them taking a Packet out of his Breast, began to read what might be called the History of their Town with more Propriety than a Petition, for it contained the Names of all the Blacksmiths, Barbers, and Attornies, that had flourished in it for many Centuries backwards. His Lordship took great Pains to suppress his Inclination to Laughter, and for a while seemed to listen with great Attention; but at length his Patience being quite exhausted, he was obliged to interrupt the Orator of the Company, saying, 'Well, Gentlemen, I won't give you the trouble to read any more; I see the Nature of your Petition extremely well, and you may depend upon my Interest; Please to leave your Petition with me, Sir, and I'll look over the remaining Part at my Leisure—— Depend upon it, Gentlemen, you shall soon be in Possession of your Desires.' His Lordship then began to enquire after their Wives and Daughters, and having ordered his Servants to bring a Salver of Sack and Biscuits, he drank Prosperity to their new Corporation, represented in the strongest Terms the Honour they did him, in making him instrumental to the Completion of their Desires, and hoped he should very soon be able to compliment them on their Success. He then conducted them to the Door, and they departed from him with the most grateful Acknowledgments of his Goodness, and the highest inward Satisfaction to think they had so gracious a Patron.

THEY were no sooner gone, than his Lordship returned into his Closet, and fell a laughing at the Folly and Impertinence of his Petitioners. 'Curse the Boobies, cries he, do they think I have nothing to do but to make Mayors and Aldermen?' and so saying, he threw down the Petition to the Dog, and began to make him *fetch and carry* for his Diversion. *Pompey* very readily entered into the Humour of this Pastime, and made such good use of his Teeth, that the Hopes of a new Corporation were soon demolished, and the Lord knows how many Mayors and Aldermen in a Moment perished by the unmerciful Jaws of a *Bologna* Lap-dog. But his Lordship soon grew tired of this Entertainment, and when he thought the Petition had been severely enough handled by the Dog, he snatched it from him, and flung it into the Fire, saying, with a most contemptuous Sneer, *So much for our new Corporation*: After which, he called for his Hat and Sword, and went Abroad; nor did *Pompey* see any thing more of him during the remaining Part of the Day.

EXPLANATORY NOTES

Page xxxix. (1) —*gressumque . . . herilem:* a reference to the dogs of Evander, *Aeneid* viii, 462, 'two menial dogs before their master pressed' (Dryden).

(2) —*mutato . . . narratur:* Horace, *Satires*, I, i, 69–70, 'Change but the name, of thee the tale is told' (Francis).

Page xliv. (1) *The late editor . . . Mr. Fielding in England:* Coventry refers to William Warburton's complete edition of Pope, which had appeared but a few months before. In a note to the *Epistle to Augustus*, l. 146, 'And ev'ry flow'ry Courtier writ Romance' (*Works*, iv, 166–8), Warburton gives a garrulous history of prose fiction and praises these two writers for 'a faithful and chaste copy of real LIFE AND MANNERS'.

(2) *he never finishes his works:* The novels of Marivaux (1688–1763), the most famous and influential being *La Vie de Marianne* (1731–5), were issued in instalments and therefore lacked proper denouements; they merely broke off abruptly.

(3) *another celebrated novel writer:* either the Abbé Prévost (1697–1763), whose *Manon Lescaut* was both admired and deplored, or (more probably) Crébillon *fils* (1674–1762), whose licentious *Le Sopha* may have suggested the plan of *Pompey*.

Page xlv. *last winter:* in February 1751. It sold for three shillings.

Page 2. (1) *discover Plots to the Government:* in 1722 Francis Atterbury, Bishop of Rochester (1662–1732), was accused of high treason in connection with a plot to restore the Pretender. His conviction resulted largely from the frequent mention in correspondence containing treasonable matter of a little spotted dog named Harlequin (said to be a code designation for the Pretender) which had been presented to him by the Jacobite Earl of Mar.

(2) *the Play-house in Lincolns-Inn-Fields:* since John Rich moved his company to Covent Garden in 1732 this theatre had been largely devoted to opera (under Porpora in the 1730s), miscellaneous entertainments, balls, and concerts.

(3) *Drury-Lane and Covent-Garden:* both were Theatres Royal when *Pompey* was written, and under the Licensing Act of 1737 the only legitimate theatres in London; but by the 1730s their programmes were much invaded by singing, dancing, and spectacles.

Page 3. (1) *The old Astronomers . . . worshipped a Dog:* Sirius, the dog-star; the jackal-headed Egyptian god Anubis.

(2) *the illustrious Theseus . . . the same Companions:* a reference to Shakespeare's Theseus; see *A Midsummer Night's Dream*, IV. i. 122ff.

(3) *JULIUS POLLUX:* a rhetorician of the second century A.D., tutor of the Emperor Commodus. His *Onomasticon*, a thesaurus of specialized terms, includes the story of Hercules' dog as a diversion for the student.

Page 4. (1) *which Lucian relates:* the anecdote of Thesmopolis the Stoic, who agreed to care for his patroness' Maltese dog, is in Lucian's dialogue 'On Salaried Posts in Great Houses'.

(2) *scattered his Image through the Land:* like King David (Charles II) in Dryden's *Absalom and Achitophel* (1681), l. 10.

(3) *His successor . . . colonel Churchill:* James II, as Duke of York, told Evelyn that he had taken a dog to sea with him during various naval engagements. On 6 May 1682, the royal frigate *Gloucester* and several escorting vessels were wrecked in a sudden storm with great loss of life while bringing the Duke and his duchess from Scotland. The Duke's conduct in this disaster was much censured by his enemies, and rumours of all sorts were circulated, one of these being no doubt the source of Coventry's story. Bishop Burnet reported: 'The duke got into a boat: and took care of his dogs, and some unknown persons who were taken from that earnest care of his to be his priests . . . .' The Earl of Dartmouth wrote in 1734 of a story 'of a struggle that happened for a plank between Sir Charles Scarborough and the duke's dog Mumper, which convinces me that the dogs were left to take care of themselves (as he did)'. See Burnet, *History of My Own Time*, ed. Osmund Airy, 1900, ii. 326–8; Evelyn, *Diary*, ed. E. S. de Beer, 1959, p. 477. For the third edition Coventry corrected his original anachronism, '*save the dogs and the Duke of M*——'. Churchill, through the influence of Lady Castlemaine a favourite of James as well as Charles, received many favours and rapid promotion from both.

(4) *Poets to write their Epitaphs:* John Gay had written an elegy on a lapdog, 'Shock's fate I mourn; poor *Shock* is now no more', which appeared in his *Poems on Several Occasions* (1720).

(5) *Bishops . . . against the Government:* the Atterbury trial; see note 1 to page 2.

(6) *Islands . . . after their Names:* the Isle of Dogs in the Thames dockside area, downstream from central London.

Page 5. (1) *an Epic Poem in Prose:* Fielding's famous definition in the preface to *Joseph Andrews* (1742).

(2) *The lowest and most contemptible Vagrants: . . . than the latter:* Coventry refers throughout the passage to actual works— *The History of Bampfylde-Moore-Carew: or, The Accomplish'd Vagabond* (1745); *The History of Charlotte Summers, The Fortunate Parish Girl* (1750); Richardson's *Pamela* (1740); the numerous hack-written 'biographies' of condemned felons and highwaymen; the pamphlets of Swift's satiric

target the astrologer Partridge; the scandalously frank memoirs of Theresa Constantia Philips and Laetitia Pilkington (both 1748); Elizabeth Thomas's *Pylades and Corinna* (1731); Colley Cibber's *Apology* (1740), mocked by Fielding; Cleland's *Memoirs of a Woman of Pleasure* ('Fanny Hill', 1748) and the memoirs of Lady Vane, inserted in Smollett's *Peregrine Pickle*, which appeared in 1751, at the same time as *Pompey*, and therefore only a few months before Coventry's revisions for his third edition.

(3) *that illustrious Mimic Mr. F—t . . . Marriages:* Samuel Foote (1720–77), a failed actor, achieved enormous success in plays of his own composition, largely improvised, in which he impersonated famous people of the day. From 1747 to 1749 at the Haymarket he evaded the Licensing Act's ban by a technicality; the tickets he issued for his performances invited the bearer to take tea or coffee; to attend an auction of pictures or a wedding, etc.

Page 6. Writer of the Life of Cicero: Dr. Conyers Middleton (1683–1750), whose particularized life of Cicero, with its fulsome dedication to Lord Hervey (1741) had been satirized at length in Fielding's *Shamela.*

Page 7. Cates: dainties, delicacies.

Page 8. (1) *Dr. Middleton . . . Dr. Ch——n:* Conyers Middleton (see note to page 6), a pioneer in Scriptural criticism, denied the credibility of miracles after the apostolic age; in the 1740's he engaged in a controversy with Dr. John Chapman (1704–84), who maintained that miracles had occurred throughout the Christian era.

(2) *N. S.:* New Style. England did not adopt the Gregorian Calendar until 2 September 1752; in 'Old Style' the year began on 25 March (Lady Day) and English dates were eleven days behind Continental ones. Coventry satirizes the precision of a pedantic historian.

Page 9. he believed . . . the Conceit: Coventry is probably punning on 'stale' in the sense of urine, and the fact that women sometimes used dogs' urine as a wash in the belief that it improved their complexions.

Page 13. (1) *Ciceroni at Rome . . . Vertù:* young gentlemen on the Grand Tour were advised by guides in the purchase of pictures, statues, etc., of artistic worth, to be displayed on their return.

(2) *the ingenious Writer of a late Essay:* Jonathan Richardson, Sr. (1665–1745), whose *Essay on the Theory of Painting* (1715) was at the time the standard work in English on the subject.

(3) *Costume:* properly *costumè*—in a painting, propriety (as to place and time) of furniture, clothing, accessories, background.

(4) *The Club at White's:* White's chocolate-house in St. James's Street, opened in 1693, soon became an exclusive club, at the time the most notorious gaming establishment in London.

Page 14. (1) *Drums:* evening card-parties, usually very crowded.

(2) *Ranelagh:* the Ranelagh pleasure-gardens in Chelsea, offering refreshments and entertainment in the celebrated Rotunda, opened in 1742, were famous throughout the century.

Page 15. *curious* ... *Shoulder-knots:* Coventry probably refers to the symbols of ostentatious folly in Swift's *Tale of a Tub*, II; *curious* has the sense of learned, technical.

Page 16. *Ridotta:* an entertainment or social assembly with music and dancing.

Page 17. *beat up his Quarters:* break in on him; visit him unceremoniously.

Page 19. *saluted:* kissed.

Page 20. *Ruelle:* a morning reception in a lady's bedroom.

Page 22. *her Character:* Lady Mary Wortley Montagu thought she recognized in Lady Tempest (see introduction, above) the character of Etheldreda (née Harrison), wife of Charles, third Viscount Townshend, who was celebrated for her gallantries, eccentricities, and wit. Lady Townshend is frequently mentioned in Lady Mary's correspondence, and was well known to her, a fact which supports the identification.

Page 23. *(for she was a very Rake at Heart):* cf. Pope's *Moral Essays*, ii ('Of the Characters of Women'), 216: 'But ev'ry Woman is at heart a Rake.'

Page 24. *Toad-eaters:* the usual slang of the period for a lady's companion, derived from the term for a mountebank's zany; origin of the modern *toady*.

Page 27. *parti-coloured Gentlemen:* servants in livery.

Page 28. *Poulcat:* polecat, i.e., stinking.

Page 30. (1) *Routs* ... *Earthquakes:* cf. Mrs. Barbauld (1779) quoted in *O. E. D.* 'There is a squeeze, a fuss, a drum, a rout, and lastly a hurricane, when the whole house is full from top to bottom.'

(2) *to shew his Collar at Court* ... *respective Orders:* Coventry refers to Pope's epigram for the collar of a dog he presented to Prince Frederick, 'I am His Highness' Dog at Kew;/Pray tell me, Sir, whose Dog are you?' and to the collars worn by knights of the Garter, Bath, and Thistle.

Page 31. (1) *Brag:* essentially identical with the modern game of poker.

(2) *the great Mr. H—le* ... *Piquet:* Edmond Hoyle (1672–1769: 'according to Hoyle') was celebrated for his many handbooks on card games, and also investigated probability theory. Piquet was a card game for two persons, using only thirty-two cards.

(3) *little Veny:* Coventry borrows here from *Spectator* No. 323 (3 November 1712) in which Clarinda records in her journal borrowing 'Lady Faddle's Cupid' to breed to her lapdog Veny, and later turns off a footman for being rude to Veny.

Page 34. *Mrs. Abigail:* a generic term for a lady's maid or waiting-

woman. See 1 Samuel 25 : 24–42 ; Abigail calls herself 'thine handmaid'.
Page 35. (1) *drowth:* drought, thirst.

(2) *Lady Sophister (for that was her name):* Lady Mary Wortley
Montagu believed that in Lady Sophister she could identify Margaret
(Rolle) Walpole, wife of Robert Walpole, 2nd Earl of Orford.
Page 36. (1) *Hobbes . . . Woollaston:* Coventry intends the names to be
taken as a list of freethinkers. All, including Thomas Woolston (1670–
1733) questioned the Resurrection and the Virgin Birth.

(2) *Killdarby:* perhaps a play on *darby,* a slang term for ready money.

(3) *Mr. Locke's controversy with the bishop of Worcester:* In 1697 Edward
Stillingfleet, bishop of Worcester, attacked *Christianity Not Mysterious*
by the Deist John Toland, which applied Locke's philosophy to
theological matters. The resulting exchange is better known as the
'Socinian controversy'.
Page 37. (1) *doctor Rhubarb:* rhubarb was much used as a carminative.

(2) *a kind of quintessence, as Aristotle observed:* this idea is not to be found
in Aristotle.
Page 38. (1) *Aristoxenus . . . tune:* a philosopher and theorist of music
(fourth century B.C.), who regarded the soul as a 'tuning' (*harmonia*) of
the body.

(2) *Descartes . . . Borri:* Coventry derives his information from the
articles 'Brain', 'Soul', and 'Sensory' in *Chambers' Cyclopaedia* in the
edition of 1738 or 1741.

(3) *wave:* waive.
Page 39. (1) *their dogs will go to heaven along with them:* A reference to
Pope's *Essay on Man,* i, 111–12:

But [the Indian] thinks, admitted to that equal sky,

His faithful dog shall bear him company.

(2) *India . . . where the Gymnosophists lived:* the term ('naked sages')
was used loosely for any Hindu ascetic or mystic.
Page 41. (1) *—sed scilicet . . . funera debet:* Ovid, *Metamorphoses,* iii. 135–7.

But no frail Man, however great or high,

Can be concluded blest before he die.   (Addison)

(2) *Rosamond's Pond:* this oblong ornamental lake, in the southwest
corner of St. James's Park, planted about with groves by Charles II,
was a favourite spot for lovers and (from an erroneous association with
Fair Rosamond) a resort of lovers in despair. In 1770 it was filled in.
Page 43. (1) *the Hours of Two and Three in the Morning:* for persons of
fashion the 'morning' extended until dinner in mid-afternoon. Fielding
commented sarcastically on this distortion in *Tom Jones,* XV. ii.

(2) *Buckingham-house:* the Duke of Buckingham's residence (1703),
purchased by George III in 1762, gradually grew into Buckingham
Palace by successive additions.

Page 46. the City: the ancient City of London, as opposed to the fashionable 'Town' to the west, was the centre of mercantile and banking activities; hence it represented sordid commerce.

Page 47. scrophulous: scrofulous—afflicted with a disfiguring disease of the lymphatic glands, the 'king's evil'.

Page 48. As in Praesenti: a section in Lily's Eton Grammar dealing with rules for forming the pluperfects and supines of verbs, so called from its first words: '[If a verb end in] -as in [the second person of] the present [tense] . . . .' The boy's studies have not progressed very far.

Page 50. Tillotson's Sermons: the two hundred and fifty-odd sermons of John Tillotson (1630–94), Archbishop of Canterbury, were enormously popular.

Page 51. (1) *Grimalkin . . . a Mouser still:* Aesop's fable of 'A Cat and Venus' figures in Sir Roger L'Estrange's Restoration rendering of selected fables, often reprinted; but the last part of Coventry's sentence is quoted verbatim from *Tom Jones,* XII, ii.

(2) *Brute the Trojan . . . Dr. S—k——y:* Brutus, son of Aeneas, was the legendary founder of Britain; Browne Willis (1682–1760) and Dr. William Stukeley (1687–1765) were both antiquaries, famous for their erudition, eccentricities, and fanciful theories about Britain's remote past.

Page 52. (1) *Gridelin . . . Grimalkin:* traditional names for cats.

(2) *another that had a Legacy . . . our English Horace:* Pope's *Epistle to Bathurst,* l. 98,: 'Die, and endow a College, or a Cat'. He refers to a story, widely believed but unfounded, about the will of the Duchess of Richmond, 'La Belle Stuart', who died in 1702, allegedly providing legacies to friends who would look after her cats.

(3) *'Tis observed . . . Cats and Women:* Addison's *Spectator* No. 209 (30 October 1711) discusses a satire of Simonides on women. 'The Cat furnished Materials for a seventh Species of Women . . . of a melancholy, froward, unamiable Nature . . . subject to little Thefts, Cheats, and Pilferings.'

Page 53. a most elegant little Ode . . . Miscellany Poems: this is the earliest known reference to Gray's *Ode on the Death of a Favourite Cat,* which appears in Vol. II of Dodsley's collection (1748), together with Gray's 'On a Distant Prospect of Eton College' and 'On the Spring'.

Page 54. Nelson's Festivals . . . Baker's Chronicles: Robert Nelson's *Companion for the Festivals and Fasts of the Church of England* and Sir Richard Baker's *Chronicle of the Kings of England* were found in every literate household; in *Joseph Andrews* Sir Thomas Booby possesses the *Chronicles.*

Page 56. Hedge-Lane: now Whitcomb Street.

Page 58. (1) *clysters:* enemas.

(2) *Abigail:* see note to page 34.

Page 59. (1) *his black solitaire:* a ring with a single stone, worn to confine a neckcloth or the tail of a wig.

(2) *scaramouch:* from the cowardly boaster of Italian farce: a rascally fop.

Page 60. *the two great field-preaching apostles:* John Wesley (1703–91), founder of Methodism, and George Whitefield (1714–70), the most famous evangelist of the period; since (among many other departures from orthodoxy) they preached in any convenient place they were fiercely attacked by the Anglican clergy and by traditionalists in general.

Page 61. *a miff . . . glowted:* a tiff; scowled or glowered.

Page 64. *lady Harridan's:* Selina, Lady Huntingdon (1707–91), daughter of Earl Ferrars, gave up a brilliant social career for Methodism in 1739, personally converted by John and Charles Wesley. In 1748–49 her mansion in Park Street became a centre for religious education, and the Methodist services regularly held there were frequented by many persons of distinction.

Page 65. (1) *small-pox . . . had* [its] *converts:* inoculation for small-pox was still rare, and those beauties who survived the disease were in almost all cases hideously scarred; thus, *faute de mieux,* they might turn to religion.

(2) —*Species . . . sororum:* Ovid, *Metamorphoses,* ii. 13–14;
Tho' various Features did the Sisters grace,
A Sister's Likeness was in ev'ry Face. (Addison)

Page 67. (1) *how Satan confined him . . . Kennington-Common:* though Coventry exaggerates slightly, these incidents are found in *A Short Account of God's Dealings with the Reverend Mr. George Whitefield, A. B.* (1740), Sect. II, pp. 33–49, and in the *Journal* which occupies the latter part of the volume, under Tuesday, 8 May 1739.

(2) *suspirious:* full of sighs or groans.

(3) *the self-same indignity that Lucian formerly offered . . . a similar impostor:* in Lucian's dialogue 'Alexander, the False Prophet', the narrator, given the charlatan's hand to kiss, bites it.

Page 69. *the Fleet . . . Smithfield:* the chapel in the Fleet Prison was the frequent scene of clandestine marriages. Smithfield was the location, among other things, of London's slaughterhouses and of the rowdy Bartholomew Fair.

Page 70. *Automedon:* the comrade and charioteer of Achilles (*Iliad,* xvii), hence generic for coachmen.

Page 71. (1) *highest Exaltation:* Coventry presumably refers to the gallows.

(2) *the illustrious Mr. F—t . . . milling Chocolate:* the Temple Exchange

Coffee House in Fleet Street was a favourite haunt of Foote's and of the law students in the Temple; see also note 3 to page 5.

(3) *the late Rebellion:* the rising in favour of the Young Pretender, Prince Charles Edward, in 1745.

Page 72. (1) *old Walpole is behind the Curtain still . . . a Correspondence between Walpole and Fleury:* Sir Robert Walpole retired as first minister in 1742; Coventry echoes a remark by the Duchess of Marlborough that if Walpole were to retire he would operate 'behind the curtain still'. Fleury was Louis xv's foreign minister.

(2) *V–rn–n:* Admiral Vernon, the naval hero who took Portobello in 1739, was also a zealous advocate of naval reform. Admiral of the White in 1745, he was deprived of his rank in 1746 because of his outspoken opposition to the government, but remained a member of Parliament until his death in 1757.

Page 74. Balmerino, and t'other Fellow, that died like a Coward: Arthur Elphinstone, 6th Lord Balmerino, was a leader in the uprising of 1745. He refused to admit treason or to plead for mercy, and was executed in 1746. William Boyd, fourth Earl of Kilmarnock, was a general for the Young Pretender. He confessed and was executed with Balmerino; his 'cowardice' consisted merely in a lack of defiance.

Page 75. Tobacco-stopper: a device for tamping down tobacco in a pipe.

Page 76. (1) *Hei . . . eris?: Epigrams,* xii. 92;

What would I do, the question you repeat,
If on a sudden I were rich and great?
Who can himself with future conduct charge?
What would you do, a lion, and at large?   (William Hay)

(2) *Agricolam . . . pulsat: Satires,* I. i. 9–10;

When early clients thunder at his gate,
The barrister applauds the rustic's fate. (Francis)

Page 77. black Silk Stockings . . . Sir John Cutler's: Cutler (1608–93), a wealthy merchant and philanthropist, became proverbial for avarice; Pope mentions him in the *Epistle to Bathurst,* l. 315. Dr. Arbuthnot, in the *Memoirs of Martinus Scriblerus,* related: 'Sir John Cutler had a pair of black worsted stockings which his maid darned so often with silk that they became at last a pair of silk stockings.'

Page 79. his Bag and Peruke: the back hair of periwigs was sometimes confined in an ornamental net bag, or snood.

Page 81. (1) *in the elegant Language of Newmarket, is called running Lives:* Coventry is commenting on the 'betting mania' of the middle and late eighteenth century; Newmarket, then as now, was a noted racetrack.

(2) *drink Champagne upon the Horse at Charing-Cross:* this escapade would have involved a huge bronze equestrian statue of Charles i, situated where the cross is now. It was cast in 1633, ordered to be

destroyed by Cromwell, hidden during the Interregnum, and set up in 1675 by Lord Treasurer Danby as a gesture to secure public support.

Page 83. (1) *a Speech in King Lear:* Edgar's speech, IV. i. 2ff. Coventry quotes Shakespeare's original text, not the Nahum Tate version that was acted in his own day.

(2) *a lean Projector:* an inventor, or would-be promoter of ingenious schemes, supposedly profitable.

Page 84. (1) *Bur:* sweetbread.

(2) *EO . . . the accomplish'd Mr. Nash:* EO was a game of chance resembling roulette, so called from the slots marked E and O. Richard ('Beau') Nash (1674–1762) was the social arbiter, master of ceremonies, and in a sense creator of fashionable Bath in the first half of the century.

Page 87, *rappee:* a coarse, rank variety of snuff.

Page 89. (1) *drank his toast on his knees:* presumably Coventry's (and Jack's) satire of extravagant lovers; but Pepys (23 April 1661) records it as a gesture of loyalty to the House of Stuart.

(2) *Hooke's Roman history:* The Roman history (1738; many reprints) of Nathaniel Hooke (d.1763) was highly esteemed. Hooke gives the wolf-story (1751 edn., i. 14) but supposes that a woman named Acca Laurentia, nicknamed Lupa, suckled the twins.

Page 91. *pair of poppers:* pistols.

Page 92. *that infernal Sir Thomas Deveil:* De Veil (1684–1746) was Henry Fielding's predecessor as magistrate at Bow Street. Knighted for his services in rounding up Jacobite sympathizers in 1745, he was zealous but extravagant and extortionate. He claimed to have made £1000 a year in executing his duties, and is probably ridiculed as Justice Squeezum in Fielding's *Coffee-House Politician.*

Page 93. *chouse:* low slang for *swindle, cheat.*

Page 94. *a hollow thing:* racing term for a decisive victory; cf. Fanny Burney, *Evelina* (Oxford English Novels, p. 294).

Page 95. *Silenus:* the tutor and companion of Dionysus, invariably depicted as old, corpulent, and drunk.

Page 108. *the great Lord Rochester:* Rochester's poem, 'Nothing! thou elder brother even to Shade', stands in a long tradition of paradoxical panegyrics on contemptible or absurd subjects. Coventry doubtless knew that Fielding had published an essay 'On Nothing' in Vol. I of his *Miscellanies* (1743), and borrowed from it the reference to a poem on nothing by 'a wit of Charles II's court'.

Page 109. (1) *the Treatises of Mr. William Wh——n . . . inexhaustible Topics?:* Whiston (1667–1752) an eccentric and unorthodox scientific investigator, popular lecturer, and clergyman who succeded Newton in 1703 as Lucasian Professor of mathematics at Cambridge but was deprived of his chair in 1710 for heresy, wrote over fifty works on controversial topics, mostly theological. Sir Richard Blackmore, a physician and the constant target of the wits (1653–1729), wrote plays and endless epics, the most notable being *Prince Arthur* (1695) and *Creation* (1712). The *Universal History* (23 vols., 1736–65) was compiled both by hacks and by authors of merit, was published by a consortium of booksellers, and was granted a Royal Privilege by George II.

(2) *the Works of Dennis . . . Divine Legations:* Coventry attacks John Dennis (1657–1734) as a critic and enemy of Pope; Descartes and the third Earl of Shaftesbury as freethinking philosophers; and William Warburton not as editor of Pope (see note 1 to page xliv) but as latitudinarian writer, controversialist, and author of *The Divine Legation of Moses* (1738–41), an innovative but obscurely written treatise on Scripture. Warburton had accused Coventry's cousin Henry Coventry of plagiarizing, in his *Philemon to Hydaspes* (which Coventry reissued in 1753 after his cousin's death), material intended for the second part of the *Divine Legation* and allegedly confided as a special favour; Henry urbanely defended himself in print.

(3) *Any News in the City, or upon Change?:* commercial and financial news; *Change* is the Royal Exchange, where securities were traded.

Page 110. *the late War:* the lengthy War of the Austrian Succession (1740–48).

Page 111. *Quicquid . . . discursus:* Juvenal, *Satires* i. 85–6;

What Human Kind desires, and what they shun,

Rage, Passions, Pleasures, Impotence of Will,

Shall this Satyrical Collection fill. (Dryden)

Page 112. (1) *over the dying Caesar:* Cicero speaks in his letter to Atticus of 27 April, 44 B.C., of 'the joy with which I feasted my eyes on the just execution of a tyrant'.

(2) *pillgarlick:* a contemptuous term for a bald-headed man.

Page 113. *a Turn-spit . . . Lustration:* small dogs were sometimes placed in a kind of squirrel-cage attached to a roasting-spit in order to turn it; lustration was the ceremonial purification used in Roman rites.

Page 119. (1) *arbitrium . . . Applause:* Horace, *Odes*, III. ii. 20.

(2) *Ridotta:* see note to page 16, above.

Page 122. *Citron Waters:* brandy flavoured with lemon or citron peel.

Page 124. *Vauxhall Gardens:* called Spring-garden in Addison's day and characterized by him (*Spectator* No. 383, 20 May 1712) as 'a kind of Mahometan Paradise', it was reopened in 1732 as an amusement park. Its formal gardens and fanciful buildings attracted Londoners until the mid-nineteenth century.

Page 125. *Lord Clarendon's celebrated Character of Lord Viscount Falkland:* Lucius Cary, Viscount Falkland, was the closest friend of Edward

Hyde, Earl of Clarendon; the character, an epitome of all the virtues, is found in the *History of the Great Rebellion* under the year 1643.

Page 127. tramontanes: a term imported from Italy: uncouth foreigners. Those coming by the 'cross post' (the east-west coach) would not be Londoners.

Page 128. in petto: in secret (lit. 'in the breast'): another of Count Tag's Italian affectations.

Page 133. (1) *Night-gown:* dressing-gown.

(2) *Father-in-Law:* often used at the time for *stepfather*.

Page 134. Cowley's Poems . . . Pamela Andrews: Coventry, like Fielding, would regard both works as pernicious, giving girls of the lower orders ideas above their station.

Page 136. Lady Townly: an extravagant, witty gadabout in *The Provok'd Husband* of Vanbrugh, completed by Colley Cibber and first produced in 1728. The part was created by the famous Mrs. Oldfield.

Page 138. at the fleet: see note to page 69.

Page 140. (1) *lord Oxford:* Robert Harley, 1st Earl of Oxford (1661–1724) was Queen Anne's first minister, 1710–14.

(2) *hermitage:* a famous and prized French wine from Valence.

Page 141. the Rev^d Mr. Wh——n . . . millennium: in 1746 and later William Whiston (see note 1 to page 109) lectured at Tunbridge Wells and elsewhere, predicting the millennium in twenty years.

Page 142. occasionally: for the occasion, or the particular circumstances.

Page 145. (1) *Khevenhullar hats:* a broad-brimmed and high-cocked hat, named for an Austrian general.

(2) *a jemmy fellow:* in sporting circles, a dandy; a *jemmy* was a riding-boot.

Page 146. Mr. Broughton's amphitheatres: John Broughton (1705–89), 'father of British pugilism', set up a theatre in Hanway Street in 1742 for exhibitions of boxing, and an academy in 1747.

Page 149. Ruckolt-house: Defoe's *Tour Thro' the Whole Island of Great Britain* (4th edn., rev. Samuel Richardson, 1748, i. 3) speaks of 'Sir *Henry Hickes's* House at *Ruckholt* (now turned into a Place of Entertainment agreeable to the depraved Taste of this luxurious Age)'. It was located in what is now Leyton.

Page 150. Cloacina . . . Bona Dea: in Gay's *Trivia* and Pope's *Dunciad* Cloacina is the Roman goddess of sewers and filth; the Roman festival of the 'good goddess' (Fauna) was celebrated by women only.

Page 155. Bristol Stones: rhinestones.

Page 157. made remarks: observed anything, took notice.

Page 158. lord Marmazet: Coventry may have borrowed the name from a deceitful character in Smollett's *Roderick Random* (1748).

Page 160. acts of seisin: symbolic acts, legally taking possession of feudal property; as receiving a sod of turf or a key.

Page 161. *in St. James's parish:* in and about the Court.

Page 162. *as Juvenal expresses it: Satires,* vi. 509.

Page 166. *flock-bed . . . jordan:* a mattress stuffed with tufts of refuse wool or cotton; a chamber-pot.

Page 167. (1) *pap and caudle:* gruel for infants and a nourishing warm gruel, especially for women in childbed, made with wine and spices.

(2) *the Heliconian maids:* the Muses.

Page 169. (1) *Shire-lane:* now obliterated; north of Temple Bar, at the boundary of the old City.

(2) *a Scotch translator:* possibly a hit at Thomas Gordon (d. 1750) who translated Sallust, Tacitus, and Cicero, wrote for Walpole, and was rewarded with a government sinecure. *a Fleet parson:* a clergyman of dubious character who would hang about the Fleet prison chapel to perform clandestine marriages.

Page 171. (1) *And I will maintain . . . in the world:* the Cartesian question of the differentia between man and beasts was crucial in the theology of the day, and was hotly debated by the leading thinkers of the Enlightenment, since it touched upon the existence of a unique human soul.

(2) *Mr. Locke's parrot . . . half an hour together:* The story, considerably exaggerated by Coventry, is quoted by Locke (*Essay Concerning Human Understanding,* 11. 27.8) from Sir William Temple. Locke points out that even such a creature could not be defined as a human being.

(3) *what-d'ye-callum . . . the capitol:* the 'translator of Greek and Latin authors' does not know that the famous story is to be found in Livy (ii. 47).

Page 172. (1) *Ulysses's dog Argus . . . the siege of Troy: Odyssey,* xvii.

(2) *the orators at Robin-Hood's ale-house:* the Robin Hood debating society moved in 1747 from the Essex Head to the Robin Hood and Little John, in Butcher Row, Temple Bar. The Monday night meetings, in Coventry's day attended by 150–225 persons, were devoted to debate chiefly on questions of religion and politics, enlivened by lemonade and porter; each speaker was allowed five minutes. The clergy attacked the society as ignorant, blasphemous, and seditious; the brisk pamphlet war that resulted in 1750 and later years revealed that among the members were 'Orator' Henley, the actors Foote, Macklin, and Derrick, and Oliver Goldsmith.

(3) *smoked him for a queer fish:* understood that he was an odd character.

(4) *some poetical strains from Milton:* presumably the Elder Brother's address to the moon in *Comus,* ll. 331–42.

Page 173. *Hartshorn:* spirits of ammonia, smelling salts.

Page 174. *Hervey's Meditations among the Tombs:* this lugubrious and macabre prose work, in the form of a letter to a lady, by James Hervey (1714–58), was immensely popular (twenty-five editions, 1746–91). The narrator wanders reflectively through a church and its graveyard: 'Promiscuous Lodgment, and amicable agreement of Corpses, suggest Humility, and Concord.'

Page 175. *to fancy herself . . . a Field of Turnips:* these effects of vapours and spleen are borrowed from Pope, *The Rape of the Lock,* iv. 49–54:

Men prove with Child, as pow'rful Fancy works,
And Maids turn'd Bottels, call aloud for Corks.

Page 178. *Premunire:* a summons; hence, a difficulty, predicament.

Page 179. *Bagnios:* originally bath-houses (Ital.), but since these were often used for assignations, a common euphemism for brothels.

Page 181. *Misses . . . a second-hand Capuchin, a white washing Gown:* Miss, earlier a pejorative term except for little girls, had by the mid-century become a badge of gentility. A capuchin was a dress with a cloak and hood; a washing gown one of washable fabric (therefore inexpensive).

Page 182. *the celebrated Fanny Hill:* Cleland's *Memoirs of a Woman of Pleasure* had appeared in 1748.

Page 183. *the Reverend Divan:* all (or most) Fellows were in holy orders. *Divan* (from the Persian) was used in the sense of *tribunal.*

Page 184. *the daughters of Cecrops . . . to the contrary:* son of Hephaestos and Gaea and in legend the first inhabitant of Attica, the infant Erichthonius was brought to the gods in a basket by Athena. The curious daughters of Cecrops, finding a serpent (in some versions, a child and a serpent) in the basket, went mad and threw themselves from the Acropolis.

Page 185. (1) *the inimitable Swift . . . suits of cloaths:* in *A Tale of a Tub,* Sect. II.

(2) *the iliac passion:* colic.

(3) *Ward . . . the poor:* Joshua Ward (1685–1761), a famous and successful quack of the 1730s and later, was noted for his 'drop' and 'pill', panaceas composed partly of antimony. Pope says (*The First Epistle of the Second Book of Horace,* l 182): 'Ward tried, on Puppies and the Poor, his Drop.'

Page 186. *Machaon:* a son of Asklepios, he cured both Menelaus and Philoctetes of their wounds (*Iliad,* ii, iv, xi); hence a generic term for physicians.

Page 187. *Another College-Character:* in the first edition this chapter, which was eliminated in the third, followed the character of Mr. Williams.

Page 194. *the Question . . . the old Lady:* in Farquhar's *The Beaux' Stratagem,* iv. i., Archer, disguised as the servant of his friend Aimwell, who is feigning illness, says to Dorinda, Mrs. Sullen, and Lady Bountiful,

'Where, where is my Lady Bountiful? Pray, which is the old lady of you three?'

Page 196. (1) *Beaux, and Belles, and Witlings:* Coventry is thinking of Pope's *Rape of the Lock,* v. 59–60:

A *Beau* and *Witling* perish'd in the Throng,
One dy'd in *Metaphor,* and one in *Song.*

(2) *Westminster-Hall:* until the middle of the nineteenth century not only the seat of the courts of Exchequer, Chancery, Common Pleas, King's Bench, etc., but contained the stalls of stationers, booksellers, and vendors of novelties.

Page 198. *ferae Naturae, Things of no Value:* Coventry lifts this passage from the argument over the legal status of Sophia's bird in *Tom Jones,* IV, iv.

Page 202. (1) *Lord Clarendon, Dr. Middleton:* see notes to pages 125 and 6.

(2) *a certain Painter:* Jonathan Richardson, Sr. (see note 2 to page 13) produced in 1734 *Explanatory Notes and Remarks on Milton's Paradise Lost . . . with the Life of the Author.* On p. ii he says:

He was rather a Middle Siz'd than a Little Man, and Well Proportion'd; Latterly he was—No; Not Short and Thick, but he would have been So, had he been Something Shorter and Thicker than he Was.

(3) *Candidate for a Ribbon:* the reference is to orders and decorations awarded to undeserving courtiers.

Page 203. *that stupendous Poll:* probably a reference to the scandalous Westminster election of 1749. In the Parliamentary investigation that followed Lord Trentham's election was sustained, but 700 votes were invalidated on each side.

Page 205. *made the Members:* controlled the votes (and the election) of Members of Parliament; see Pope's *Sixth Epistle of the First Book of Horace,* l. 106: 'That makes three Members, this can chuse a May'r'.